The Fifth Passenger

The Fifth Passenger

By Edward Young

PERENNIAL LIBRARY
Harper & Row, Publishers
New York, Cambridge, Philadelphia, San Francisco
London, Mexico City, São Paulo, Sydney

THE FIFTH PASSENGER. Copyright © 1963 by Edward Young. All rights reserved. Printed in the United States of America. No part of this book may be used or reproduced in any manner whatsoever without written permission except in the case of brief quotations embodied in critical articles and reviews. For information address Harper & Row, Publishers, Inc., 10 East 53rd Street, New York, N.Y. 10022. Published simultaneously in Canada by Fitzhenry & Whiteside Limited, Toronto.

First PERENNIAL LIBRARY edition published 1981.

ISBN: 0-06-080544-7

81 82 83 84 85 10 9 8 7 6 5 4 3 2 1

For Mary
dear wife and invaluable critic
an aperitif

The Fifth Passenger

1

The naval staff car pulled away from the officers' block and came smoothly along the sea road toward the main exit gate. A bunch of sea gulls rose complaining from the shingle beach, soaring upward in a vertical glide against the freshening Channel gale. At the head of the flagstaff by the gate the white ensign cracked like a whip, slatting the halyards against the mast.

A chief petty officer stepped out from the guardhouse, called the sentry to attention and signaled the car to a standstill.

"It's O.K., Chief," said the seaman driver, jerking his head backward. "Captain Howard."

The C.P.O. looked into the back seat and saw that it was indeed the ginger-bearded Captain Howard. He was not in uniform but in his usual shoregoing rig: gray-green dogtooth tweeds and green trilby hat. Two brown travel-worn leather suitcases were in the front passenger seat alongside the driver.

"Good morning, sir," said the C.P.O., saluting and raising his voice a little against the blustering wind. "Nice fresh day for going on leave, sir!"

Captain Howard smiled and raised his hand in casual acknowledgment. The car drove on through the old brick archway and almost at once swung left onto the road leading toward the town. The captain, his frosty blue eyes alert with anxiety, looked back through the rear window at the familiar gateway and the white signboard with its forbidding warning:

ADMIRALTY RESEARCH ESTABLISHMENT
ALL PASSES TO BE SHOWN

Losing sight of it as the car turned the corner by the water reservoir, he leaned back with a sigh of relief.

First hurdle over.

He combed the ginger hairs of his mustache with his fingernails—sure sign that he was on edge—and looked at his watch. "Step on it a bit, Wilson, if you can," he said. "I haven't got too much time to catch my train."

"Aye, aye, sir."

In fact Howard knew he was in good time for the train he intended to catch. It was just that he wanted to get away from the base as quickly as possible. He had a sickening fear that he had almost left it too late as it was.

They were running into the busy part of the town now, and the driver was enjoying himself, nipping in and out of the traffic, cutting in under the noses of the Corporation buses. Opposite the Town Hall they were held up by the traffic lights. Straight ahead was the railway bridge. They had only to go under the bridge and turn right and they would be in the station yard.

Captain Howard turned to look behind. A stab of alarm contracted his bowels: he fancied he caught a glimpse of the fawn-colored hood of a black Zephyr convertible, some way back in the traffic lane. But whatever it was, it was hidden at once by the stream of lorries and buses. He could easily have been mistaken. Tony Gardner was his oldest friend, but he was the last person he wanted to see at this particular moment.

It was a well-known trick of fear, this: it gave you halluci-nations, made you imagine the thing you dreaded most.

The lights turned to green and the traffic moved forward. Even if it had been Tony's car, thought Howard, it didn't necessarily mean he was trailing him. There were many other places in the town he could be aiming for.

As they drove under the railway bridge and turned into the station yard he looked back along the line of traffic. There was no sign of the black convertible so far as he could see.

His driver stopped the car by the entrance to the booking hall, jumped out and opened the rear door.

"You go in and get your ticket, sir," he said, "and I'll look after your gear."

"No, it's all right, Wilson, I can manage on my own, thank you. You push off back to the base."

"Very good, sir. Hope you enjoy your leave, sir."

Howard picked up his two suitcases and walked across the booking hall to the first-class ticket window.

"Single to Brixham, please," he said.

As he waited for his ticket he happened to glance across to the other side of the hall and saw, reflected in the mirror of a weighing machine, Tony's car entering the station yard. He turned hurriedly back to the ticket window and rapped loudly on the wooden shelf.

Commander Tony Gardner had in fact been following him all the way from the naval base to the railway station, at what he had intended to be a discreet distance. But the traffic was heavier than he had allowed for, and before they reached the Town Hall he lost sight of his quarry altogether.

He turned in to the station yard just in time to see Wilson driving away in the staff car. He pulled up short of the entrance and jumped out. He was in uniform, but his brass hat, three rings and two rows of medals were somehow at odds with his youthful appearance. He was a small, compact man, dark-haired, lean-faced, and with restless whimsical eyes which under their dark lashes seemed aware of everything that was going on about him.

As he came round one of the flanking pillars he saw Howard hurrying away toward the platforms. At the same moment Howard glanced briefly over his shoulder. Gardner stepped quickly back out of sight, cursing himself for not having changed into plain clothes.

When he looked again, Howard had vanished.

Gardner didn't think he had been seen. He hurried forward across the hall toward the ticket window. To his annoyance a rather deaf elderly Scotsman had got there before him and was now taking what seemed an interminable time to buy a through ticket to Inverness. Gardner waited at his elbow with ill-concealed impatience, but at last the old gentleman picked up his ticket and moved away.

Gardner spoke rapidly to the ticket clerk. "There was a fellow with a red beard buying a ticket a moment ago."

"Yes, that's right, sir, there was."

"I wonder if you could tell me what train he booked on, please?"

"Well, sir, it's a bit irregular. . . . Would he be a naval gentleman like yourself?"

"Yes, I . . . have an important message for him."

"As a matter of fact, sir, he didn't seem to know *which* train he wanted. First he booked a single ticket to Brixham—"

"Brixham!"

"Yes, sir, Brixham . . . and then he suddenly changed his mind and asked the time of the next train to London. I told him there was the fast leaving in three minutes, so he took a return to London and dashed off without waiting for his change."

"Leaving in three minutes, did you say?"

"Yes, the 10:43. Did you want a ticket yourself, sir?"

"No thanks, I'm not traveling."

"You might just catch him if you run, sir." The ticket clerk raised his voice as Gardner began hurrying toward the trains. "Platform 3, sir. . . ."

Gardner dodged in and out of the bustling crowd amidst the noise of escaping steam, engine whistles and rumbling baggage trolleys. The big overhead clock showed only seconds to go.

As he arrived at the ticket barrier to Platform 3 the gate was shutting. The guard blew his final whistle, and the train began moving slowly out of the platform.

Gardner had to know whether Howard was on that train or not.

He waited. The ticket collector reached up and pulled the "Waterloo" indicator board out of its slot, replaced it with the board for the next train and unlocked the gate.

Gardner said, "Did you happen to notice if a man with a red beard got on that train?"

"Yes, sir, about two minutes ago. You could hardly help noticing him. More ginger than red, I would say—I've seen him on this station several times. A naval officer, by the look of him."

"That sounds like him all right. The train doesn't stop anywhere before London, does it?"

"No, sir, it's fast nonstop to Waterloo."

"And when is it due in?"

"Twelve twenty-two, if it's on time. It might be delayed a bit by the track repairs the other side of Woking, but it should make that up all right."

Gardner thanked him and walked back to his car, sick at heart at the thought of what he must now go and tell the admiral.

And what the devil was all this about Brixham?

What a bloody day this was turning out to be! He slid into the driving seat and started the engine.

"Damn, damn, damn," he said as he let in the clutch.

Back at the naval research base Gardner parked his car in its usual place behind the torpedo workshops and went at once to the staff block on the seaward side of the parade ground. Low clouds were scudding across a threatening sky. Typical end-of-September weather. "Gale's freshening up a bit," he thought, and the wind was already so strong that he had to hang on to his cap as he climbed the outside stairway to the admiral's office.

Lieutenant Pawson, the admiral's secretary, surrounded by filing cabinets, was sitting at his desk, patiently immersed in documents.

"Hullo, Scratch. The Old Man in?"

The secretary looked up from his work. "Hullo, sir. He's a bit tied up at the moment, I'm afraid. The weekly report of proceedings has to go off tonight."

"I have to see him at once, Scratch. It really is terribly urgent and hush-hush."

"All right, sir, I'll tell him."

Gardner was shown in immediately.

Even when he was sitting behind his wide leather-topped desk Admiral Sherwood looked imposingly tall with his massive shoulders and large square head. The gray-blue eyes that looked piercingly out of his granite face had clearly lost all their illusions except an abiding faith in the Royal Navy. He waved Gardner toward a crimson-leather armchair and greeted him in his rasping voice.

"Well, Gardner, how's Naval Intelligence getting along? Any clues yet about this damned leakage?"

"Nothing absolutely positive yet, sir, but that's what I wanted to see you about. At the moment I've nothing more than a hunch to work on, but I've got to move fast if I'm to follow it up. And it's so fantastic I can hardly believe it myself."

Admiral Sherwood slid a silver cigarette box across the desk. "Tell me all about it."

"Well, sir, as you know, this new homing atomic depth charge you're working on down here—once you've ironed out all the present teething troubles—is expected to revolutionize antisubmarine warfare. And you know that our information at the Admiralty is that a surprisingly accurate outline of the project has already reached Moscow."

The admiral got up from his chair and began pacing up and down the room.

"Yes, I know that's supposed to be so, but frankly I just don't see how it's possible. Our security arrangements in this base are almost Gestapo-like in their thoroughness."

"All the same, sir, I understand our information comes from an unimpeachable source."

"Well, Gardner, you came down here to investigate this supposed leakage. Have you discovered any weak spots?"

"No, sir, I've checked in every possible way. Your distribution list for top secret signals and information is a hundred per cent watertight, and I've gone through your personnel screening reports with a fine-tooth comb."

The admiral stopped his pacing and stood in front of Gardner in his best quarterdeck manner, hands behind back, chin jutting aggressively forward.

"Well, then?"

"Last month, sir, I arranged with my department in London for the deliberate leak of three separate items of plausible but misleading information. These leaks were confined to this base and to a carefully restricted distribution channel. Every one of these items is known to have since reached the Kremlin."

"Go on."

"This has narrowed my suspects to a very small circle indeed. The result of the tests, plus the very strictness of your security precautions, points almost certainly to someone in a highly responsible position—someone, in fact, in the staff office itself."

"Look here, Gardner," said the admiral quietly, "I hope you realize the implications of what you're saying. Frankly, I think you're barking up the wrong tree. Commander Phillips has been staff officer here for four years or thereabouts. He's a man I would trust to the very limit. As for Fortescue, you couldn't ask for a more loyal officer to have as your number one."

"I'm not thinking of Phillips—or Fortescue, sir."

The admiral stared at him in silence.

"Well," he said, after a pause, "that leaves Captain Howard . . . and myself."

"I do not include *you* among my suspects, sir."

Admiral Sherwood moved over to the window and stood with his back to Gardner, looking out across the foam-streaked sea with his hands dug deep into his jacket pockets.

"What you are trying to tell me, Gardner, is quite, quite impossible. Off and on I've known Captain Howard for over twenty years. His war career in submarines was quite outstanding . . . two D.S.O.s, a D.S.C. and God knows how many thousand tons of enemy shipping sent to the bottom. The first time he was in the zone for a brass hat, he got one. I myself asked for him to be put in charge of this vitally important research project. It would be difficult to imagine anyone less likely to be your . . . traitor."

Gardner stubbed out his half-smoked cigarette, leaned forward in his chair and clasped his hands between his knees. He hesitated for a moment and then, staring at the carpet, began speaking in a voice so strained that the admiral turned to look at him.

"Sir, a few days ago I would have agreed with you. Bill Howard is, I suppose, one of my oldest friends. We were in the same term at Dartmouth. We did our big-ship time in the same cruiser. We joined submarines together—a few months before war started. We did our C.O.'s qualifying course together, and when we got our own commands we often found ourselves in the same submarine flotilla——Beirut, Malta, Algiers, and so on. I would say we've been about as intimate as two normal men could be. Bill is one of the few N.C.s I've ever met whose minds are interested in other things besides naval shop. He knows a lot about music, plays the flute extraordinarily well, and he's something of an expert on sea birds. We used to talk for hours together about every subject under the sun——you know, art, philosophy and so on. Unfortunately, since the war we've rather drifted apart. I went off to do my three-year job with the New Zealand Navy, and when I got back he had been posted to West Berlin. Bill, of course, with his technical knowledge, began specializing in research and got his brass hat long before I did. Since then he's kept more or less a stripe ahead of me, and we haven't seen much of each other."

The admiral sat heavily down at his desk and began toying with a carved-ivory paper knife. He was whistling softly through clenched teeth.

"Go on," he said.

"When I came down here on this Intelligence assignment I looked forward to picking up the old threads again. But there seemed to be some barrier between us that I couldn't break through. Bill seemed changed in some way, more withdrawn, almost evasive. I just couldn't pin it down. And then something rather odd happened. He knew, of course, what I was doing here, and one day he asked me how my investigations were going. I told him I was worried because it was beginning to look as though my quarry was someone in a very responsible position with legitimate access to highly restricted information."

The admiral looked up sharply.

"Was that wise of you, Gardner? Surely, in your position, that was a breach of security in itself?"

"Looking back at it now, sir, I suppose it was. But Bill is my oldest friend, and after all he's actually in charge of the

whole project. As it turned out, my telling him may actually
have given me my first important clue. He didn't bat an eye-
lid when I told him, but he looked at me very hard in a
rather peculiar way and then changed the subject a bit
abruptly."

"Not very conclusive evidence, surely?"

"Maybe not, sir, but knowing him as well as I do it was
very odd behavior. And then three days later I heard he was
unexpectedly going off for a week's leave."

"Yes," said the admiral, "he came along to me and said he
was feeling a bit under the weather and could do with a
break. He's certainly been looking rather strained and over-
worked lately, and I thought a spot of leave would do him
good. There's nothing particularly sinister about that."

"Well, sir, as I said before, I haven't proof of anything, but
I have a ghastly hunch it all adds up to something. This
morning, when he went off on leave, I took the liberty of following him to the station. I gather from the booking office
there that first of all—and this is another very curious thing—
he booked a ticket to Brixham, of all places, and then suddenly changed his mind, took a ticket to Waterloo and hopped
on the London train that was just due to leave. Whether he
spotted me arriving at the station or not, I don't know, but
something mighty peculiar seems to be going on."

He looked at his watch.

"His train arrives in London in three-quarters of an hour.
With your permission, sir, I'd like to ring Admiralty and get
them to put a man on his tail just in case he's up to something. If we lose track of him in London I'd better go to Brixham myself and see if anything odd's going on there."

The admiral was staring blankly at the middle of his desk.
He had the sagging look of a man who had just been told of
the death of someone very close to him.

"I don't believe it, I just don't believe it," he said, clearing
his throat noisily. "If you must, you must, I suppose. But on

the evidence you've produced so far I couldn't possibly authorize any more positive action."

He picked up the telephone. "Scratch, get me on to Admiralty, as quick as you can . . . on the scrambler."

He waited until the call was through, and then handed the receiver across to Gardner.

"Hullo . . . Admiralty?" said Gardner. "Put me through to Department 503, please. Urgent . . ."

2

The man sitting at the left of the rear bench opposite Platform 6 on Waterloo station was not a criminal on the run. If he had been, he would have been the despair of the police, for he looked so ordinary that he was almost impossible to describe. Medium height, brownish hair, nondescript eyes, fairish complexion, wearing a plain navy-blue suit, white shirt, sober tie of indeterminate pattern, dark gray socks, black shoes, no hat. Distinguishing features—none. Mr. Fisk's appearance was ideally suited to his job.

He had been waiting there since just after twelve o'clock, glancing from time to time over the top of his outstretched *Evening News*—now at the jerking minute hand of the station clock, now at the platform where the train was already seven minutes overdue, and sometimes at the faces of the anonymous crowd hurrying back and forth or sitting patiently, like himself, waiting for someone to arrive.

It suddenly occurred to him that, for all he knew, he might not be the only person on that station waiting for Captain Howard to arrive.

Almost exactly at twelve-thirty the train could be seen entering the platform. Mr. Fisk made no move to get up as the train braked to a standstill and began to disgorge its passengers. From where he was sitting he could look straight down the platform past the ticket collector. Presently among the bobbing heads and shoulders he picked out a figure with a trim ginger beard and a green hat, carrying a suitcase in each hand.

As Howard gave up his ticket and came through the barrier he looked quickly around him, half expecting trouble. But he did not notice the unobtrusive man absorbed in the middle page of the *Evening News,* nor, as he went on through the booking hall to find a taxi, did he observe him quietly fold up his newspaper and unhurriedly get to his feet.

For once there were plenty of taxis, and Howard got one almost immediately. He handed the suitcases to the driver, said, "United Services Club, please," and got in.

Outside the station the taxi turned left along York Road, threaded its way past St. Thomas's Hospital and crossed the river by Westminster Bridge. Big Ben was striking the three-quarter hour as they came to a halt at the traffic lights before turning right onto the Embankment. Howard looked back at the following traffic. Immediately behind were two or three taxies, a bus and other miscellaneous vehicles. It all looked innocent enough. The driver of the nearest taxi caught his eye, but only because the man happened to be wearing dark glasses. The traffic moved on, and they turned east along the Embankment past Scotland Yard. Surrounded by the roar and bustle of London, Howard began to feel more at his ease.

They turned first left and then right again into Whitehall. Opposite the Whitehall theater, with Nelson's Column looming ahead of them, they were again held up by the lights. Howard, glancing back through the rear window, found the same taxi close behind him. The driver with the dark glasses was leaning back and talking to his passenger.

It was ridiculous, of course—hundreds of taxis every hour must use this same route from Westminster Bridge to Trafalgar Square—but Howard suddenly had a hunch that he was, after all, being followed.

He decided to put his hunch to the test.

As the lights changed and the traffic surged forward into Trafalgar Square he tapped on the driver's window. "I'm sorry," he said, "I'll have to go back to Waterloo. I seem to have left my glasses in the train."

"O.K., sir." Instead of continuing left into Cockspur Street as he had intended, the driver turned up toward the National Gallery. To get back into Whitehall he had to follow the one-way circuit round Trafalgar Square. Through the rear window Howard saw the other taxi following on their heels. But still that didn't mean anything; this was a perfectly legitimate route for Charing Cross Road or the Strand.

Opposite the National Gallery Howard rapped again on the window. "As you were! I've found them in another pocket. So sorry!"

"I don't mind, sir," grinned the driver. "I'm quite happy to go on making rings round Nelson till midnight so long as you'll pay the fare."

Soon they were heading west again into Cockspur Street, having made a complete circuit of Trafalgar Square. The same taxi was still close behind them, and Howard was now thoroughly alarmed. It could mean only one thing—Tony Gardner had tumbled onto the truth, and the hunt was on.

He must make an immediate and drastic change of plan. Somehow he had to shake off this immediate pursuer. It would be foolish to go to the United Services Club now—it would be stiff with fellows he knew. Yet it was essential to get rid of his luggage—he couldn't cart it about with him all afternoon. No good dropping it in at the club or a railway cloakroom; he would only be setting a trap for himself when he went to pick it up again. He wondered what a professional spy would have done in the circumstances. The most important thing was to keep calm and think quickly.

"Another change of plan," he called to the driver. "Don't go to the United Services. Take me to Brown's Hotel instead."

"Anything you say, sir."

The taxi continued along Pall Mall, turned up St. James's, wriggled left and right into Arlington Street and was brought to a halt by the traffic lights by the side door of the Ritz.

"What's on the clock?" asked Howard.

"Four and ninepence so far, sir."

"Well, look, here's ten bob. I'm late for my lunch appointment, and I'm going to hop out here. Could you take my bags on to Brown's Hotel and tell them to hold them for me? I haven't booked, but tell them I'll contact them early this afternoon. Keep the change."

"Thank you, sir. What name shall I say?"

"Tell them . . . Mr. Hitchcock."

"Mr. Hitchcock. O.K., sir, you leave it to me. Better hop out now, the lights are changing."

As the traffic began moving forward into Piccadilly, Howard jumped out of the taxi, skipped dangerously between a Daimler and a Harrods van, and gained the pavement on the Ritz corner. He became aware of an irritated hooting of car horns behind him, and out of the corner of his eye he caught a rapid glimpse of the pursuing taxi stationary in the middle of the traffic like a half-tide rock in a turbulent river. The driver with the dark glasses was leaning across the driving seat, somewhat astonished, as his fare, a hatless man in a dark suit, got out, slammed the door and hurriedly thrust a fistful of silver into his hand.

For a moment Howard hesitated, combing his mustache with his forefinger, wondering whether to slip quickly into the bar of the Ritz or cross over to the other side of Piccadilly. He walked briskly along the shadowed pavement under the colonnade, scarcely able to resist the temptation to look behind him. Beyond knowing that his pursuer was wearing a dark suit he still had no idea what he looked like, and he felt this put him at a disadvantage. On the other hand, it appeared that he had only one pursuer to contend with—for the moment—and he had at any rate drawn the scent away from his luggage.

He decided against the Ritz. He walked on past its front entrance, crossed Piccadilly by the traffic lights at the beginning of Green Park, and jumped onto an eastbound Number 14 bus as the lights changed to green.

He went up to the top deck and sat in one of the rear seats. No one followed him up the stairs, but it was possible of course that his pursuer was riding inside, on the lower deck. As the bus drove past Burlington House toward Piccadilly Circus, Howard had a few moments to review the situation. The thought suddenly struck him that if the game was really up he would simply have been arrested as soon as he arrived at Waterloo. The fact that he had not been arrested must mean that, so far, he was merely under suspicion. If that were so, then he must avoid giving any impression that he was behaving unnaturally. All his actions must appear normal and unhurried.

The thought made him feel considerably better, as though he had been granted a temporary reprieve. He realized he was hungry. The bus was now swinging round Piccadilly Circus and entering Shaftesbury Avenue. He remembered an excellent little French restaurant less than a stone's throw away. At the next bus stop he got off, sauntered across the road and turned the corner into lower Wardour Street, forcing himself not to look back as he pushed open the restaurant door.

Gravely the proprietor inclined his head toward him from behind his desk. *"Bon jour, m'sieur."* An elderly waiter, smiling as though he remembered him as an old and valued customer, showed him to a table at the far end of the room. Howard ordered a simple meal of rump steak and salad followed by cheese, a half bottle of Pommard to go with it, and a glass of Amontillado as an *apéritif*.

No one that could possibly be identified as his pursuer had yet followed him into the restaurant. He did not deceive himself into thinking he had so easily thrown off the hunt, but there was no sign of it for the moment. He leaned back in his chair, stroking his pointed beard with the finger tips of his right hand, savoring the promising aromas of honest French cooking and the decent, unpretentious atmosphere of the room.

The steak proved to be tender and succulent. He deliberately lingered over his food and wine, reflecting that it might well be his last really civilized meal for a very long time. It provided him, too, with a breathing space in which he could, in comparative calm, make his plans to meet the new situation.

The first and most important thing he had to do was to ring the Paddington number and get in touch with the horrible little man whose name he did not know but whom he had privately nicknamed "Ratface." He must arrange a meeting and warn him of the way things were going. He must also telephone Brown's Hotel about a room for the night. Sometime during the next couple of days, he supposed, he would have to drop a line of explanation to poor Marjorie. . . . Then his appearance was altogether too conspicuous: for one thing, his gray-green tweeds were not quite the thing for a man about the West End. Then . . .

He pushed away his empty plate and frowned into the luminous crimson depths of his wine glass. The more he thought about it, the more he realized he had a busy afternoon ahead of him. With such a tight schedule it was important to do everything in the right order. He pulled a box of matches out of his pocket and began making notes on the back of it in his neat calligraphic writing:

Ratface
Browns
Clothes
Barber
Chemist

He considered the list thoughtfully, and then put a ring round "Barber" and with an arrow moved it up to third place. Presently, struck by a sudden idea, he smiled to himself and added: "Phone harbor master." Finally satisfied, he put the box back in his pocket and signaled to the waiter for his bill. It was time to get moving. He wondered if "the enemy" was waiting for him outside. If so, he must dispose of him before he did anything else. The situation reminded him of one of his more unpleasant wartime episodes in submarines. During the German invasion of Norway he attacked an enemy cruiser through a heavy destroyer screen just before midnight and had to spend the rest of the night and all the next day being intermittently depth-charged, creeping slowly away with a nearly flat battery. Every time he thought he was clear and came up to have a look, there was a destroyer so close it seemed to be looking straight down his periscope.

Standing at the cash desk waiting for his change, he looked across to the window. Above the lace curtain he had a clear view of the other side of the street.

"I hope you enjoyed your meal, monsieur?" said the proprietor, placing the change on the front of the desk.

A hatless man in a dark blue suit was standing on the opposite pavement, looking into a tobacconist's window—a little too casually, Howard thought. He seemed to be eating something, a bar of chocolate perhaps. Howard smiled, turning toward the proprietor.

"Yes, indeed I did, thank you. It's made me feel a different man."

He put on his hat and went out into the street. With deliberate unconcern he paused to light a cigarette, watching the back view of Mr. Fisk over the flame of his match. That his emergence from the restaurant had been observed in the reflecting window of the tobacconist's was indicated by a scarcely perceptible freezing of Mr. Fisk's shoulders and a momentary cessation of the movement of his jaws. With the comforting sensation of good food and wine under his belt Howard felt a distinct psychological advantage over an opponent whose tactical situation had obliged him to content himself with a mere snack. He even felt an amused sympathy for him.

On a sudden impulse he decided to press home his advantage. He crossed the street and entered the tobacconist's shop, almost brushing Mr. Fisk's shoulders as he did so. There were no other customers in the shop, and it took him under a minute to buy a packet of cigarettes and come out again. Mr. Fisk had moved out of sight, but looking neither to right nor left Howard recrossed the street, turned into Shaftesbury Avenue and began walking at a brisk pace toward Piccadilly Circus. It was a lovely afternoon. There was a bit of a breeze about and the sky held a threat of more wind, but the sun was shining and the air had a delicious late-September mildness. Howard was surprised to find he was almost enjoying himself. If he had read the situation correctly, his last move would have disconcerted his pursuer and convinced him that Howard was unaware of being followed. He must continue to let him think so. But time was pressing, and he must somehow get rid of him before very long.

At the Circus he dived into the Underground. There were a lot of people milling back and forth, and there seemed a good chance of losing his pursuer in the bustling movement of the crowded mezzanine booking hall. But when he re-emerged into daylight on the south side of Piccadilly and stopped to buy an evening paper from the newsvendor on the corner, a quick sideways glance showed him that Mr. Fisk had already reached the top of the subway stairs, less than five yards behind him.

Howard tucked the newspaper under his arm and continued westward along Piccadilly. He had no particular plan of action in mind. He was working from hand to mouth, as it were, hoping that chance would provide an opportunity of throwing off the pursuit without exciting suspicion by unusual behavior. Perhaps this wasn't going to be so easy as he had imagined.

At the same time he began to be aware of a growing discomfort in his intestinal regions. With a wry smile he reflected that in all the books of fictional espionage he had ever read, the characters never appeared to be under the necessity of attending to the body's natural functions. Yet here he was in real life, and, pursuit or no pursuit, something would have to be done about it—and pretty soon.

The elegant display of men's suits, underwear and sporting apparel in Simpson's windows suggested an opportunity of solving at least one, and possibly both, of Howard's problems. He turned into the doorway, walked quickly down the few steps into the front shop and went straight through to the shirt department opposite the staircase and the lifts. He was about to inquire of one of the shop assistants when, halfway up the first flight of stairs, he saw the door he wanted. He took the stairs two at a time and disappeared into the "Gentlemen's Toilet."

Mr. Fisk saw his quarry turn toward the staircase, but when he reached the foot of the stairs Howard was not to be seen. He could not tell whether he had entered the toilet or gone on up toward the next floor. But Mr. Fisk was no fool. He had no intention of getting involved in a game of hide-and-seek through the building and running the risk of letting Howard slip between his fingers. From his present position he could see the staircase and the lifts and both the Piccadilly and Jermyn Street exits.

He went across to the shirt counter and spoke to one of the assistants.

"I've arranged to meet a friend of mine who's doing some shopping somewhere in the building. If I go upstairs and try to find him I may miss him. Presumably I would do better to wait for him down here?"

"I would think so, sir. He couldn't leave the building without passing through here."

"There are no other exits besides the two I can see from here?"

"No, sir."

"Thank you very much."

When Howard emerged from the toilet five minutes later he failed to spot his pursuer mingling with the customers in the shirt department. Deciding to leave by the back exit, he walked down the steps into the shoe department and came out into Jermyn Street, fairly confident that he had shaken free at last. To make sure, he turned the corner into Duke of York Street and crossed over to the book-lined window of Herbert Jenkins, the publisher. But here, reflected in the glass, he observed to his dismay the brief movement of someone stepping abruptly backward out of sight round the corner behind him. It happened so quickly that in the next moment he wondered if it had really happened or was merely a fabrication of his heightened imagination.

With a mounting irritation he walked on down the street toward the greenness of St. James's Square. He was beginning to feel a pricking sensation in the back of his neck, and although it was not a particularly warm day a trickle of sweat ran down under his shirt from his armpit. He looked at his watch. It was after 2:45, and the afternoon was already slipping away.

At the bottom of the hill he turned right. Facing him, in the northwest corner of the square, he observed the entrance to the London Library, and immediately remembered that a cousin of his, a rather dry-as-dust military historian, had once taken him into it. He decided to go in. Quite what he would do once he was inside he did not know, but he had a vague memory of a confusion of dimly lit corridors and thousands of books on many floors; surely in the intricacies of that labyrinth he could somehow shake off this maddeningly efficient bloodhound.

He walked up the steps, ignoring the "Members Only" notice which faced him, pulled open the inner swing door and went in. Through the tall window of the entrance hall he looked back into the sunlit square and saw the now familiar figure of his pursuer approaching along the pavement. He crossed to the center of the hall and made a pretense of looking up a book in one of the drawers of the "Author Catalogue" card-index cabinet. A few seconds later Mr. Fisk came in. Howard immediately shut the drawer and walked unhurriedly to the back of the room, mounted the short flight of stairs and disappeared through the door leading to the "Science and Miscellaneous" section of the library proper.

3

Mr. Fisk was now faced with something of a dilemma, as Howard had hoped he would be. He was still not sure whether his quarry was aware of being followed or not, and he had seen him enter the library with so much assurance that it did not occur to him that Howard was anything but a bona fide member. Never much of a book reader himself, he was rather overawed by the hushed, august atmosphere and felt uncomfortably conscious of being an outsider, a non-member, trespassing in an alien world of literature and learning. Experience told him that his best move was to stay near the entrance, yet he could not be absolutely sure that there was no other exit somewhere at the back of the building. He did not want to call attention to himself by making the sort of inquiry which had been natural enough in a store like Simpson's but would seem extremely odd here. He came to a quick decision to follow Howard up the stairs.

Reaching the doorway at the head of the stairs he found himself confronted by an apparently endless series of narrow corridors walled with metal shelves and intersected by transverse gangways. For a moment he hesitated, taken aback by the sight of more books than he had ever seen in his life. The whole scene struck him with a singular eeriness. A few naked bulbs provided a minimum of permanent illumination, the lighting to each corridor being separately controlled by an individual switch. Prominent signs requesting members to "switch lights off after use" appeared to be strictly obeyed, for the corridors were tunnels of darkness and confusing shadows.

Mr. Fisk's sense of being a trespasser came on him with redoubled force. There was no one in sight, but he could hear Howard's footsteps moving rapidly away down one of the farther corridors, clanging on the metal gratings which served as footplates between each floor. He moved to his right along the first gangway until he reached the end corridor. He was just in time to see Howard momentarily caught in a distant pool of light as he vanished through a doorway into what appeared to be another section of the library at the rear of the building.

He heard him climbing a short iron staircase—and then silence.

Reason told him that Howard was probably looking for some book or other, and that he was now standing in front of the relevant shelf browsing through its pages. Yet the tingling on Mr. Fisk's scalp indicated a growing apprehension that Howard might be leading him into some kind of trap. For the moment, it seemed, he and Howard were the sole inhabitants of the library—or at any rate of this particular section of it. So far he had been the hunter and Howard the quarry, but he was beginning to have an uneasy feeling that the tables might have been turned. Beyond the bare facts he had been given at the Admiralty that morning he knew very little about Howard, and it occurred to him for the first time that Howard might be a dangerous man who was prepared to use force if necessary. Supposing he had lured him into this empty library in order to dispose of him?

For perhaps a quarter of a minute he stood where he was, listening intently. He could hear nothing but his own breathing and the muffled hum of distant traffic. By looking up between the gratings overhead he could see through to the floor above him. He was not normally a particularly imaginative man, but he now had a sudden nightmare vision of floor upon floor mounting endlessly to the sky and descending below him into the bowels of the earth, a bibliographic Tower of Babel from which he could never escape and in which he was condemned to live in perpetual terror, playing cat-and-mouse with Howard throughout eternity.

He shivered and pulled himself together. He reminded himself that his mission was simply to keep an eye on Howard and report on his movements, and so far, he had to admit, Howard had done nothing that could be regarded as particularly suspicious.

He walked boldly down the corridor in Howard's wake, his footsteps clattering on the gratings with a loud metallic sound which reminded him of the engine room of a large ship. When he reached the doorway through which Howard had disappeared he found that he was, as he had expected, in another section of the library exactly similar in plan to the other—with the exception that the floors here were not metal gratings but smooth slabs of a semi-opaque greenish composition. On floors like that a man on tiptoe could walk very quietly indeed.

Mr. Fisk turned to his left and mounted the iron staircase to the floor above, and as his eyes reached floor level he observed that the lights were on in the farthest corridor. A brief flicker of shadow moved on the bookshelves at the far corner, and there was a rustling sound as of someone turning the pages of a book.

No sooner had Mr. Fisk reached the top of the stairs than the rustling abruptly ceased. In the silence which followed, his fingers unconsciously tightened on the cold iron of the handrail. Then, with a slow deliberation, soft footsteps began moving up the hidden corridor. The shadow on the corner grew larger in rhythmic jerks. Somewhat alarmed, Mr. Fisk stepped quickly across the gangway and flattened himself as well as he could in the darkness of the nearest corridor.

As he did so, the footsteps halted. There was a loud click, the far corridor lights went out, and then the footsteps resumed their deliberate approach. In a moment they would reach the corner of the corridor in which Mr. Fisk was concealed. He was aware of a dryness in his throat and a rapid increase in the rate of his heartbeats. He intended not to let Howard see him if possible, but he was tensed and ready for action if necessary.

When the figure emerged across the end of Mr. Fisk's corridor, illuminated by the overhead light above the staircase, he saw that it was not Howard after all. It was an elderly gentleman with a yellowing white mustache and a sharply-boned, aristocratic nose surmounted by an old-fashioned pince-nez. As he walked slowly along, his lips moved, silently mouthing the words of a book held close to his face. At the head of the stairs he shut the book abruptly, tucked the pince-nez into his waistcoat and went shakily down to the floor below.

Where, then, was Howard?

Mr. Fisk's deflated alarm was succeeded by a new anxiety. Had Howard already given him the slip? Had he managed to climb unheard to a higher floor and somehow got back to the front of the building? Or was he even now lurking in the shadows behind him, waiting until the old gentleman was out of earshot?

In all the years he had been doing this job Mr. Fisk had never met a situation he disliked more than this.

He moved stealthily down the darkened corridor toward the back of the building, walking on the balls of his feet, often holding his breath to listen, turning his head sharply at imagined sounds. At the end he turned and came back along one of the parallel corridors. By the time he had returned to the harsh light by the staircase he had worked himself into a state of near panic. With the unnerved instinct of a man who, unable at last to stand the strain of the unseen, breaks rashly out into the open to attack his hidden foe, he now ran along the line of corridors, switching on every light he could find. But still Howard was nowhere to be seen.

Mr. Fisk was about to beat a retreat back to the entrance hall when he heard the sudden sound of rapid footsteps somewhere overhead. Standing by the staircase, he looked up. A man had begun climbing the stairs—two floors, perhaps three floors, above him. He could not see him clearly, but he had a distinct impression of greenish tweed trousers. He felt sure it was Howard. Ashamed of his momentary outbreak of panic, Mr. Fisk pulled himself together and began to climb the stairs after him.

Of course . . . the roof!

A building of this sort would be bound to have some sort of roof escape in case of fire. If he could catch Howard trying to get away by the fire escape that would prove that he was acting suspiciously.

He went on climbing steadily, and as he climbed he could hear the ringing sound of Howard's feet on the staircase some two flights above him. The building was higher than he had expected. In passing he noted the signs at the top of each flight—Third Floor, Fourth Floor, Fifth Floor. . . . He was nearly at the Sixth Floor when he realized that the sound of the footsteps above him had ceased. He looked up. The stairs appeared to continue upward for one more flight and then stop. Howard had reached the top floor.

For perhaps ten seconds Mr. Fisk stood and listened. His heart, pounding from the effort of the climb, was thudding like the propeller of a ship in ballast. A distant car horn, wafted plaintively on the air from somewhere in the direction of Piccadilly, served only to emphasize the silence and isolation of this upper floor. Of Howard there was not a sound.

More slowly now, and with eyes and ears alert for the slightest sign of his quarry, he continued his climb up the last flight to the Seventh Floor. When he got there Howard had vanished.

Mr. Fisk's eyes fell at once on a glass-paneled doorway not

six feet away from the head of the stairs. The fire escape. He looked out of the window and saw that the door opened onto a sloping catwalk built over the adjoining roof and presumably connecting with some other portion of the library building.

He tried the door. It was locked—and the key was on the inside.

Howard was still inside, too, then. And this time Mr. Fisk *knew* that he must be somewhere on this very floor. A slight chill ran down his spine.

He moved over to the nearest shelf, took down a book at random and stood apparently absorbed in reading. He stood thus for some five minutes, fighting down the returning tide of apprehension. He was beginning to wonder how much longer he could stand this sort of thing when he was startled by a new sound, a sound he had not expected to hear—the clanging of a metal gate.

Cursing himself for a fool, he put the book away on its shelf and hurried down the corridor in the general direction of the sound. It was somewhere to his right and toward the far end of the room. When he reached the middle gangway dividing the corridors he stopped dead in his tracks. At the end of the gangway, tucked against the far wall, was the enclosed shaft of a small lift. Its entrance was hidden from him, but he could see the light streaming out of it toward the back of the room. How was it that it had never occurred to him there might be a lift at the back of the building? If only he had not lost his head he would surely have spotted it downstairs.

Even as he sprinted toward it he heard the click of the operating button and the hum of the machinery as the lift began its descent. He reached the gate in time to get a clear view of Howard's head and shoulders descending to floor level. For a second their eyes met, but Howard's face was expressionless as his head sank rapidly out of Mr. Fisk's sight.

But not yet would Mr. Fisk accept defeat. He ran back to

the head of the staircase and began clattering down the stairs at breakneck speed. By the time he reached the Fourth Floor he heard the clang of the gate as Howard got out of the lift several floors below him, but without a pause he continued his rapid descent, intent only on reaching the front door of the library as soon as possible. Somewhere toward the bottom of the building he turned through a doorway into what he supposed was the front section of the library, and then realized that he had forgotten the way he had come in. Which floor was he on now?—all these damned corridors looked the same! For a moment he was utterly lost. Then, discovering another iron staircase, he took a chance and rattled down to the foot of it. Looking to his left he saw at the end of the corridor a large open doorway which appeared to lead into a big room at the front of the building. He sprinted on tiptoe along the corridor, slowed abruptly to a casual walk at the doorway, and found himself to his surprise in the front entrance hall. Immediately over his left shoulder was the short staircase by which he and Howard had entered. To his relief he saw out of the corner of his eye that Howard had only just emerged from the library proper and was even now descending the steps into the hall. Mr. Fisk, who had fully expected Howard to be ahead of him, crossed the foot of the stairs, went over to a table covered with specialized monthly journals and made a pretense of browsing amongst them.

Howard, for his part, was equally astonished to see Mr. Fisk. He had thought it unwise to hurry unduly, it was true— and he too had taken a wrong turning on his way from the lift —but he really thought his gambit had given him a clear enough lead. He had not reckoned with Mr. Fisk's determined speed and agility. So, after all that, he was back where he had started. The situation was getting rather desperate.

But as he reached the foot of the stairs he had an inspiration.

To the left of the high front window was the long desk at

which members were required to enter the titles of the books they were taking out. Howard went up to one of the three clerks sitting behind the desk.

"You know, someone ought to keep an eye on who comes in and out of this library."

The clerk, a polite, fair-haired young man in his early twenties, looked surprised.

"Why, how do you mean, sir?"

"Well, I don't want to make a fuss, but there's a man over by the table under the back window who's been following me about all over the place and generally behaving in a most peculiar manner. I don't know what he's up to, but I'm quite certain he's not a member. My guess is he's probably a book thief."

Without turning his head, the clerk looked conspiratorially toward the back of the hall.

"Which man do you mean exactly, sir?"

"Medium height, dark hair, navy-blue suit."

"Yes, I see the one you mean. I certainly don't know his face. Just a moment please, sir."

He went over to the senior clerk and spoke in an undertone. Then he came back to Howard and said:

"Thank you, sir, leave it to us."

"Good, but for God's sake don't bring me into it. I just thought you ought to know."

Howard raised a cheerful hand and went to the exit. Pushing open the swing door he could not resist a backward glance. Mr. Fisk, red in the face, was being politely ushered toward the secretary's office at the back of the hall.

Outside, Howard was lucky enough to find a taxi at once.

"Piccadilly Underground Station, please, in a hurry."

As the taxi swung out of the square into Charles Street he chuckled to himself. He wondered how long it would take his pursuer to talk himself out of that one. Long enough, at any rate.

At Piccadilly Circus he paid off the taxi, went down the

steps into the subway and slipped into a telephone call box. Before starting to dial, he held the receiver to his ear and carefully surveyed the booking hall for a full three minutes. I really think I've thrown the bugger off at last, he thought. He put four pennies in the box and dialed Paddington 2354. Almost immediately a high-pitched continuous buzz filled his ear. He rang off and tried again, but again he got the "unobtainable" signal. Irritably he put the receiver down, picked up the A-D telephone directory and looked up the number of Brown's Hotel. He rang the hotel and spoke to the girl on reception.

"Hullo, Brown's Hotel? My name is Hitchcock. My taxi driver should have left some luggage of mine with you this morning."

"Mr. Hitchcock? Just a moment . . . Yes, sir, I have a note here to say you would be getting in touch with us."

"Good. Can you give me a room at such short notice?"

"Single or double, sir?"

"Single."

"And how long for?"

"Just the one night."

"Very good, Mr. Hitchcock. A single room for one night only. That will be quite all right."

He rang off and tried the Paddington number again. But he still got the high-pitched continuous buzz. He dialed 100 and spoke to the operator. She came back with the answer that his Paddington number was temporarily unobtainable; a burst main had flooded a junction box and put a whole group of numbers out of action.

"Oh," he said. "Have you any idea for how long?"

"The engineers say it will be at least a couple of days."

"I see. . . . Thank you very much."

He put the receiver down, extremely perturbed. It sounded genuine enough, but just to be on the safe side, just in case Ratface had been rumbled and M.I.5 were tracing all calls made to Paddington 2354, he decided it would be advisable to leave the call box. He walked up the steps into Regent

Street and set off toward Austin Reed's. The sooner he did
something about making himself less conspicuous the better.
He didn't want that detective fellow on his tail again.

As he walked he pondered on the new setback. That his
"contact's" phone should be out of order today of all days was
a fantastic, disastrous coincidence. Now he had no means of
getting in touch with Ratface. He had never been allowed to
know his address; whenever he had had a message for him he
would ring the Paddington number and Ratface would give
him a rendezvous—always a different one, usually in some
teashop in one of the more genteel of the outer suburbs or in
some extremely busy center in the heart of London. But the
idiots had never visualized a simple contingency like a telephone breakdown! The most important rendezvous of all, and
he had no way of getting through. It was incredible. He could
not wait around in London for two days. In two days' time . . .

He would have to amend his plans—and that wasn't going
to be easy at this late stage.

At Austin Reed's he went straight down to the barbershop.
There were about a dozen customers sitting in the waiting bay, but the receptionist assured him that he would have
to wait only about ten minutes. He took a number tally, picked
a copy of *Punch* off the table and sat down. Flipping over the
pages of the magazine he suddenly thought of a possible solution to his problem.

He pulled out his diary and looked up a telephone number.
There was a telephone cabinet on the other side of the room,
but he could see it was occupied. He moved to a chair nearer
the cabinet and tried hard to distinguish what the caller was
saying. He was glad to find it was reasonably soundproof.

Presently the man put down the receiver and came out.
Howard stepped in, pulled the door to, and dialed a Chancery
number.

"Good afternoon," answered a woman's voice. "Prebble,
Smith and Carrington."

"Could I speak to Mr. Carrington, please."

"Mr. Carrington senior or Mr. Carrington junior?"

"Mr. Peter Carrington."

"That would be Mr. Carrington junior, sir. Who's speaking, please?"

"Captain Howard."

"Hold the line, please."

A moment's pause, and then an eager voice from the past.

"Hullo, Bill, this *is* a pleasant surprise."

"Hullo, Pedro," said Howard. "How are things?"

"Fine, thank you. Are you in London? How long are you up for? What about a drink this evening or—"

Howard cut it abruptly.

"Look, Pedro, I haven't much time. I want to ask you a big favor."

"Yes, of course."

"I've got myself into a spot of trouble, Pedro. Can't tell you what it's about on the telephone—it's just that I've done something rather stupid and got myself involved in something that's become too big for me. Don't worry, I don't want to borrow any money."

"You know I'd do anything to help you, Bill," said Carrington, speaking quietly and seriously. "What do you want me to do?"

"Get down to Brixham as soon as you can."

"Brixham . . . did you say Brixham?"

"Yes, I'll meet you there tomorrow evening or sometime the day after. But keep it under your hat at all costs. Don't try to find me, don't make inquiries about me, don't tell anyone you're expecting to meet me."

"O.K., Bill, of course I'll come . . . but . . . where shall we meet and so on?"

But Howard had already hung up.

4

Peter Carrington slowly put his receiver down and sat with his elbows on his desk, staring out of the window. In her chair at the side of the desk his secretary, young Miss Stephens, grateful for any chance, however temporary, of sinking back into her cloudland of romantic dreams, lowered her shorthand notebook onto her lap and began chewing the end of her pencil. Although he was entirely unaware of it, one of her dreams included the nice Mr. Carrington himself. Somehow, she thought, he didn't seem at all like a solicitor. Certainly he wasn't stuffy like the other partners. He had been in the Navy during the war, she had been told, and perhaps that accounted for it. She liked taking letters from him; he had an attractive deep voice, and it had none of the usual Public School affectations.

Waiting for him to emerge from the reverie into which the telephone call had plunged him, she studied his half-turned profile. The afternoon sunlight, slanting across it, emphasized the compact sculpture of cheek and jaw. His slightly protruding lower lip might have given him an air of sullenness if it had not been for the ironic wrinkles at the corners of his mouth. His eyes fascinated her. They were dark, brooding, skeptical. From the hints dropped by Mrs. Wharton, who worked on the switchboard downstairs, she gathered he had plenty of girl friends. She wondered if he made love to them all.

A warm blush spread slowly up to her face as she recalled her recurring daydream concerning Mr. Carrington. If he wanted to, she said to herself, I'd have to let him. She felt a sudden desire to run her fingers through his dark hair and rumple those untidy locks. She wondered why he had never married. He's too old for me, I suppose, she thought; he must be forty at least, nearly twice my age. The dream faded a little.

"Not bad news, then, I hope, Mr. Carrington?" she said.

Peter Carrington turned his gaze from the window, cupped his chin in the palm of his right hand and looked directly at his secretary, absent-mindedly clenching his little finger between his teeth. A sexy little thing, he thought, and as empty headed as they come. "What did you say?"

"I said I hoped it wasn't bad news—your telephone call, I mean."

"Oh," he said, smoothing the back of his head. "No . . . no, not bad news. Let's see, we were in the middle of a letter to the tiresome Mr. Ellis. Where had we got to?"

Miss Stephens looked down at her notebook. "Mutually convenient arrangements as to your taking possession."

"Yes. Er . . . taking possession of the property. New paragraph. We enclose herewith the replies to our preliminary inquiries, capital P and I, for your information and perusal. Would you kindly return them to us in the enclosed envelope, together with any observations you may have. Yours faithfully, and don't forget to put in a stamped envelope addressed to us. That will be all for the moment, Miss Stephens, but I shall probably need you again shortly as I may be going away for a day or two."

"Right you are, Mr. Carrington." Miss Stephens stood up

and went to the door. In the doorway she paused and glanced back at her boss, using the slant-eyed look she had been trying out lately, but he had already returned to his window gazing. Sighing, she shut the door.

Carrington picked up the telephone. "Mrs. Wharton, do you happen to know if my uncle is busy at the moment?"

"No, sir, as far as I know Mr. Carrington senior has no one with him. Shall I put you through?"

"Thank you."

His uncle's precise, scraping voice crackled in the receiver. "Peter?"

"Uncle, can I come in and see you for a moment about something rather urgent?"

"Yes, my boy, come along."

Mr. Albert Carrington's room was twice as large as his nephew's, but it was cluttered up with so many obstacles— filing cabinets, black metal deedboxes with the names of their owners in white letters, assorted piles of Law Reports, ancient newspapers, years-old correspondence parceled in brown paper and string—that it was difficult to move about the floor. In the far corner under one of the tall windows, against a background of bookshelves full of red-bound sets of Chitty's *Statutes,* the *Encyclopaedia of Forms and Precedents,* Gibson's *Conveyancing* and so on, sat Mr. Albert, blinking through steel-rimmed spectacles and making sucking noises through an empty pipe which curved down from his pursed-up lips. His rosy, shrunken figure, strangely like a Cox's pippin that has been stored too long, lent an exaggerated perspective to the great worn mahogany table which served as his desk. This table, too, had almost disappeared under an ever-rising tide of papers in wire baskets and documents tied in pink ribbon. Dust lay everywhere.

Peter Carrington picked his way toward a faded brown armchair, removed a sheaf of papers from the seat and sat down.

"Well, my boy," said his uncle, without removing his pipe, "what's the trouble?"

"I've just had a rather odd phone call from my old submarine commanding officer. He seems to be in some sort of trouble and wants me to go down to Brixham and meet him there tomorrow."

"Why in Brixham? Couldn't he have met you in London?"

"I don't know. He rang off before I could find out any more."

"But Brixham's right down in Devon, isn't it?"

"Yes, next door to Torquay and Paignton."

"Well, I must say it seems rather unreasonable to expect anyone to drop their business at a moment's notice and go off to Devonshire without so much as a word of explanation. What did you say to him?"

Peter took out a pipe and a tobacco pouch from his pocket and began packing the bowl with deliberate care.

"I don't know if I ever told you," he said, "about that rather grim episode off the coast of Malaya when I nearly got nabbed by the Japs?"

"I've heard something about it, of course, but you've never told me the full story."

"I was frightened as hell at the time, and since then I've done my best to forget about it. It was during July, 1944, when the Japs still held the whole of the Malayan peninsula and the Dutch East Indies. We were patrolling in the Malacca Straits and having rather a quiet time, with very little enemy shipping about, when Bill Howard, our C.O., suddenly got a signal from our base in Trincomalee telling him to go into a little bay somewhere north of Penang. A couple of Australian Fleet Air Arm boys had made a forced landing in the jungle, and we were to pick them up. The arrangement was that the Australians would go to a little promontory at the north end of the bay and precisely at midnight begin flashing a torch out to seaward. We were to take the submarine in as close to the shore as Howard thought safe, and then send in a rubber dinghy. We were given two successive nights for the pickup, and if the rendezvous was not made by the second night the operation was to be abandoned.

"Well, we found the spot all right, and spent a day looking through the periscope and reconnoitering the layout of the land from close inshore. The jungle came right down to the water's edge all along the shore, and at the head of the bay, some five hundred yards to the right of the pickup point, we could see a village of thatched huts under the palm trees, with Malayans going about their daily affairs. At midnight we were in position, about a mile off shore, waiting on the surface with the rubber dinghy ready on deck. I was in charge of the dinghy, and I was to take one leading seaman in with me."

He paused to light his pipe. Leaning back in his chair he watched the blue haze of smoke hovering in the air, as if seeking the reality of his memories in the dissolving mists of time.

"I hope I'm not boring you?" he said.

"No, on the contrary. I'm curious, though, to know what bearing this has on your telephone call."

"You'll see that presently, I hope. I'll keep it as short as possible."

"Go on," said his uncle.

"Well, no signal came. Howard decided to give them an hour's grace and then retire until the following night. Suddenly, at exactly *half past* midnight, we saw a flashing signal from the shore. But there was something odd about it. For one thing, it wasn't coming from the right place. It was coming from the head of the bay, very close to the position where we'd seen the village. And it wasn't the correct signal. We'd been told to expect the letter R—dot, dash, dot in the Morse code—but the signal flashing from the shore was dot, dot, dash—the letter U. Bill Howard and I had a quick discussion on the bridge, and he finally decided that there were so many fishy aspects of the situation—wrong time, wrong place, wrong signal—that it would be better to call it off and try again the following night. So we retired to seaward. During the next twenty-four hours, of course, we thrashed over all the possible explanations. The sinister explanation was that the Aussies had been captured and forced under torture to spill the beans. If so, perhaps they had tried to warn us by giving the Japs the wrong place and the wrong signal letter. Perhaps, we thought, it was no coincidence that in the International Code the single letter U stands for *You are standing into danger*. The curious exactness of the half-hour delay in the appearance of the signal could have been due to the Japs keeping a 'zone time' half an hour behind ours, so that midnight to them would be half past midnight to us. On the other hand it was quite possible that the Aussies had reached the coast a little late, and had not been able to find the correct rendezvous position in the dark—and perhaps there had been a misunderstanding about the signal letter. Anyway, we all agreed that we must give them the benefit of the doubt and put in an appearance on the second night.

"So, the next night, once again, we were waiting offshore at midnight, expecting trouble this time—guns' crews closed up, lookouts doubled, and so on. And at midnight—again, no signal. I don't know how often I looked at my watch during the next half-hour, but certainly during the last two minutes of it my heart was thumping away like hell. Then, sure enough, at half past twelve exactly the flashing started up again. It was still the same wrong letter, but at least this time it was a good deal nearer to the correct position. Bill Howard said to me: 'Well, Pedro'—he always called me Pedro—'you're the one who's going in. What do you make of it all?' I didn't like it at all, of course, but we obviously couldn't just feebly chuck in the operation on a mere *suspicion* of treachery. So it was decided we should go ahead. Howard took the submarine slowly in until we were only about a quarter of a mile from the shore. He made me take a rocket pistol to fire as a signal if anything went wrong, and then we slid the rubber dinghy into the water and the leading seaman and I started rowing toward the shore. The land looked horribly black, but the torch was flashing all the time. When we got to within a hundred yards or so of the beach I thought I could hear the sound of feet crashing about in the undergrowth, so we stopped rowing and listened. Suddenly a voice came out of the darkness, calling, 'Here we are. Bring the boat here.' But the owner of the voice was no Australian. It was high-pitched, rather excited, and I thought it had a distinctly 'oriental' flavor. 'Come on,' I said to the leading seaman, 'I don't like the smell of this. We're getting out of here.' We turned the dinghy around and started rowing like hell out to sea.

"And then suddenly all pandemonium broke loose. Machine-gun fire opened up on us from all angles. After the silence it was a shattering noise. I fired off my rocket pistol, and a couple of lovely red Roman-candle fireballs soared up in the air—a rather superfluous signal in the circumstances! Tracer bullets were coming at us from all over the place, whinging past our ears. One shot in the rubber dinghy and it would be all over for us. Then the submarine opened up with the four-inch and the Oerlikon, firing blind at the shore with nothing much to aim at but guesswork. But at least it attracted some of the machine-gun fire away from us. And then some larger gun suddenly opened up from the shore. I could hear its shells roaring past overhead—aiming for the submarine. This was a nasty surprise, for a submarine on the surface is terribly vulnerable—one direct hit on the pressure hull and she'd be done for, unable to dive. And the thought of this made me quite sick, because I knew that now Howard, by all the accepted rules, ought to dive and get the hell out of it.

"All this time we were rowing frantically. We were both out of condition, as we'd been nearly a fortnight at sea cooped up in the submarine with no exercise. It was going to be a question whether we could last the pace. I know I was praying feverishly. 'Please let them wait,' I thought, 'please let them wait for us.' Luckily we must have been invisible to the shore by now, or they would surely have hit us. The machine-gun fire was getting wilder. If only we could keep going, and if only Howard could wait for us!

"And then the submarine stopped firing. That could mean only one thing—Howard had decided he couldn't risk the submarine any longer. I looked over my shoulder. It was a pitch-black night, and there was no sign of her. We seemed to have been rowing for so long that I felt sure we ought to have been near enough to see her by now if she was still there. I must admit I was close to tears, I was so done in and desperate."

He stopped to wipe his handkerchief across his damp forehead. His uncle coughed and looked at Peter sympathetically over the top of his glasses.

"It must have been a nasty moment."

Peter relit his pipe, waited until it was going well, and continued.

"Yes, it certainly was. But worse was to come. A minute or so later the Jap machine guns also stopped firing. The big gun was still booming away, firing out to seaward, but apart from that there was this uncanny silence. And then the leading seaman suddenly stopped rowing and called out, 'Sir, can you hear something?' I stopped too and listened. It was the sound of a motorboat, and it was coming from the direction of the shore. And a moment later we saw a searchlight groping about in the water between us and the shore. That was why their machine guns had stopped firing! They were coming out to look for us. 'Come on,' I said, 'keep going,' and we started rowing again, though this time I really thought the situation was hopeless. They were coming nearer all the time—and then the searchlight caught us. Immediately a machine gun opened up on us from the motorboat, closing the range very fast. It would only be a matter of moments before the dinghy was punctured or one of us was hit, and then it would be all over. They would pick us out of the water, and that would be that."

He paused for a moment, puffing rapidly at his pipe, staring unseeing at the marble fireplace. He was several thousand miles away.

"Go on," said his uncle, "you can't keep me in suspense like this."

"It needed a miracle—and suddenly, out of the darkness over my right shoulder, the miracle happened. A cracking burst of machine-gun fire, a stream of tracer pouring into the motorboat and smashing its searchlight, and the dark shape of the submarine very close, swinging across to put herself between us and the enemy. A minute later we were alongside and being helped over the saddle tanks by Dicky Seymour—he was our gunnery officer. 'Don't worry about the dinghy,' he said. 'Leave it.' How we found the strength to climb up to the bridge I shall never know. By this time, of course, the shore guns had opened up again, and there was a hell of a racket going on. I heard Howard shouting down the voice pipe, 'Hard-a-port, full ahead together, dive dive dive,' and then we were tumbling down the conning tower, treading on each other's fingers.

"When we had got safely away to deeper water and had time to recover, I heard Bill Howard's side of the story. He had stopped firing because it was hopeless trying to compete with half a dozen machine guns spread over a wide arc, and he saw no point in letting the gun's crew get mown down to no purpose. He couldn't see the flash from the bigger gun, so he could only guess at its position, whereas his own gunfire was helping to pinpoint his position. So he sent everybody down below except himself and Dicky Seymour. He knew he ought not to risk the submarine, but as the big gun showed no sign of getting an accurate range on him he decided to chance closing in and see what was happening. And just as well for us that he did."

Mr. Albert took off his spectacles and began polishing them with his handkerchief.

"So," he said, clearing his throat, "you've agreed to meet him in Brixham."

"Bill Howard saved my life, uncle. He needn't have done, but he did, and he took a hell of a risk to do it. I can never forget that. Now *he*'s in some sort of trouble. No matter what that trouble is, if he thinks I can do anything to help, then I've got to do it. It's the least I can do."

"Well, yes, my boy, I think you're right. What about the work, what's on your plate this week?"

"Let's see. Today's Monday. Tomorrow afternoon I'm supposed to be seeing old Mrs. Winkworth—she wants to add another codicil to her will."

"Not again! The old trout will be changing her will right up to the day she dies. Ring her up and say you've been called away on urgent business."

"Then on Wednesday I'm due to attend at the Law Courts in the Hodge v. Hodge divorce case. I've handled this one personally all the way through, and I ought to be there really."

"I forget the details of the case. Is it complicated at all?"

"No, perfectly straightforward, undefended, usual evidence all tied up. I don't anticipate any trouble."

"Young Cartwright could handle that. Good experience for him. Your client doesn't have to appear, does he? If you caught a train sometime about the middle of tomorrow morning, you could come in first thing and brief Cartwright. Anything else?"

"Well, there are several things in progress, of course, all by correspondence. But I've no doubt a couple of days' delay won't hurt any of them."

"What about that company formation problem? How are you getting on with that?"

"Oh, the Dring Development Trust. Yes, there are a lot of different interests involved there, and I'm finding it pretty heavy going at the moment. I've done a first draft of the objects clause for the Memorandum and Articles, but I'm not satisfied with it. It's not an easy thing to sort out in the office with the phone going all the time, and I'd rather planned to spend next week end on it."

His uncle's eyes twinkled. "Well, now," he said, with a

barely concealed smile, "what could be better than a nice long train journey for a job like that? No interruptions, and you may easily find some time on your hands in Brixham. I suggest you take the papers with you and do a bit of homework on them."

Peter Carrington looked up at his uncle and grinned. "All right, uncle. Just as you say. Anyway, thanks for being so understanding. By the way, Howard asked me to keep all this very confidential."

"No one else shall know. I'll tell everyone you've been called away on urgent private affairs."

Peter stood up. "Well, thank you once again. I'll get back as soon as I can. Sometime on Thursday, I imagine."

As he reached the door, his uncle said, looking very seriously at him over the top of his glasses: "You're a solicitor, Peter, so I don't need to tell you to be careful. Just because a man has saved your life, it doesn't mean you owe him your soul. Don't allow yourself to get involved in anything that's —what shall we say?—on the wrong side of the law."

"Don't you worry, uncle. Bill Howard's not that sort of chap at all."

Mr. Albert took his pipe out of his mouth and waved it affectionately at his nephew. "Best of luck!"

5

Promptly at twelve-thirty the next morning the Tor Bay express began moving out of Paddington Station. Carrington checked the time against his watch, settled back in his corner seat facing the engine and prepared to enjoy the journey. One of the luxuries he always allowed himself was first-class travel on railways. A bachelor, living in London as he did, he had long ago given up owning a car of his own; he fretted at the waste of time involved in driving in London traffic, and it had become increasingly difficult to park outside his ground-floor flat in Campden Hill Square. Taxis and the Underground proved adequate for most of his transport requirements. To cope with the few occasions when he really needed a car he found it cheaper to hire one. He loathed flying, and for long journeys preferred to travel by rail.

Slowly gathering speed the train swung round in a slow curve through the back streets of Westbourne Park, Acton and Ealing and finally settled down to a westerly course for its long run to Devon—first stop Exeter. Carrington lit a cigarette and opened his midday *Standard*. On the seat beside him lay a copy of a new Graham Greene novel and a couple of paperbacks by Simenon. He certainly had no intention of allowing the Dring Development Trust to ruin the pleasure of the entire journey. And from the look of the only other occupant of the compartment, a rather timid little man in a black suit who, to Carrington's mild irritation, had joined the train at the last moment, just when he was beginning to think he had the compartment to himself, he did not expect the journey to be occupied in lively conversation.

A dining-car steward passed along the corridor announcing the serving of first luncheon. With nearly three hours to go before Exeter, Carrington decided to wait for the second sitting to help break the journey, and went on reading his paper. Presently the little man in the opposite corner opened a black briefcase, pulled out a packet of sandwiches wrapped in greaseproof paper and began eating in an apologetic, almost furtive manner.

Carrington groaned inwardly.

Without raising his head he glanced over at the offender. Inadvertently catching Carrington's censorious eye, the poor man dropped several egg crumbs in his embarrassment. This was too much. Carrington changed his mind in favor of the first luncheon after all, got up and went out into the corridor, sliding the door shut behind him with unnecessary vigor. There ought to be a law against it, he decided, and suddenly remembered an occasion in Venice two years earlier when a loud party of German hausfraus at an adjoining table had ruined a heavenly day in St. Mark's Square by eating sandwiches out of brown paper bags.

He walked forward along the corridor and entered the restaurant car. It appeared to be already full. He had almost decided he would have to retire to his compartment and endure the beastly man and his sandwiches when, at the far end of the coach, he spotted an empty seat at a table for two. The young woman occupying the other place at the table was sitting with her back to him, leaning on her elbow and looking out of the window, but in the short time it took him to reach the table he noted with approval the smooth line of a delicious shoulder under her blouse, a graceful neck and the deceptively simple but probably expensive cut of her hair.

"Excuse me," he said, "but is this seat reserved?"

She turned her head and met his question with frank blue-gray eyes and a friendly but impersonal smile.

"Not so far as I know."

"May I?"

"Of course. I'll move my clutter out of your way." She took her handbag off the table and put it on the floor beside her chair. Carrington sat down and began studying the menu. It took him less than half a minute to make his choice from the limited selection of alternatives, but he continued to hold the menu in front of him, casting surreptitious glances over the top of the card at the unusually attractive woman opposite him.

She's an absolute honey, he said to himself, putting the menu down, and then, attracted to her hands by the sparkle of a diamond ring, saw that she was wearing a plain gold wedding ring on the same slender finger.

He caught the waiter's eye and called him over to give his order. The girl, it appeared, had already given hers.

"And anything to drink with your meal, sir?"

"Yes, can you do me a bottle of Beaujolais, or something like that?"

"Yes, sir, we have a nice Beaujolais. A whole bottle or a half bottle, sir?"

He was about to order a half bottle, but changed his mind. "Bring me a whole bottle," he said.

When the waiter had gone he looked across at the girl. Her face was half turned, gazing out of the window, her eyes flicking across the wheeling countryside. She had the beginnings of a smile at one corner of her mouth.

He said, "There's something about half bottles I don't like."

She turned her head and looked directly at him. "Oh?"

"Well," he continued, "they're mean, unfriendly, unsociable things. If you order a half bottle you immediately set a limit to conviviality—it means you don't intend to drink any more than that one half bottle. If you order a whole bottle there's no reason to suppose you aren't going to follow it up with another. Besides, a half bottle clearly indicates that you mean to drink it by yourself, whereas . . ."

She smiled. "It's very kind of you, but I'm really very happy with my glass of water. Thank you all the same."

"Your Beaujolais, sir." The waiter had brought two glasses. As he set them down on the table there was a moment of hesitating confusion.

"Do change your mind," said Carrington.

"No, really . . ."

The waiter, now aware of his mistake, stood looking from one to the other, one hand half raised, not sure whether to remove the second glass or not.

"Please," urged Carrington, "you'll be doing me a favor. If I drink it all, it will send me to sleep after lunch, and I have some work to do. Besides, two glasses have miraculously arrived on the table."

She surrendered, laughing. When she laughed she had an odd and delightful way of wrinkling her nose.

The waiter uncorked the bottle and, after Carrington had sampled it and nodded his approval, poured out two half glassfuls. The wine, glowing in a moment of sunlight, trembled with the motion of the train. Carrington raised his glass.

"*Santé!*"

"Cheers."

"Perhaps I should introduce myself. Peter Carrington."

"How do you do! I ought to make it clear, Mr. Carrington," she said with mock formality, "that I'm not usually in the habit of drinking wine with strange men. Is this one of your standard opening gambits?"

"As a matter of fact," he replied, matching her bantering tone, "it's one I've never used before. It came to me on the spur of the moment."

"It's a good line. You must try it again."

"Now you're laughing at me."

"I'm sorry. I'm being beastly and ungracious. Ah, here's our soup. I'm absolutely ravenous."

Really, he thought, she has a terribly attractive voice. For no reason that he could think of, he had at this moment a sudden vision of a deep trout pool he had once fished in, many years ago, in the Wye valley.

"But I don't yet know *your* name," he said, between spoonfuls.

"I'm sorry. . . . Day. Jane Day."

"A lovely name, if I may say so."

"Oh, I don't know, it's always seemed rather 'plain Jane' to me."

"No, really, I mean it. It's the kind of name you might find in an old English ballad."

"Thank you very much!"

"You know, this sort of thing . . . 'Jane Day sat weeping at her window bow'r, as her soldier went off to the wars. . . .' Why, what's the matter?"

She was looking a little startled. "What on earth put that into your head?"

"I'm sorry, what have I said? It was just a bit of nonsense I made up as I went along. Now I've upset you."

"No, it's all right. My husband was killed at Arnhem three weeks after we were married, and your little ballad brought it all back to me for a moment." She looked out at the passing Berkshire farmlands. Strong winds were tossing trees and sending cloud shadows racing across the patchwork earth. In the middle distance a tractor was plowing a chocolate furrow in a field of stubble.

Carrington glanced up at her. Her eyes were a little sad.

Feeling a stirring of compassion, he looked down at his empty plate. "I'm sorry."

"Don't worry, it all happened a long time ago. Now, tell me about yourself. What do you do?"

"Oh, I'm just a dreary old solicitor. I batten on the more unpleasant sides of human nature. Our stock in trade is anger, jealousy, spite, greed, insecurity, mistrust. . . . We're stoppers-up of loopholes, purveyors of verbal quibbles, debasers of the Queen's English. Our motto is: 'I'm covered—are you?' We . . ."

She was laughing. "Steady on! I don't believe a word of it, and nor do you."

"Well—" He smiled and shrugged. "It's the family business, so I became a solicitor. As a matter of fact I rather enjoy it. Sometimes it's extremely interesting, and funny things are happening all the time. . . ."

And for the next half hour, while they ate their meal and the train ran steadily westward, he kept her entertained with stories about some of the more unusual legal cases that had passed through his hands. She was a good listener, watching his eyes with grave concentration as he rambled on, sometimes wrinkling her nose with amusement. Everything about her delighted him. She was—perhaps not beautiful in the classic sense of the word, but undeniably and disturbingly attractive. Flattered by her interest, he felt, and indeed was, in splendid form.

But when the waiter served their coffee he realized he had been talking too long. Leaning across to light her cigarette, he apologized for monopolizing the conversation.

"Not a bit. I've enjoyed listening. You seem to have an amusing life."

"Well, of course I've picked out the best bits. A lot of my work is just damned dreary. But enough about me. What about you? What do *you* do with yourself?"

"Me?" She hesitated for a moment, smiling down at her

coffee. "My job's very dull compared with yours. I work in a government office."

"One of the ministries?"

"Mmmm . . . sort of."

"Well, I'm quite sure you're not just a little fish in a great typists' pool. I'll bet you're personal private secretary to some pompous bigwig."

"It's not quite that, but . . . yes, I suppose you might call it something of the sort."

He smiled at her. "I must say you're giving me a wonderfully vivid idea of your job!"

"I'm sorry. The civil service, you know . . . forms, documents, memoranda, diplomatic papers, red tape . . . and we're not encouraged to talk about our work outside. Not that mine is particularly exciting or important, but . . . well, you know how it is."

"Forgive me. I'm being horribly inquisitive."

She signaled the waiter for her bill. She was still smiling, but he was conscious of a distinct drop in the temperature of their conversation. It was as though someone had left a greenhouse door open. He cursed himself for a stupid ass.

There was silence between them as the waiter made out their separate bills. Desperately he sought for something to say that would lead back to the sunnier mood of five minutes ago.

"Well," he said, "I hope it's pleasure and not business that's taking you down to the west country."

"Entirely pleasure. We've been working all-out in the department lately, and they've very kindly given me an extra week's leave. Isn't that nice?"

She was gathering her handbag and gloves together. Clearly the episode which had begun so promisingly was coming to a most disappointing conclusion.

"And you?" she said.

For a moment he was tempted to regain her interest by telling her about the strange telephone call which had occasioned his present journey, but remembering Howard's urgent injunctions to secrecy he decided to match her discretion with his own.

"A mixture of both, with me," he said. "I've a knotty problem over a new company formation, and there are so many interruptions in the office that my uncle—he's the senior partner—suggested I take a day or two off to work out the details in peace and quiet."

She stood up, holding out her hand. "Well, Mr. Carrington—"

He took her hand and held it. "Don't go," he said, "it's a long journey. . . ."

"No, after all that lovely wine I must go and have a good snooze, and I know you have some work to do. Thank you very much for entertaining me, and I hope your work doesn't take up *all* your time." Withdrawing her hand, she smiled. She was as lovely as ever, and friendly, but cool and poised and tantalizingly remote. He felt a clumsy fool.

"Good-bye, Mrs. Day," he said, lamely. "I hope we shall meet again."

"Well—you never know. Good-bye."

He watched her sadly as she moved toward the door at the front end of the dining car, moving with a grace that even the jolting of the train could not disturb. In addition to everything else, he now observed, she had beautiful legs and a figure that caused him to utter a sigh of infinite regret.

He sat down and lit a cigarette, looking gloomily out of the window, allowing his eyes to be hypnotized by the swooping of the telegraph wires, his thoughts wandering despondently amid the ruin of his enchantment. Halfway through his cigarette he suddenly stubbed it out, grinding it angrily in the ash tray, and returned to his own compartment.

He was relieved to find that the little man in the black suit had finished eating sandwiches and was now immersed in the *Daily Telegraph* crossword. Stepping over to his window corner he took the Dring Development file out of his suitcase, sat down, lit a pipe and stretched his legs. He tried to concentrate on the intricacies of legal phraseology, but the vision of his luncheon companion insisted on obtruding itself between his eyes and the impersonal typewritten pages. Presently he found himself nodding with drowsiness. Pulling himself up with a start he put the Dring file on the seat beside him, picked up the Graham Greene novel and began to read.

He woke up to find the train entering Exeter station. It was 3:17 by the clock; they were running only two minutes late. He was delighted to see that the man in the opposite corner was putting on his coat and hat, and when the train resumed its journey five minutes later, turning south now for the Tor Bay peninsula, Carrington had the compartment to himself. He stood up, yawned and stretched his arms. He felt an unpleasant dryness in his throat. He went along to the dining car and ordered a pot of tea. For some time he lingered over it, watching the farther door in the hope that Mrs. Day might appear and be persuaded to join him. But she did not appear, and when the train began slowing down for its scheduled stop at Torquay he paid his bill and returned once more to his compartment, feeling rather depressed.

He looked out of the window, but there was no sign of her among the disembarking passengers on the platform. Deciding that she had probably left the train at Exeter, he tried to put her out of his mind. In this he was only partially successful, but with a mere twenty minutes to go before the train was due to arrive at Churston, the junction for Brixham, he now began thinking, with a mounting sense of curiosity, about the mysterious rendezvous ahead of him.

As soon as he stepped down onto the platform at Churston he saw Mrs. Day getting out of a carriage further up the train. His spirits rose like a submarine surfacing into sunlight from a deep dive. She was wearing a loose bottle-green mohair coat with wide sleeves, and carrying a white suitcase. The blustery wind was blowing her hair all over her face.

She's quite, quite adorable, he decided, watching her for a moment with tender amusement as she put down her suitcase and pulled an orange scarf over her head, knotting it deftly under her chin. He walked along the platform toward her, a little hesitantly, not quite sure of his reception. As she picked up her suitcase again she suddenly saw him.

Their exclamations were simultaneous.

"Well . . . !"

She had to laugh. "Don't tell me you're going to Brixham too!" she said.

"Yes, I'm afraid I am. Here, let me take your bag."

"That's very kind of you. Is that our connection over there, do you think?"

"I imagine so."

They followed the half-dozen passengers who were now making their way across to the archaic little shuttle train that was waiting on the other side of the platform to take them on the seven-minute run to Brixham. Behind them, the express was already moving out of the station on the last lap of its journey, and soon it had become no more than a steadily diminishing roar in the distance.

They had a compartment to themselves. She took off her scarf, shook her head and began combing her hair back into shape.

"What marvelous air it is down here," she said. "Now that other train has gone I feel I've really shaken off the dust of London at last."

"Yes, you can smell the sea already."

A whistle blew, and the train started with a jerk.

"Do you know Brixham well?" he said.

"No, I've never been there in my life."

"What on earth made you choose Brixham for a holiday—at this time of the year?"

"Well, it had to be somewhere. Why *not* Brixham?" She had opened her handbag, and now brought out a lipstick and compact and began applying a little color to her lips. "Excuse me for doing this, but we arrived at Churston before I expected. As a matter of fact I have a couple of dear old aunts living in Torquay whom I haven't seen for ages, so I thought I'd have a few days in Devon, which I love, and pop in and see them. I don't like Torquay very much—too big for me—and I've always thought Brixham sounded a nice little place. So here I am."

She looked gravely into her mirror for a final appraisal of her make-up, returned the compact and lipstick to her handbag, crossed her legs and sat back in her corner, folding her coat over her knees and regarding him with a faintly challenging smile.

"If it comes to that, what about you? It seems a long way to come just to get away from the hurly-burly of the office for a couple of days."

"Yes . . . I suppose it is." He hesitated for a moment. To gain time he began filling his pipe. I must be careful here, he thought. "Keep it under your hat at all costs," Howard had said; "don't tell anyone you're meeting me." He had no idea what Howard might be afraid of, but if his former commanding officer, the man who had saved his life, said "anyone," he meant *anyone*. And that included especially anybody in, or on their way to, Brixham. Brixham was a small place.

"The thing is," he continued, glad to be able to tell her at least a half truth, "I used to know Brixham fairly well. I don't get much opportunity for sailing these days, but at one time I did a good deal and I used to put into Brixham quite often. You said yourself a moment ago that you felt you'd shaken off the dust of London. I feel the same. It's one of the few remaining unspoiled places on the South coast. The trippers come in here a good deal during the summer, I know, but out of season it settles back into the quiet routine of being just an honest little fishing port. I love it, and I'm sure you will."

"Funny, it didn't strike me you were a sailor. I thought all sailors were supposed to have blue eyes."

"Well, the Navy never made it a condition of entry."

"You were in the Navy, were you?"

"Not the regular Navy, just R.N.V.R. Hostilities only, as they used to say."

He lit his pipe.

"I'm terribly sorry," he said, suddenly remembering his manners. "Will you have a cigarette?"

"Not just now, thank you. We'll be arriving any minute." She picked up her scarf from the seat beside her and re-arranged it carefully over her hair. "Tell me," she said, "what sort of ships were you on? Or should I say in?"

He was about to tell her that he had been a submariner, but instinct warned him that he might be treading on dangerous ground. If, as seemed possible, Howard was in danger from someone, or running away from someone, a chance word dropped innocently in conversation by Mrs. Day, and over-heard in the wrong quarter, might indirectly link Howard with himself.

He stood up and looked out of the window. "I started the war in destroyers," he said, truthfully, and then abruptly changed the subject. "Hullo, I think we're arriving."

The train was indeed slowing down.

"How are you getting to your hotel?" he said. "By the way, where are you staying?"

"I'm booked at the Anchor. I imagine there'll be a taxi around."

He laughed aloud.

"Well, well, well—so am I. We'll share a taxi."

Sea gulls were screeching and wheeling overhead as they got out of the train.

They had given him a room on the first floor, overlooking the harbor. He threw his suitcase and his overcoat on the bed and flung open the window, filling his lungs with sea air. There was a smell of salt and seaweed and gutted fish. Smiling with pleasure he leaned out to survey the well-remembered scene.

Below him was the inner harbor, the very heart of the little port. Around it clustered the houses of Brixham with their gray slate roofs, climbing up and overtopping each other on the steeply rising ground, their windows looking down on the harbor like boxes in an amphitheater, spectators of an unending drama that was always the same yet always changing, and whose backcloth was the long stone wall of the outer harbor and, beyond it, the wide sweep of Tor Bay with Torquay to the north. The modest Anchor hotel was roughly in the center, facing northeast and out to seaward, separated from the inner harbor by only a narrow road and a low wall. Below Carrington's window the wall formed an embrasure which gave parking space for three or four cars. Looking to his right he could see where the road turned seaward, climbing past a row of narrow stone-fronted houses and then swinging right to disappear from view. To his left were the long sheds of the fish quay, and beyond them a frontage of miscellaneous houses and shops, including a small café and—most prominent of all —the Dolphin inn. Carrington smiled again, wondering if the beer was still as good as it used to be.

Against the fish quay half a dozen small trawlers were moored together, their wooden hulls grinding gently against the rope fenders. There were evident signs of preparation for sea, with a good deal of coming and going, careful stowing of nets, cleaning of port and starboard lights, singling up of ropes, and cheerful shouting across the decks. A young fisherman in a red woolen cap threw a bucketful of gash over the side, and a flurry of squawking sea gulls descended on it, quarreling loudly over the choicest scraps.

Beyond the sea wall, riding to anchor in the outer harbor,

was a large two-masted schooner with a black hull. Carrington admired her beautiful lines, wondering idly who she might be.

He decided to go for a walk round the town before dinner. Howard might be trying to find him; the more he showed himself about the place the better.

He washed his hands and face in the hand basin, changed into a blazer and slacks, and went downstairs. He half thought of finding Mrs. Day and trying to persuade her to come with him, but decided against it.

As he went out of the door he noticed a black Zephyr convertible with a fawn-colored hood parked on the other side of the road. It must have just arrived, for it had not been there when he looked out of his window upstairs. Its owner, a slightly-built man of about forty, was taking a suitcase out of the boot. Shutting the lid, he turned toward the hotel. Carrington had a sudden feeling that he had seen him before. For a second their eyes met. The man hesitated, looked hard at Carrington, opened his mouth as though he were about to speak, changed his mind and pushed open the door of the hotel.

Carrington, feeling vaguely disturbed, turned to his left and walked thoughtfully toward the fish quay.

6

The gale had almost blown itself out. Ragged clouds were still drifting steadily northeast in the wake of the storm, but the sky beyond was blue and clean. The sun, now flaming in a diffused crimson glory behind the town, threw long shadows across the road and warmed the faces of the old men lounging on the quayside. They were standing in little groups, leaning against bollards and empty fish crates, the peaks of their ancient caps pulled well down over their eyes, smoking their short-stemmed pipes and talking in quiet Devon voices, watching without envy the younger fishermen preparing for a rough night at sea.

Carrington strolled past the old men to the edge of the quay and stood looking down on the trawler decks. Catspaws of wind still ruffled the black water between the rounded hulls. One of the boats was already under way, going astern from the wall and swinging her bow toward the harbor mouth. While she was still turning, a ruddy face appeared at the side of her bridge and shouted some incomprehensible message across the water. A young woman walking along the road past the Anchor hotel, dressed in plain black with a green shawl over her hair, turned her head, laughed and raised her hand. At the same moment Carrington's eye was caught by the sight of Jane Day standing at an upstairs window, two or three rooms along from his own. He waved, but she was already in the act of shutting the window and did not see him.

Feeling a little chilly, he left the fish quay and began walking up the road toward the cliffs. When he had gained a little height he stopped and looked back. The trawlers were going out in single file, the rapid pup-pup-pup of their motors echoing quietly over the bay. The leader was already abreast of the anchored schooner Carrington had seen earlier from his bedroom window and of which he now had a fine bird's-eye view.

Suddenly the conviction came to him that the presence of this schooner had something to do with Bill Howard.

She was certainly a beauty, with her two tall masts, her taut shrouds and stays, and her raking bow curving forward into the long, tapering bowsprit. She combined grace and latent strength like a thoroughbred stallion. Gleaming with fresh paint and picked out with a single gold line along the rubbing strake, her black hull reflected the lapping of the waves at her waterline. She was lying to the wind with her elegant bowsprit pointing toward the town, and she had a boom out on the port side with a couple of tenders lifting to the gentle swell. Flapping lazily at her stern was a blue-and-white-striped ensign whose identity Carrington for the life of him could not recognize. It was, he suspected, one of those South American "flags of convenience" which give no clue to the real nationality of the owner.

This schooner, surely, was the reason for his summons to meet Bill Howard in Brixham. If his surmise was correct, it must mean that Bill was getting out of the country—and by an unorthodox route. What the hell could he have been up to? Clearly he was avoiding somebody, or afraid of somebody. "Don't try to find me, don't make inquiries about me," he had said. He must be expecting someone to be in Brixham who would try to prevent him from going. But who? The police? C.I.D.? Naval Intelligence? M.I.6.? Had he embezzled the mess wine fund, cheated at cards, run his ship aground while drunk, got mixed up with a fellow officer's wife, made improper advances to some sailor . . . committed murder—or treason?

None of the possible answers seemed at all feasible. As Carrington had said to his uncle the day before, Bill Howard just wasn't "that sort of chap."

Yet his experience as a solicitor had made Carrington aware of the Jekyll-and-Hyde, schizophrenic nature of the human animal, aware too of the improbable things even the most respectable citizen can be driven to under the stress of extreme pressure. What pressure, he wondered, could have brought an upright naval officer like Bill to the desperate point of fleeing the country?

He probed among his wartime memories for some clue to a possible weakness in the seemingly invulnerable character of his former commanding officer. He remembered him standing in the control room, a man of iron, decisive, imperturbable, calmly giving his orders as the sea around them resounded to the crash of depth charges. He remembered him poring for hours over the chart at night while the submarine was carrying out its surface vigil over the enemy's shipping route; often, lying in his bunk in the wardroom, he had watched him as he leaned his elbows on the chart table, the dim red bulb on the bulkhead casting a fiery glow over his ginger beard.

Yet he recalled, too, an occasion in the Mediterranean when they had fired torpedoes at an Italian tanker. He was watching Bill's face at the periscope as the first torpedo struck the target; he had never thought about the incident since, but he now remembered vividly how Bill had turned ashen white and jerked his head away from the sight of the explosion, drooping his arms over the periscope handles in an extraordinary gesture of despair. "Poor bastards," he had said, in a barely audible voice.

Certainly Bill had an introspective side to his character, but it was this aspect of him, combined with his passion for music and his delight in philosophical argument, which had made him more interesting than the average extrovert naval officer.

Carrington continued his walk up the hill, but then remembered that as Bill might be looking for him he must not wander too far from the center of the town. He turned and retraced his steps toward the harbor.

Now that the trawlers had gone, the fish quay seemed sad and deserted. He walked back round the harbor road and past the hotel. The sight of the black Ford car, still parked opposite the entrance, set him wondering again where he had seen its owner before. In the course of his legal work he came into contact with a large number of people—his own clients, the opposing parties in court, witnesses, press reporters, and so on. There was no doubt that the stranger, whoever he might be, had recognized *him* as someone he had once met. But rack his brains as he might, he could not place the man.

He began to have an uneasy feeling that the stranger might represent some danger to Howard's plans. It was about time Bill turned up and put him into the picture; he was floundering in dangerous waters—with no chart and no echo sounder to warn him of the shoals and rocks ahead of him. If the man was staying in the same hotel, as he appeared to be, Carrington was certain to run into him again. He would have to be careful. But he wished he knew what it was all about.

He strolled on, feeling rather low in spirits, meandering up and down the narrow streets adjacent to the harbor, his mind agitated with innumerable questions. He could be wrong, of course, and the schooner anchored so proudly in the roadstead might have nothing to do with the situation. But if not, why had Bill brought him all the way down to Brixham? Had he already arrived? Was he already on board the schooner? How would he make himself known to him? If he wasn't already here, how and when would he arrive? What sort of help did he want from Carrington—legal advice of some kind, perhaps?

And who was he afraid of?

The September evening was turning chilly. Carrington wondered what Jane Day was doing, and cheered himself up with the thought that he was bound to see her at dinner. He walked up the hill along the Berry Head road, then turned back when he had reached Uphams' boat yard. As he came into view of the harbor again, he looked across and saw that the door of the Dolphin was now open. He made his way back past the fish quay and went into the public bar.

He was the first customer. The landlord was new to him, but the room was exactly as he remembered it. He ordered a pint of bitter and remarked that it was a lovely evening.

"Yes, it's a little better now the wind's dropped."

He took his beer over to the window and stood looking out across the harbor.

"That's a fine schooner out there," he said.

"She came in a couple of days ago from Holland. Been refitting there, I understand."

"She's not a Dutchman, though, is she? I couldn't make out her flag."

"Well, she's flying the Uruguay flag, but that means nothing these days. I believe her owner's an American, but I'm not sure. They say she spends most of her time in the Caribbean, running luxury cruises for Yankee millionaires."

"She's a lovely ship, all right. What's her name?"

"The *Black Pearl*, they call her."

Carrington sat down at a table near the bar and began drinking his beer. The landlord wiped the counter, rolled a cigarette and propped his elbows on the bar.

"You on holiday here, then?" he asked, making conversation.

"Just a couple of days," said Carrington.

"You've missed the best of the weather, I'm afraid. Lovely spell we had a couple of weeks ago. Very busy we were then, with the trippers coming over on the boat from Torquay."

"All right for business, I suppose, but I must say I've always preferred Brixham quiet like this."

"You know Brixham, then?"

"Before your time, I think. I used to put in here sometimes sailing down Channel on the way from the Solent to the Helford River. But the last time I was in here was—let's see—six or seven years ago."

"Ah, yes, we only came here four years ago last July. If you're interested in sailing ships, now, you ought to get out and have a look at that schooner. They say she's a real luxury job down below—state cabins, bathrooms, white and gold paint and everything."

"Nothing would please me more. I'll have to try and arrange it."

"Well, they're usually in here of an evening. Come in later on—you'll find half the crew here—skipper, mate and all. I don't think you'd have much trouble wangling an invitation aboard."

"Thank you, I'll do that." He got up and pushed his beer mug across the counter.

"Same again, sir?"

"Please—and what about yourself?"

"That's very kind of you, sir. I'll have a half pint of ale, if I may."

"Well, the beer hasn't changed," said Carrington, watching him fill the glasses. "It seems to be as good a brew as ever."

"It's not a bad drop of beer. Of course, it's the way it's looked after that counts. . . . Well, your very good health, sir."

"Cheers."

They drank together in silence.

"It's quiet in here this evening," said Carrington presently.

"Usually is at this time of evening, when the season's over.

They'll start drifting in presently, though. And of course the schooner boys liven the place up a bit."

"What's the captain like?"

"Great big fellow with fair hair—a Swede by the look of him."

"And the crew? They're Swedes too, I suppose?"

"One or two, maybe, but the rest are a pretty mixed bag, mostly darkies—Jamaicans, I dare say."

"When are they off, do you know?"

"Ah, that I don't know. I did hear something about them picking up one or two passengers, but I don't suppose they'll be stopping more than a day or two. More's the pity."

Carrington finished his drink and put his empty glass down on the counter.

"Well, I must be getting along. May see you later, then."

"Yes, sir, they're usually in here by about half past eight. Cheerio, sir."

Carrington walked back to his hotel with the name of the schooner ringing in his mind. The *Black Pearl* . . . The *Black Pearl* . . . A romantic name, he thought, with a whiff of coral reefs and dark deeds about it.

He decided to have a drink in the hotel bar before dinner, hoping he might find Jane Day there. He pushed the door open and looked in.

To his disappointment she was not there. In the corner of the room was a small cocktail bar. Serving behind it, and looking a little theatrical under the concealed lighting, was Mrs. Porter, the buxom proprietress whom Carrington had already met when he first arrived at the hotel. She was talking to a shortish, dark-haired man perched on a stool at the bar. It was the owner of the black Ford.

Otherwise the room was empty.

Carrington was about to withdraw when the man turned his head and saw him.

"Good evening!" he called. "Come and have a drink."

And suddenly Carrington remembered who he was.

The last time he had seen him was in the wardroom of the submarine depot ship *Adamant* in Trincomalee. He was then commanding officer of one of the submarines operating from the sister depot ship *Maidstone* across the bay. He had never known him personally, partly because he was considerably senior to Carrington, and partly because his particular submarine had gone on to Australia shortly after Howard's had arrived out from England. For the moment he could not even recall his name.

His presence here in Brixham could hardly be a coincidence.

"It's very good of you, but . . . " Uneasy, Carrington hesitated. "I won't, if you don't mind. I've just had a couple of pints round the corner."

"Well, have a short one—a pink gin or something."

It would have been too pointedly ungracious to refuse.

"Well, if you insist. I'll have a gin and tonic, thank you."

As she was pouring the drink Mrs. Porter said, "Do you gentlemen know each other? Mr. Gardner . . . Mr. Carrington."

Gardner . . . of course, Lieutenant Tony Gardner, D.S.O., R.N. Carrington remembered now that he had sunk a Japanese submarine on his first patrol in the Malacca Straits.

"You know, Mr. Carrington," said Gardner, handing him his gin and tonic, "I've a strong feeling we've met somewhere before."

"Oh?" Carrington was polite, noncommittal, alert. "I don't think so."

"During the war perhaps, in the Navy?"

"Well, it's possible, I suppose, but I'm afraid I . . ."

But Gardner was relentless.

"Surely," he said, "you were in submarines?"

Useless to deny it—the man's memory was too good. "Yes, as a matter of fact I was."

"Trinco, I think, about the middle of '43? I was driving *Stingray* at the time."

"Yes, of course, I remember now," said Carrington, feeling rather hypocritical; and then, as if to excuse himself for not having remembered him, he continued: "But I think you went on to Australia fairly soon after I got out there."

"That's right. I was one of the first boats to go on to Fremantle. Well," he said, raising his glass, "it's a small world. God bless."

"Cheers."

Carrington was acutely aware that Gardner was watching him closely over his glass. He wished to God he had never come into the bar.

Gardner took out a silver cigarette case. "Cigarette?"

"Thank you." Carrington fumbled in his pocket for matches.

"Here you are—save the match." Leaning forward with his lighter, Gardner said: "You were Bill Howard's third hand, weren't you?"

Carrington felt like a chess player who has stupidly allowed himself to be checkmated in the opening moves of the game. Gardner had got him, well and truly—pinned down like a specimen butterfly in a showcase. There was an ironic smile on the lean face, and the eyes, regarding him intently under their long lashes, were cold and watchful.

"Yes," said Carrington, "I was."

To change the subject he knocked back his gin and said, "What about the other half?"

"Thanks, I will."

At that moment, to Carrington's relief, Jane Day walked into the bar. She had changed into a charmingly simple jersey suit of light gray. Carrington was delighted to see her, for more reasons than one. He waved a greeting.

"Hullo, come in! What are you drinking? I'm just in the chair."

"What a lovely idea," she said. "Could I have a whisky and soda?"

"May I introduce you?" said Carrington. "This is Mr.—

sorry, Commander is it now?—Commander Gardner . . . Mrs. Day. We met coming down on the train this afternoon."

Gardner smiled politely and shook hands with her. "How do you do?"

Carrington ordered a round of drinks.

"Do you live in this part of the world," said Gardner to Mrs. Day, "or are you just on a visit?"

"Just visiting," she said. "A few days' holiday, pottering about and calling on one or two relations. I'm very fond of Devonshire, but funnily enough I've never been to Brixham before. And you?"

"As a matter of fact," said Gardner, smiling, "I'm not sure that I ought to be here at all. I . . . I've bought a little yawl from a chum of mine in Falmouth, and he's sailing her round to pick me up here so that we can take her up Channel together. He should have got here this afternoon, but I dare say the gale has held him up. I must ring up presently and see if I can find out if he's started or not. If not, I may go on to Plymouth and join him there instead."

"You ought to get Mr. Carrington to go with you," she said. "You used to do quite a bit of sailing, you were telling me, Mr. Carrington."

"Ah, if only I could," said Carrington, feeling extremely skeptical of Gardner's story. "Alas, I've come here to concentrate on some legal work. Otherwise I'd have loved to."

"Mr. Carrington and I have just discovered we were in submarines together," said Gardner, addressing Mrs. Day but looking at Carrington.

Mrs. Day turned her head quickly.

"Oh!" she said, rather surprised, "I thought you said you were in destroyers."

Inwardly cursing Gardner for bringing the subject up again, he laughed and said: "Fortunately for you, the train arrived at Brixham before I could bore you with a full account of my naval career. I did start the war in destroyers, but when I heard they were taking reserve officers in submarines I rashly volunteered."

"Funnily enough," said Gardner, "he served under a fellow called Bill Howard who happens to be one of my oldest friends. Brilliant submariner. I never understood why he didn't get a V.C. for sinking those two Italian cruisers through a heavy destroyer escort. Were you with him then?"

"No,-I didn't join him until the beginning of '43. But of course I'd heard all about it."

"Do you ever see Bill these days?" Gardner's manner was perhaps a little too elaborately casual.

"No," said Carrington, thinking: Really, this fellow's being a bit of a bore. Mrs. Day couldn't possibly be interested in all this naval shop. "No, I haven't seen him for three or four years. We send Christmas cards to each other, but I'm ashamed to say that's the full extent of our correspondence."

"I remember once reading in one of his patrol reports about some cloak-and-dagger show in which one of his officers nearly got left behind with the Japs. That wasn't you, was it?"

"As a matter of fact it was, and if it hadn't been for Bill I don't suppose I'd be alive today."

"That sounds rather alarming," said Jane Day, turning to Carrington. "What happened?"

"One night I had to take a dinghy ashore to pick up some Australian airmen whose plane had pancaked in the jungle. When we got to the beach we ran into a Jap ambush. If Bill hadn't brought the submarine close inshore at great risk to himself, I'd have been a sitting duck."

"You must feel pretty grateful to him," said Gardner.

"Yes."

"And you haven't seen him for some time, or heard from him? Not even a phone call?"

Carrington looked at him straight in the eyes.

"No . . . Why are you so interested?"

"Nothing. I only wondered, that's all. . . ."

At this point Mrs. Porter announced that, though there was no immediate hurry, dinner was now being served in the dining room. Gardner at once suggested that the three of them might as well share the same table. Carrington, who had been hoping to have Mrs. Day to himself, was inwardly furious, but there was nothing he could do about it. When they had finished their drinks they went through to the dining room. They were shown to a table in the window bay, looking out onto the harbor. It was beginning to get dark, and the table lamps were already lit. As the season was over, the hotel was almost empty, and the only other diners were a honeymoon couple who sat at a corner table at the back of the room talking to each other in undertones.

The meal *à trois* was a distinct failure. Carrington, for his part, was in a foul mood. He was angry with himself for having, however unwittingly, allowed this situation to develop. He felt pretty certain by this time that Gardner knew, or at least strongly suspected, that Howard was going to be in Brixham, if he wasn't there already. Judging from Gardner's inquisitorial manner, he felt sure he boded no good to Howard's cause—whatever that cause might be. And now that Gardner had so unerringly identified him as one of Howard's wartime officers he would obviously assume that Carrington was in Brixham for some reason connected with Howard.

Carrington was angry, moreover, because he had been looking forward to seeing Jane Day again—and now here was this tactless fellow butting in where he wasn't wanted, boring everybody by insisting on talking shop all the time. Several times in the course of the meal Carrington tried to change the trend of the conversation, but remorselessly Gardner brought him back to the subject of Bill Howard. Carrington grew increasingly morose and monosyllabic. He kept glancing at Mrs. Day, trying to guess at her reactions to Gardner's boorishness, but her expression remained bafflingly neutral. She was amused, impartial, inscrutable, enchanting; half smiling, with her eyes fixed on her plate. He could not tell what she was thinking.

By the end of the meal he felt he could stand Gardner no longer. He excused himself, declined coffee, and stood up to go, saying he was going out to get a breath of fresh air. Mrs. Day made no move to join him. She and Gardner sat smiling up at him, waiting for their coffee . . . almost as if they were waiting for him to go. He felt he was cutting a somewhat ridiculous figure.

"Well," he said, addressing Jane Day, "may see you later, perhaps."

She continued smiling, but said nothing.

He left the dining room, sprinted upstairs for his overcoat, and went out.

7

It was a night of brilliant stars. He walked round the fish market to the outer arm of the quay and leaned his elbows on the sea wall, looking gloomily toward the outer harbor. The schooner's hull was now a barely distinguishable smudge in the darkness, but her two riding lights shone like newly risen stars of the first magnitude. Although the wind had dropped to a dead calm after the gale, from the sound of it there was still a bit of a sea running outside. Even in the inner harbor a gentle swell surged uneasily like the breathing of an exhausted whale, slapping against the lower landing steps at the end of the quay with a mournfulness that seemed in tune with Carrington's mood.

He was beginning to feel a little irritated with Bill Howard. If only Bill had warned him that he might run into Gardner! It was possible, he supposed, that Bill had had no idea that Gardner was going to be in Brixham. Perhaps he was finding it difficult to make himself known to Carrington now that Gardner had appeared on the scene. Or perhaps some unforeseen complication had made it impossible for him to get here at all. There were altogether too many ifs and buts and perhapses in this situation, and Carrington wished fervently that Bill would turn up and give him some kind of a lead as to what he wanted him to do.

The only thing he could do for the moment was to avoid Gardner as much as possible, and so give Bill every opportunity of making contact. For Gardner had now clearly put two and two together: *he knew, in fact, that Carrington could lead him to Howard.*

Meanwhile Gardner had managed—whether deliberately or not, he was not sure—to make him look ridiculous in front of Mrs. Day. He had to admit to himself that he had behaved badly during dinner, had made no effort to conceal his ill temper. Now she would have written him off as a churlish boor. The thought of this depressed him intolerably, for it was a long time since any woman had attracted him so strongly.

Out in the roadstead there was a sudden glow in the darkness, the switching on of a floodlight on the schooner's deck, and a moment later there came across the water the varying pitch of a motor launch maneuvering alongside her gangway. The crew coming ashore to the pub, thought Carrington, and he wondered if by any chance Howard would be in the boat. He could make out several figures descending the gangway, the sound of distant voices, and then the throbbing of the motor as the launch drew away and began moving toward the shore. He could see both its red and green side lights as it came toward him, veering slightly as it rode the swell, making for the entrance to the inner harbor.

Suddenly he was aware of light footsteps to his left, approaching him along the quay. Turning his head and peering into the half darkness, he saw that it was Jane Day, walking alone. As she came into the pale light of one of the quayside lamps he could see she was bareheaded and wearing a light raincoat. She came straight toward him.

"Is that you, Peter?" she said, using his Christian name for the first time. "Where on earth have you got to? You deserted me!" Her voice was quiet and friendly.

He was delighted, and rather surprised, to see her.

"Hullo, Jane," he replied, gladly accepting her move toward informality. "I didn't mean to desert you. I somehow got into a filthy mood and thought the sooner I cleared off the better."

"Well, you were a bit grumpy, certainly, but that was no reason to run off and leave me to cope. . . . He's a bit of a bore, your friend, isn't he?"

"No friend of mine," said Carrington, suddenly feeling cheerful again, "but I agree with you, he's a bore all right."

She looked out across the sea wall. "Isn't that a boat out there?"

"Yes, it's a launch from the schooner. The crew coming ashore for a drink, I imagine."

The boat was close in now, the green starboard light reflected brilliantly in the oily water. They stood together, watching the boat in silence as it came abreast of the wall and turned in toward the quay, going hard astern to take the way off and then gliding up to the steps. A gentle bump, a gruff command from the man at the wheel, and the grating clink of a boathook finding a hold on a ringbolt. Several men clambered out of the boat and up the steps and began making their way noisily along the quay toward the Dolphin. Carrington could not recognize Howard in any of them. Striding ahead of the rest was an unusually tall, well-built man wearing his peaked cap well forward over his face. He was smoking a large cigar. As he passed Carrington and Jane, the lamplight shone on his pale blond hair, stubble-cut almost to baldness at the back of his head. The aroma of the cigar came deliciously to Carrington's nostrils.

"That," he said, "must be the Swedish captain."

"How do you know he's Swedish?" asked Jane. "He could just as easily be German or Dutch from the look of him."

"Well, that's what the landlord of the Dolphin told me."

"You haven't wasted much time getting around! Is it a nice pub?"

"Depends what you mean by a nice pub. It's bare boards and no fancy trimmings, which is what *I* think a pub ought to be."

The launch was pushing off to return to the schooner. By now the shore-leave party had reached the door of the Dolphin and were silhouetted against the warm light streaming out onto the road from its long window. As they opened the door a sudden crescendo of laughter and noisy argument burst on the night air.

"Sounds like a good session brewing up," said Carrington. "Shall we go and see what's going on?"

"Come on, let's." As they fell into step Jane took his arm as naturally as though they had known each other for a long time. Carrington looked down at the softness of her hair with a quizzical smile of mingled surprise and affection, and as he did so a hot gush of emotion took him unawares somewhere in the pit of his stomach, coinciding subtly with the sudden and violent stirring of physical desire. For a moment he could not trust himself to speak. He drew his breath in sharply and looked up at the sky. He thought he had never seen it so full of stars.

They reached the door of the Dolphin and went in.

The light and the noise and the fug hit them with a staggering impact, and for a moment or two they stood blinking and smiling by the door. There was scarcely room to move. The bar, which had obviously been pretty full before, had now become uncomfortably crowded with the sudden invasion of the schooner party. The local fishermen had tactfully conceded to them the long table in the farthest corner from the door, and here four Jamaican members of the crew had already ensconced themselves, along with a couple of pale-faced middle-aged men in ordinary suits. The Jamaicans were at once perfectly at home in the midst of this noisy cheer-fulness, grinning at the locals with shining chocolate faces and brilliant teeth. The two landlubbers seemed out of their depth: they had the slightly sweaty look and uneasy smile of men who are not sure of their welcome. These, Carrington guessed, were two of the passengers, and he made a mental note to get around to talking to them before the evening was out.

The captain, by virture of his powerful voice and sheer bulk, had had no difficulty in reaching the bar. He was in-deed a somewhat alarming figure with his square jaw, beetling brows and protuberant eyes.

"Plenty glasses an' two bottles whisky!" he boomed, with-out removing the cigar from his mouth. He pulled out a five-pound note and slammed it down on the counter with the flat of his enormous podge hand. The landlord set up a tray of tumblers, and a young fair-haired officer standing at the cap-tain's elbow, whom Carrington took to be the mate, picked up the tray and balanced it high above his head on the tips of his outstretched fingers. Pushing his way through the crowd to the accompaniment of ironical cheers he brought it swiftly down to a perfect landing on the table in the corner. The captain followed, holding the two bottles of whisky to his enormous chest, moving ponderously through the packed bar with the inevitability of an icebreaker shouldering aside the outer fragments of an ice field. Standing at the table he emptied one of the bottles into the glasses in recklessly generous meas-ures, pushed the glasses round the table, and then turned to the rest of the room, holding the other bottle high above his head.

"Drink, my friends!" he cried, and started pouring whisky into the glasses of everybody within reach, regardless of what they were already drinking, brushing aside their protests. "Blooddy bilge water—that's no drink for a man. Come on, come on, have a real drink!"

The noise had become deafening.

Carrington had now managed to get to the bar and order two large Scotches for himself and Jane. He was feeling tremendously elated. He shouted to the landlord above the din: "Looks like dirty weather blowing up!"

The landlord turned his eyes to the ceiling in a gesture of mock despair. "What did I tell you? But who am I to complain!"

As Carrington handed Jane her whisky, the captain suddenly caught sight of her across the room.

"God in heaven! A woman, a beautiful woman!" he roared, holding the whisky bottle aloft. "Come over here, my dear, and join the party!"

Jane flashed an unspoken query at Carrington, but he only shrugged his shoulders and opened his eyes wide in an expression which clearly disclaimed all responsibility for the future course of events.

"Give a bit of sea room there to the lady!" cried the captain, waving a huge arm in her direction. Somehow the fishermen standing crushed almost shoulder to shoulder managed to open up a gap that was as miraculous as the parting of the waters of the Red Sea. Clutching Carrington's hand to make sure he went with her, Jane squeezed her way across the room.

"Move up there, boys, and mind your blooddy language!"

A moment later Carrington and Jane were sitting at the table between the captain and the mate, facing the cheerful Jamaicans and the two nervous passengers. The mate went through the motions of making introductions all round. There was so much noise that Carrington failed to catch a single name except that of Captain Gustavsen. The captain, who evidently fancied himself as something of a lady-killer, was soon engaging Jane in a heavy-handed flirtation, but Carrington found her hand reaching for his under the table. He gave it a protective squeeze and continued to hold it on his knee while he talked to the mate. The two passengers, when they spoke at all, spoke quietly to each other, but for the most part they smiled bravely and gazed glassily around the room.

One of the Jamaicans produced a guitar from under the table and began softly plucking the wires, lowering his head to listen to the first tentative chords. He was a tough fellow with a broken nose, and under his jacket he wore a dark jersey with the words BLACK PEARL in white letters across his chest.

Captain Gustavsen crashed his fist on the table.

"That's the way, bos'un. Come on, give us a song and liven this place up a bit."

The bos'un grinned at his captain, twanged a loud introductory chord which brought a sudden hush to the room, and launched into a West Indian calypso. Like puppets suddenly brought to life on invisible strings, the other Jamaicans began to jerk and sway, snapping their fingers, improvising harmonies, drumming their oyster-pink palms on the table. Soon the lilting rhythm of the music was running through the bar like a prairie fire. Through the haze of smoke the weather-tanned faces of the fishermen began to shine with pleasure, and even the older men were nodding their heads to the infectious thrumming of the guitar.

Carrington turned to the mate, yelling to make himself heard. "Looks like a good fellow, that bos'un of yours."

The mate had one of those chubby faces which seem creased in a perpetual smile. Unlike Captain Gustavsen, he spoke indifferent English. "Ja, ja," he said, "very goot fellow. Very strong wit' his hands . . ." and he held up his own hands, crooking the fingers to demonstrate his meaning. "Very strong, very goot fellow, ja."

"I was admiring your schooner this afternoon."

"Please?"

Carrington put his head close to the mate's ear. *"Black Pearl*—very fine ship!"

"Oh, ja! Very goot ship. Very strong, very quick, very fine ship."

"When do you sail?"

"Tomorrow night . . . maybe next morning."

"You've just come from Holland, I believe?"

"Amsterdam, ja. Now we go back to West Indies."

"You go a long way south, I expect, before you cross the Atlantic?"

"Please? . . . oh, ja, ja, to get the Trade Winds. That's right. First we go to Tangier, then Tenerife . . . then Antigua. You like to come?"

"Ah!" said Carrington, laying his hand on the mate's shoulder. "If only I could! But work and all that . . . you know. But I'd love to come aboard and have a look at her before you sail. Is there any chance of that?"

"Ah, ja! Tomorrow. Tomorrow evening maybe. That's right, come and have drinks on board tomorrow evening. I tell you what. We send boat at five o'clock for Mr. Hitchcock—"

"Who's Mr. Hitchcock?" said Carrington, pricking up his ears.

"Mr. Hitchcock, he is the fifth passenger. He will arrive from London on the train, and we pick you up at the same time. O.K.?"

"O.K.," said Carrington, picking up his whisky. "Five o'clock tomorrow. Well—*skoal!* and a good voyage to you."

"*Skoal!* and . . . how do you say? . . . bottoms up!"

They clinked glasses and emptied their drinks at one swallow. The mate reached across for one of the bottles and refilled the glasses. Carrington noticed that the bottle was nearly empty. He leaned over and spoke in Jane's ear.

"Back in a second. Must contribute my whack to the party!"

He got up, resisting the protests of the mate, and fought his way to the bar. He returned with another bottle of whisky and plonked it down on the table. By this time the mate had closed up alongside Jane, so Carrington edged round to the other side of the table and squeezed in beside one of the passengers. He was now facing the room and looking obliquely across the table at Jane, who was at this point firmly resisting Captain Gustavsen's attempts to top up her whisky.

"Captain!" cried the mate, indicating the new bottle and waving a hand in Carrington's direction. "My friend here—he buy another bottle."

Gustavsen stood up and leaned forward with his fists on the table, looking at Carrington with an aspect of terrible ferocity.

"You should not have done that!" he roared. "This is my party, and when Captain Gustavsen gives a party . . . What is your name, sir?"

Carrington wondered what he had let himself in for, but he met the captain's eye without flinching. "Carrington," he said.

"I like your face, Mr. Carrington. You are a good fellow, and I thank you. Have a cigar."

Carrington accepted the cigar with a silent sigh of relief.

"And your lady is charming and beautiful," continued Gustavsen, resuming his seat and turning to Jane. "You are a very lucky man!"

Jane looked across at Carrington with a mischievous smile and slightly raised eyebrows. Once again he noticed that attractive way she had of wrinkling her nose. He returned her smile, looking steadily into her eyes while he struck a match and lit his cigar. A faint blush came to her cheek, and she turned her head and began talking to the mate.

The calypso had come triumphantly to an end, and for a few moments there was a welcome lessening of the din. Carrington picked up the bottle and passed it to the passenger on his right. "Fill up and pass it round," he said. His neighbor, a pallid, loose-fleshed man with bleary eyes, aged somewhere between fifty and fifty-five and already almost completely bald on the top of his head, passed the bottle straight on. He half turned toward Carrington and smiled. "Thank you," he said, with only the merest trace of a foreign accent, "but I cannot drink these days like you young men."

"Well, it's turning out quite a party," said Carrington. "You're one of the passengers in the *Black Pearl*, I take it?"

"Yes, I am indeed. May I introduce myself—my name is Brünner—Carl Brünner."

"Peter Carrington." They shook hands. "Are you from Germany?"

"No, no, no," said Brünner, raising a hand in mild protest, "I am a Swiss lawyer, and my home is in Lausanne. You know it perhaps?"

"No, I can't say I know it. I've driven through it, but that's all. But tell me, how did you come to take passage on this schooner?"

"Well, I saw an advertisement in your London *Times*—I see *The Times* in my club at Lausanne every day. I have been working very hard this year—too hard, perhaps—and my doctor had been advising me to take a holiday. 'Go on a long cruise,' he said, but unfortunately, you know, I don't like big ships. Then I saw this advertisement. It seemed to be the answer. I am a good sailor, and I have always wanted to sail in a sailing ship. So I wrote to the address in Amsterdam—and here I am! Are you a passenger too, by any chance?"

"Oh no," said Carrington, "I wish I were. How many passengers can she take?"

"I understand there are to be five on this voyage, but one has still to arrive. There is Doctor Friedhof, who is a Dutchman, and an Englishman called Ramsey, who has just suffered a sad bereavement, poor fellow—they have stayed on board tonight—and there is myself, and my friend here who comes from Rotterdam. Perhaps I may introduce him. . . ."

He took his neighbor's arm.

"Mr. Van Krimpen . . . meet Mr. Carrington."

Carrington, reached across and shook hands. Mr. Van Krimpen had a long, hard-boned face and rimless glasses, and when he smiled his eyes shone eagerly through the enlarging lenses.

"I am very fond of your country, Mr. Carrington," he said, speaking rapidly and easily, but with a staccato emphasis on consonants. "In fact my wife is English. I have often been in your pubs in London, but never have I seen an evening like this. The noise! It is quite fantastic!"

And indeed the noise had once more been steadily increasing to the pitch where ordinary conversation had become impossible. In the midst of it all Carrington was suddenly aware of Gardner standing by the bar. He had a pint of beer in his hand, and he was smiling at Carrington. The smiler with the knife, thought Carrington, wondering how long he had been standing there, but feeling confident and genial from all the whisky he had been drinking he waved him a vague invitation to join them. Gardner pushed his way across and stood by the table, looking down at Carrington under his long eyelashes.

"Well, well!" he said. "Quite an evening!"

"Meet my friend from the *Black Pearl*," said Carrington, introducing him to the mate. "This is Commander Gardner, Royal Navy, and . . . but I'm afraid I didn't hear your name. . . ."

The Swede grinned and shook hands. "Jan Isaaksen," he said, moving up to make room for Gardner.

"Very beautiful ship, the *Black Pearl*," said Gardner.

"Oh, ja, ja, very fine . . ."

This is where I came in, thought Carrington, who was beginning to feel he had drunk more whisky than was good for him. He turned to Jane. Gustavsen was standing up and roaring for another bottle.

"How's it going?" said Carrington, offering her a cigarette.

"Hard work, but fun," she said, laughing. "But I don't know that I can stand the atmosphere in here much longer."

"Well, let's go."

"No, no, I'm all right really. We'd be terribly unpopular if we left now."

"No, dammit, it's nearly ten o'clock already. You leave it

to me." He stood up, went round the table and put his hand on Isaaksen's shoulder, interrupting his conversation with Gardner.

"Jan," he said, "please excuse us—the lady is a little tired after her train journey."

"No, no, you must not go," protested the mate, half rising from his seat.

"Really, we must," insisted Carrington. "But Jan, I'd love to come and see your ship. Does your invitation still stand?"

"Ja, ja, tomorrow evening. Ja, that's right, come and have drinks on board, all of you."

"Well, we'd love to," said Carrington.

"Yes, thank you very much," said Gardner, "that sounds splendid." He was looking up at Carrington as he said it.

"Don't forget," said the Swede, "we send boat at five o'clock, O.K.?"

"O.K. Five o'clock," repeated Carrington. "Good night, then. See you tomorrow."

Jane made a move to stand up, just as Gustavsen was putting the new bottle on the table.

"What is this?" roared the captain. "You are going?"

"Yes, we really must be off," said Jane.

"Nonsense. It is not yet—how do you say in England?—closing time! I will not hear of it."

"No, we really are going, Captain," interjected Carrington. "It was a long journey down from London today, and Mrs. Day is very tired, you understand?" And from behind Jane's head he gave the captain a deliberate wink.

"Ahaaah!" cried Gustavsen, closing one eye and prodding a thick finger into Carrington's shoulder. "Gustavsen understands. You are a naughty man, a very lucky fellow! Gustavsen would not interfere. . . ."

"Well, good night, Captain, and thank you for a grand party. But we shall be seeing you tomorrow evening on board. Mr. Isaaksen has invited us for a drink."

"Good, good! Good night, my children and—" with another

exaggerated conspiratorial wink—"sleep well!" And he slumped down at the table roaring with laughter.

Waving good night to Gardner and everyone at the table, Carrington and Jane made their escape, fighting their way to the door.

The cool night air smelled glorious. They stood for a moment taking deep draughts of it into their lungs. Then Jane tucked her arm into Carrington's, and they walked slowly, and a little unsteadily, back to the hotel.

They went upstairs together. In the first-floor corridor, outside her bedroom door, they stopped. She leaned against the door, smiling up at him.

"Good night, Peter."

"Good night, Jane." His voice was a little husky. He took her hands and pulled her toward him. She made no resistance, allowing her arms to slide up and lie relaxed on his shoulders. His hands, surprisingly strong, held her behind her body, urging her breasts against him. Her eyes were shut as she raised her face. Her subtle perfume and the indefinable scent of her hair affected him powerfully as he bent his head to kiss her. For the full space of two minutes their mouths, slightly parted, lay motionless together. It was a long and tender kiss, and when it was over she touched his cheek with her fingers. "Good night, Mr. Carrington." Then she turned abruptly and vanished into her room, shutting the door gently but firmly in his face.

He walked to his own room two doors farther along the corridor. Without turning on the light he went to the window and drew back the curtains to reveal the star-filled sky. With his hands in his trouser pockets he leaned his forehead against the cool glass of the window pane, feeling an ecstasy in his brain that he could not remember experiencing for many years.

He undressed in the dark, climbed into bed and fell asleep almost at once.

8

Blinking his way to consciousness he was puzzled by an unusual whiteness about the morning light on the ceiling. For a moment he thought it was the reflection of snow, but then realized this was hardly likely at the end of September. He turned his head on the pillow so that he could listen with both his ears for a sound he had been only dimly aware of as he emerged from sleep, a low sustained boom like a bass note on a tuba or the long moo of a cud-contented cow. The customary impacts of footfalls and voices in the street were unusually muffled. He sat up in bed. The view of the harbor he had expected to see was obscured by a white blanket of mist. And a moment later, vibrating through the moisture-laden air, came again the sound he was waiting for, the deep-throated siren of a large ship somewhere out in the Channel.

He got out of bed and went to the window. It was an astonishing change in the weather. The mist was coming in from the sea, advancing, rearing up, swirling forward like breaking waves in slow motion. He could see the parked cars opposite his window, the low wall beside them, and halfway across the inner harbor, but of the sea wall and the schooner in the outer harbor he could see nothing. The lace curtains at the sides of his window hung damp and limp, and a cobweb on the corner of the sill was jeweled with minute drops of moisture. The air was distinctly chilly.

He turned away from the window and went to the hand basin. He cleaned his teeth, washed, sluiced his face in cold water and rubbed it vigorously with a towel, making faces at himself in the mirror. He regarded with some distaste his tangled hair, his blue chin and the sagging lines under his eyes. "You unpleasant-looking bastard," he said aloud, "you drank too much whisky last night."

And yet, he thought as he lathered his face with shaving soap, she kissed me. Surely I'm not falling in love—at my age? Just an infatuation, he decided, frowning sternly at himself in the mirror, but he began humming loudly and cheerfully as the safety razor cut swaths in the stubble. He was one of the few men who actually enjoy the process of shaving. It made a clean start to the morning, and he found it conducive to thought. This was the time he liked to make his plans for the day. Now, in his mind's eye, he ran over the events of the previous evening, the disturbing meeting with Gardner, the unexpected and delightful access of warmth on the part of Jane after dinner, the noisy session in the Dolphin, and the news of the fifth passenger expected on the afternoon train.

I must meet that train, he decided, buttoning up his shirt.

When he left his room to go down to breakfast he almost bumped into Gardner coming up the stairs.

"Good morning," said Carrington breezily, feeling absurdly cheerful. "That was quite a party last night. By the way, any news of your boat from Falmouth?"

He was watching Gardner carefully, but there was scarcely a flicker of hesitation before his reply: "No, not really . . . I rang S.N.O.'s office last night and they thought he'd sailed but weren't sure, and of course it was too late to ring the boat yard. I'm going to try again this morning."

"I suppose this mist will hold him up a bit too."

"More than likely. Of course, if it doesn't clear up I don't imagine the *Black Pearl* will sail tonight either. Well, enjoy your breakfast. . . . I can recommend the kidneys and bacon." And he turned to open his bedroom door, facing Jane's room on the opposite side of the corridor.

"Thanks for the tip, I'll try them," said Carrington, grinning cheerfully. Honors even in that little skirmish, he thought as he skipped down the stairs to the dining room.

He breakfasted alone, taking his time over it. There was no sign of Jane, and he presumed she was treating herself to a lazy morning. She was, after all, on holiday. She must look marvelous when she's asleep, he thought, and tried to imagine what it would be like to wake up and find her hair tousled on the pillow beside him. It was a line of thought he found delightful but much too disturbing, so he made a deliberate mental switch and turned his mind onto the problem of Bill Howard. As he had heard nothing from him, he felt pretty certain now that the fifth passenger, the mysterious Mr. Hitchcock, would in fact turn out to be Bill himself. He must meet the train and warn Bill about Gardner. On the other hand, it might not be Bill. But if he was already in Brixham, perhaps already on board the schooner, why hadn't he contacted him by now?

He decided to go for a short walk, and then come back and do some work in the hotel lounge. There weren't all that number of hotels in Brixham, and if Bill wanted to contact him it would be easy enough for him to find him there.

He lit a pipe and went out of the hotel. Turning right he walked briskly along the front, bore left up the hill and followed the road past the boat yard toward the Berry Head hotel, puffing at his pipe, enjoying the exercise, taking a positive pleasure in observing the effects of the mist. Garden gates, stone walls, the road surface—everything was covered in a film of condensation. He could feel the moisture in his nostrils as he breathed. Pine trees loomed out of the whiteness with the delicate charm of a Japanese print. All sounds seemed woolly and distorted; and it was difficult to judge their direction.

Suddenly he had an instinct that he was being followed. Surely those were footsteps he could hear somewhere in the mist behind him? He stopped abruptly in his tracks and stood listening for a moment. He heard one belated footfall—and then silence. His pursuer had stopped too—or perhaps that had been the echo of his own last footstep? He wasn't sure. He went on, walking more briskly, but beyond the sound of his own feet he was certain he could detect another set of footfalls keeping in step with his own. When he reached the Berry Head hotel he stopped again and looked back along the road, but could see no one within the short range of visibility. And again that uncanny silence, broken only by the repeated moan of a foghorn out to sea. Yet he was convinced there was someone there in the mist.

Could it be Bill Howard? He waited for the full space of a minute, and then began walking slowly back the way he had come. Presently he came once more to a halt, hearing the now unmistakable sound of approaching footsteps. A moment or two later a dark figure emerged from the mist. Carrington's tensed muscles relaxed: it was a man in a dark jersey wearing a fisherman's cap, and as he passed Carrington he nodded his head and said, "Good morning." But, even as he passed, Carrington heard a new sound on the road ahead of him, the diminishing sound of a man sprinting softly on tiptoe in the opposite direction. Carrington continued walking, baffled by these indications of alternate pursuit and flight. Presumably whoever had been following him had now realized he was coming back on his tracks and had decided to beat a hasty retreat. In that case it could hardly be Bill Howard. But who was it? Gardner keeping tabs on him in case Bill contacted him? Perhaps someone else altogether?

He got back to the hotel without seeing or hearing anything more of his shadower, and at once went up to his room to collect the file on the Dring Development Trust. From his window he saw that in spite of the mist two or three of the trawlers had managed to nose their way back into port and were now beginning to unload their catches at the fish quay under a wheeling, screaming umbrella of sea gulls. Resisting the temptation to linger over the busy scene he took out the file from his suitcase and went downstairs to the lounge. It was an unexciting room furnished with green basket chairs, a few round wicker tables, a couple of oval wall mirrors and a large potted fern, but at least he had it to himself. He refilled his pipe and settled down to concentrate on his work.

About twenty minutes later the door opened. It was Jane.

"Hullo," she said. Her voice was low and conspiratorial. She was wearing the same loose green coat she had worn on the train, and was looking fresh and radiant.

"Hullo, Jane," he said, putting down his papers and rising to his feet. "Where are you off to?"

"Just going for a look around the town."

"You won't see much in this mist. I'll come with you."

"No, I know you've got some work to get on with, and there's a bit of shopping I must do. How about some coffee later on?"

"Good idea. There's a little café about four doors this side of the pub which looks reasonable from the outside. Meet you there at half past eleven?"

"Lovely." She blew him a kiss and vanished.

When he walked along to the café he felt the air had become noticeably warmer. The visibility had improved a good deal during the last hour; already he could see as far as the beginning of the outer breakwater, and overhead was a wide area of intenser brightness where the sun was trying to break through the mist.

Jane had not arrived. Except for a couple of stoutish elderly women and a solitary, studious youth reading a book through metal-rimmed spectacles, the café was empty. Carrington chose a table near the window, a vantage point from which he had a view of the whole harbor area. Almost at once he saw Jane coming along the road toward him. She walked beautifully, and he felt a tide of excitement rising within him.

She came in with a toss of her hair and a swirl of her coat, smiling when she saw that he was already there.

"Oh, this sea mist plays the devil with a girl's hairdo," she said as she joined him at the table.

"Nonsense, your hair looks marvelous. In fact I think you're looking particularly lovely this morning."

"Thank you, kind sir."

"You know, I think any minute now it's going to turn into a perfectly beautiful day."

"Do you really think so? I *would* like today to be a lovely day."

"Why today particularly?"

"It happens to be my birthday."

"No! Why, that's wonderful. . . . Hell, if only I'd known, we could have arranged some special celebration. Tell you what, I'll get Mrs. Porter to lay on some little extra for dinner tonight and we'll have the best bottle of wine we can find in Brixham."

She put her elbows on the table and cupped her chin in her hands, puckering her forehead with affectionate amusement at his boyish enthusiasm.

"That will make the second bottle of wine I've shared with you," she said. "But what about your commander friend? He seems to have established himself at our table."

"I'll tell him we are having a very private celebration and particularly want to dine alone tonight. I might even drop a hint, in a man-to-man sort of way, that I was planning to propose to you over dinner. Come to think of it, I might even do that very thing."

She laughed, stirring her coffee.

"Hullo, talk of the devil," he said, "there *is* the commander. Let's hope he doesn't spot us. Damn the fellow, I do believe he's coming in!"

Gardner entered the café, looked around and walked over to their table. It was almost as if he knew he was going to find them there. "Mind if I join you?" he said, sitting down without waiting for an invitation.

The waitress brought him a coffee.

"How's the legal homework coming along?" he asked, with an edge of mockery in his tone which Carrington found exceedingly irritating.

"Well, I managed to get in a useful hour on it this morning, and I hope to have another session this afternoon. And what about you? Have you found your boat yet? Did you manage to get through to Falmouth?"

"Yes, I got on to the boat yard after breakfast, and it seems my friend left at the crack of dawn this morning. Though with no wind to speak of I doubt if he'll make much headway against the ebb tide."

Carrington found himself distrusting Gardner's story about the boat more than ever. "It must be very tiresome for you to hang about like this," he said coldly.

Gardner had a way of always seeming to be smiling at some secret thought beyond the words he was speaking. "Oh, I don't know," he answered, "I rather enjoy mooching around. And Brixham seems to me to be the kind of place where anything might happen at any moment."

"What sort of thing do you expect to happen?"

"Don't you ever get that feeling about a place?"

"Sometimes," said Carrington. "Let's have some more coffee."

The conversation now became more general, with long uncomfortable pauses. Jane hardly spoke a word, and Carrington felt so irritated with Gardner for having interrupted their *tête-à-tête* that he was in no mood for making an effort at sparkling repartee. Yet in a particularly maddening way, even the awkward pauses seemed to be affording Gardner considerable quiet amusement.

Finally Carrington looked at his watch and called for the bill. "Well, the pubs have been open for some time," he said, looking at Jane; "what about a quiet glass of something along the road?"

"Splendid idea," said Gardner, bluntly including himself in the suggestion. "And the first round's on me."

Carrington raised his eyebrows at Jane, shrugging his shoulders in resignation. As she bent to pick up a glove that had fallen on the floor, she seemed to be having some difficulty in concealing a smile.

They walked along to the pub. The air had turned pleasantly warm. The sun was now clearly visible as a golden disc, and there were promising patches of blue sky overhead. At the door of the Dolphin, Carrington put his hand on Jane's elbow and said, "I'm just going to slip back to the hotel and have a word with Mrs. Porter about this evening."

"You're not leaving us?" said Gardner.

"I'll be back in five minutes. If you'd like to have a cool light ale waiting for me on the bar when I come back, that will be very nice."

When Carrington rejoined them they were engaged in a game of table skittles. Jane was standing at the table, about to make her throw. As Gardner walked over to the bar to collect Carrington's light ale, Carrington moved close to Jane and murmured: "All fixed. Mrs. Porter's producing some smoked salmon for us, and I've arranged for a bottle of Château Latour 1955 to be decanted and *chambré* in time for eight o'clock."

"That sounds delicious," she said, propelling the little wooden ball forward on its elliptical flight.

"You two sound as though you're hatching some plot," said Gardner, returning with Carrington's drink.

"As a matter of fact, we are," rejoined Carrington, speaking with the decisive, louder-than-usual voice of a man who has decided to say something unpalatable and feels he might as well say it now as later. "We're planning a little private dinner party tonight, for a very personal celebration—just the two of us. I—we—hope you won't mind if we . . ."

Gardner laughed and put his hand on Carrington's shoulder. "Don't worry about me, my dear fellow. I quite understand. I wouldn't dream of butting in."

"It's very rude of us, but—well, you know how it is."

"My dear Carrington, think nothing of it."

Jane was setting up the fallen skittles on the board, biting her lower lip to conceal her suppressed amusement.

They played a few more games of skittles, and had two or three more rounds of drinks, one of which Jane insisted on buying. Presently Gardner looked up at the clock over the bar.

"Luncheon is now being served at the Anchor," he said. "I'm feeling pretty hungry. Are you people coming?"

"Actually," said Carrington, looking at Jane with a mute appeal for support, "Jane and I had planned to make do with a sandwich lunch. I've already broken the news to Mrs. Porter."

Jane was standing near the window in a shaft of sunlight, holding her unfinished drink and smiling at them both with amiable neutrality.

"Oh," said Gardner, a little taken aback. "Well, it looks as though I shall have to eat my sausage-and-mash, or whatever it is, in solitary state. Never mind, have a lovely time, you two."

And then, just as he was closing the door, he turned back and said, "Don't forget, we all have a date on the jetty at five o'clock. *Au revoir, mes enfants!*"

When he had gone, Carrington said, "I hope you don't mind. Somehow I couldn't face spending another whole hour or so listening to that fellow talk."

"No, I'll be very happy with some sandwiches. Why don't we go and picnic somewhere by the sea? It's lovely and warm out now."

"Marvelous idea! Let's see what the landlord can find for us to eat."

They found a sheltered spot under the cliffs of a small bay on the other side of the peninsula. When they had eaten their meal they lay side by side enjoying the unexpected heat of the sun. They had taken off their coats to make pillows for their heads. She was wearing a simple dress of mingled deep-hued blues and greens.

The landlord of the Dolphin had done them well: four rounds of fresh ham sandwich, two bottles of beer and a few apples; and his wife had insisted on lending them a basket to carry them in and a rug to sit on.

Carrington could feel the sun burning through his shirt and trousers. The insides of his eyelids were a pale crimson, and when he half opened them the sun sparkled through his eyelashes with prismatic brilliance.

"Mmmm!" murmured Jane. "This is heaven."

"We ought to have brought our swim suits," he said.

"I've got mine back at the hotel, but I never dreamed it was going to turn out as hot as this."

"If it's like this tomorrow we must have a bathe. If you're still here tomorrow."

"So far as I know, I will be."

"What about your aunts in Torquay—when are you going to see them?"

"I don't know. Plenty of time for them. What about your work?"

"Oh, to hell with the work. It needn't stop me from bathing with you."

After a long silence she said, "You don't like Commander Gardner very much, do you?"

He considered this for a moment.

"I suppose he's all right, really, but he seems to have a genius for not realizing when he's not wanted."

"He goes on a bit sometimes, I agree, but I suspect he's quite a lot nicer than you think."

"You're probably right. But he has a maddening way of getting *at* me all the time."

She sat up and clasped her hands in front of her knees.

"You're a funny pair," she said, laughing and turning her head toward him. "You both seem to be waiting for something to happen, and you scratch at each other like a couple of fighting cocks sparring before the real fight begins. What's it all about?"

He did not answer at once, but lay with his eyes shut, wondering what to say next. He was terribly tempted to take her into his confidence and tell her the whole situation. It would be comforting to have someone to talk to about it. But again he hesitated, held back by the respect for secrecy which wartime discipline had rooted into him. Until he saw Howard he must abide by his wishes and keep his mouth shut.

"What's it all about?" he said, echoing her question. "I wish to God I knew. Tell me, do you believe this story of his about waiting for a boat to arrive from Falmouth?"

"Why, don't you?"

"I don't know. It seems an odd thing to do, to hang about here and wait for the boat to pick him up. The natural thing would have been to join his chum in Falmouth and do the whole trip up Channel together."

"Well, I hadn't thought about it. I don't know anything about sailing, but it would seem quite reasonable to me to wait and join the boat here. He probably couldn't get to Falmouth by the time he expected the boat to start. He wasn't to know it would be held up by the weather."

"Well," he said grumpily, "it sounds a bit fishy to me."

"As a matter of fact," she said, "I have a feeling he doesn't believe *your* story about coming down here to do some work."

"I don't care whether he believes it or not," he said belligerently. "It's true. The Memorandum and Articles for the Dring Development Trust—I'll show you the file, if you like."

She patted his arm. "Don't worry. *I* believe you."

For several minutes they did not speak, soaking themselves in the scorching rays of the sun. Then she exclaimed:

"This heat's terrific! I've got far too many clothes on. Would you mind if I took off my dress?"

"No, of course not."

"Can you undo me at the back?"

He freed the little hook at the top of her dress and pulled the zipper down to her waist. He was about to lean forward and kiss the nape of her neck when she stood up and began wiggling the dress over her hips and down to her feet. For a moment, as she stood there in her close-fitting black nylon slip, kicking off her shoes, the whole of her body made a dark silhouette against the sun. Leaning on one elbow he gazed up at her with admiration. Then she kneeled on the rug, laying her dress carefully on the ground beside her.

"There, that feels better."

"I think I'll follow your example," he said, and pulled off his shirt, leaving the upper part of his body exposed to the sun.

For a long time they lay on their backs, their arms relaxed full length at their sides, surrendering themselves to the embrace of the late-summer sun, saying not a word but supremely aware of each other's physical nearness. Presently Carrington moved his hand so that it lay under hers, palm to palm. She did not stir. She was lying so still that he wondered if she had fallen asleep. He began moving his hand slowly backward and forward, caressing the flat of her palm, and still she did not move. Scarcely breathing, she seemed in a blissful state of suspended animation, conscious of no other world beyond this radiant sun, the eternal murmur of the sea, and the magical ecstasy now flowing through her palm to the innermost fibers of her body. Gradually, as he continued to stroke her hand, he allowed a finger to press more firmly upward against the bowl of her palm, sliding between her fingers with the delicate insinuation of desire. The spell was broken. She clenched his hand, shuddering.

He raised himself on one elbow, looking down at her. Her eyes were open now, and she was looking up at him with a strange expression of sadness.

"You're very lovely," he said.

He lowered his head and kissed her on the mouth, without passion, and then buried his face in her hair. His hand, cradled on her waist, moved slowly up the side of her body until it came to rest on her shoulder. For several minutes they stayed motionless. Presently he moved his hand along her shoulder, pulling her strap gently but deliberately down her arm to the elbow. She made no resistance, but when he curved his hand over the naked roundness of her breast she gave a little moan and pulled his face toward her, kissing him with a vehemence which took him by surprise. Thrown off balance he shifted his arm to prevent his weight from falling onto her. As he did so, out of the corner of one eye he was suddenly aware of his hand braced on the rug beyond her shoulder, of the sunlight etching the individual hairs on his tensed forearm, and of his wrist watch with its black face and its green hands pointing to five minutes past four.

"My God!" he exclaimed, drawing himself away from her. "I'd no idea it was so late. Darling, I'm terribly sorry, but I've got to fly." And he sat up and began pulling on his shirt.

"What's the trouble?" she said, very near to tears, pulling her strap over her shoulder.

"I've got to be at the station at four-thirty to meet the train."

"Why—are you meeting someone?" She was kneeling on the rug and picking up her dress.

He had prepared his excuse beforehand, but now that he

knew he was in love with her he was finding it wretchedly difficult to lie to her.

"My firm are sending down an urgent packet by passenger train," he said, bending down to tie his shoelaces. "It's an important legal document which has to have my signature, and they didn't want to trust it to the post."

He felt he was making a very bad job of it. He glanced round at Jane. She was still kneeling, but she was now fully dressed and making up her face.

"Well, you mustn't be late," she said, pulling herself together. "You go ahead. I can look after myself."

"I wouldn't dream of it. The least I can do is to see you back to the hotel."

They walked back in silence, arm in arm. When they reached the steps of the hotel she turned and smiled at him.

"Thank you for the nice picnic."

"It was your idea. Sorry I had to break it up like that."

"Shall I come to the station with you?"

"No, it won't take me a minute to run up there and back. You go in and have a nice cup of tea. If I'm back in time I may even come and join you."

"All right, but don't forget we have a date for drinks on the schooner."

"Yes, five-o'clock boat. I'll be there. And don't you forget our birthday date tonight."

"I won't. Off you go, then, or you'll be late."

The smoke from the approaching train was already in sight as Carrington arrived at the station. Before going onto the platform he made a quick survey of the situation. The one thing he had been afraid of was that Gardner also might have decided to meet the train. To his relief the platform was empty.

In a few moments now he would find out whether, as he fully expected, Mr. Hitchcock and Bill Howard would turn out to be one and the same person. After all the uncertainty of the past twenty-four hours it would be a relief to learn what sort of trouble Bill was involved in, and why it was he had asked him to come all this way to meet him.

The train was entering the station. Suddenly, above the noise, he heard Gardner's voice close behind his shoulder:

"Come to meet the fifth passenger, Carrington?"

9

Concealing his surprise and irritation, Carrington forced his lips into the semblance of a bland smile and turned to Gardner.

"As a matter of fact I've come to pick up a small packet my office said they might be sending down from London. What are *you* doing here anyway?"

Gardner took out a cigarette case and offered it to Carrington. "Are you smoking?"

"Thank you. Not just now."

Gardner lit a cigarette and inhaled deeply. "A long shot, really," he said, allowing the smoke to escape through his nostrils. "There's just a possibility that an old friend of mine might be arriving on this train to join me in my trip up Channel. He wasn't sure he could make it, but I thought I'd come along on the off-chance."

They were both smiling, each certain the other was lying. They stood uneasily together, looking down the platform. Carrington was thinking hard. By delaying his arrival at the station until the last moment, Gardner had trapped him neatly. He cursed himself for his stupidity. Bill Howard would certainly not want to meet him here, with Gardner standing by. Yet Bill himself must have foreseen the possibility that Gardner—or whoever it was he was trying to avoid—might have guessed that he was the schooner's fifth passenger and might meet this train.

Once more Carrington wished to God he knew more about what was going on. He tried desperately to think of some diversion, some means of getting Gardner out of the way. But it was too late. So far as he could see, there was now only one thing he could do if Bill *was* on the train: he must get out of the way himself. The guard's van, he observed, was at the front of the train, immediately behind the engine; he would have to dive into the van and pretend to look for the mythical packet from London.

The train drew to a standstill with a grunting of brakes. Two carriage doors opened. Three rosy-faced schoolgirls in black gym tunics and white blouses came up the platform, swinging their satchels and chattering loudly together, followed more slowly by a couple of local women with heavily laden shopping baskets.

But that was all. There was no sign of anyone else.

A minute later, apart from Carrington and Gardner, and the guard, who was depositing a small mail bag and a bundle of newspapers on the platform, the scene was deserted.

The anticlimax was so surprising that the two men had to laugh. Gardner put his hand on Carrington's arm. "Don't forget your parcel, old man," he said with mock gravity, and turned away toward the exit. Although he was aware that Gardner was making a fool of him, Carrington nevertheless felt obliged to go through with the motions of making the necessary inquiries.

"Carrington, Carrington?" repeated the guard, shaking his head doubtfully. "No, sir. The only items for Brixham off the London train were what you can see on the platform there.

Still, I'll have another look round inside just to make sure, if you like."

"No, no, don't worry. I'm sure you'd have known if it was there. It may come tomorrow. Thank you very much."

"That's all right, sir. Sorry I couldn't help you."

Carrington was about to turn away and follow in Gardner's footsteps toward the exit when his eye was caught by an unexpected movement at the other end of the platform.

The door of the rear compartment of the train had just opened.

Emerging backward, stepping down from the carriage with some difficulty, was the figure of an elderly lady, heavily clothed almost to her ankles in black and gray. Her face was hidden behind a brown veil and large round dark glasses, and she supported herself on a heavy stick.

Carrington stood watching her, struck by a fantastic thought. A quick glance in the opposite direction showed him that Gardner had already left the platform and was out of sight.

He looked back at the old lady. She was now standing safe on terra firma, an erect, gaunt, formidable presence, rather tall for a woman, and she was in the process of draping an incongruously vivid yellow scarf about her neck. Then she looked up the platform and gave an imperious wave of her stick, calling loudly for a porter.

Carrington looked about him, but the guard had momentarily disappeared into his van and there was no one else in sight.

"Young man!"

The voice had a high-pitched north-country nasal boom, and it carried an unmistakable air of authority. Carrington began walking down the platform, convinced that this redoubtable figure of a woman was in fact Howard in disguise. He was fascinated by the attention to detail which had evidently gone into the preparation of the disguise: the black velours pancake hat, the single touch of color in the yellow scarf, the long black alpaca coat with its large shiny buttons, the high white collar in *broderie anglaise* ringed with a frayed velvet ribbon, the strings of jet beads, the thick dark-gray stockings, and the felt gaiters buttoned over the sturdy but slightly down-at-heel shoes. It was a magnificent tour de force, though he could not help wondering if Bill hadn't overplayed his hand a little. Was the disguise—especially the veil and the dark glasses—just a shade too elaborate to be utterly convincing?

As he drew closer to her he was actually smiling; at any moment he expected to hear some quiet word of recognition uttered in Howard's voice from behind the all-concealing veil.

"Can I help you carry your bags, madam?" he said, gazing intently at her.

"I don't know what's the matter with the railways these days," boomed the same dominating voice. "No one tells you when you've arrived at your destination, and you can never find a porter when you need one. Thank you, young man, yes, if you could help me with my bags I'd be grateful." And she pointed her stick at the carriage door.

He jumped up into the compartment and brought out two large brown leather suitcases, both of which had seen better days and now had to be secured with straps, and finally a string bag which appeared to contain nothing but knitting needles and balls of wool.

"I can manage that one," she said, taking the string bag and holding it in her left hand along with her black morocco handbag, "if you can manage the suitcases."

Slowly they made their way up the platform, she hobbling a little, taking the weight of alternate steps on her stout rubber-ferruled walking stick, and Carrington purposely keeping a little way behind her so that he could amuse himself by trying to find fault with the details of the disguise. He had to admit that it was brilliantly done. The fine gray hair, beautifully brushed and swept back to a neat bun at the nape of the neck, was the work of an artist. Where on earth did one go, wondered Carrington, if one needed a disguise as thorough and expert as this? And when did Howard learn to be such a damned fine actor? He was certainly putting up an impeccable performance. The voice especially . . .

They had nearly reached the ticket barrier when the woman turned to Carrington and said, "Shall I be able to get a taxi, do you think?"

"There's usually one waiting," he replied, "and if there isn't you never have to wait more than five minutes for one to come back."

When they came to the exit Carrington saw that there were two cars waiting.

One was a taxi. The other was Gardner's convertible, with Gardner sitting in the driving seat.

Carrington at once hailed the taxi and took the two suitcases straight over to it. The driver got out and began strapping them onto the roof rack. Carrington, observing Gardner climbing out of his car, turned quickly to the old lady.

"I wonder if you would mind if I shared this taxi with you?"

"Not at all, young man, you're being most helpful."

Gardner was hovering. He was looking very hard at the old lady. "I waited to give you a lift, Carrington," he said.

"Oh, I didn't realize you were waiting for me! I'm so sorry. Actually, I've already arranged to go with this lady and give her a hand with her luggage."

"Where to, madam?" asked the taxi driver.

"Well," boomed the old lady, "what I'm really looking for is a ship called the *Black Pearl*. Do you know where I can find it?"

Carrington cleared his throat loudly and put his hand under her elbow to urge her into the taxi. "I'm going there myself, madam, and I'll take you there," he said. He got in after her and shut the door.

Winding down the window as they drove off, he called out cheerfully to Gardner, "Sorry about that, old man! See you at the jetty!"

Looking back through the rear window he saw Gardner hurriedly getting into his car.

The old lady now began untwisting the knot of the veil from under her chin. Quickly she rolled it up to the rim of her hat. And as she lowered her hands she removed her smoked glasses in one deft movement, turning her head toward Carrington at the same time.

"Tell me, young man—what sort of ship is this *Black Pearl?*"

Carrington was staring at her, flabbergasted—staring at the faded gray eyes set deep in a nest of wrinkled pouches, the palely mottled parchment skin sagging a little over the rigid cheekbones, the prominent Roman nose and the scraggy folds of the skin below what had once been a chin of the utmost determination. It was the face of an elderly lady of strong character, of one who must have been known, perhaps twenty years earlier, as a "handsome woman." It was certainly not the face of Bill Howard.

"Are you quite well?" she asked, a little sharply. "You look as though you'd seen a ghost. Is my face so ugly?"

"I'm terribly sorry," he said, recovering himself, and made the first excuse that came into his head. "For a moment I thought you were an old friend of my mother's whom I haven't seen for many years. But I was mistaken—please forgive me, it was very rude of me."

"Well, now, perhaps you can give me some information about the *Black Pearl*."

"The *Black Pearl,* madam, is a sailing schooner which came into Brixham two or three days ago and is due to sail for the West Indies sometime tonight. In fact, there she is." He pointed out of the window. They were about to descend the hill toward the harbor, and the *Black Pearl* was lying below them in the blue water.

"Ah, so I'm just in time."

"Just in time?"

"My son-in-law is a passenger, I understand, and I thought I'd come and see him off. My daughter married a Dutchman, you see—a Mr. Van Krimpen. . . ."

"Ah, yes, I met him last night. Does he know you're coming?"

"No, I thought I'd make it a surprise. I haven't seen him for two years or so, though my daughter has been over to see me more recently. I only heard from her about his trip two days ago. I wasn't sure when he was due to sail, and coming all the way from Norfolk I was afraid I might be too late."

"Well, it so happens that I'm going out to the schooner myself in about fifteen minutes. You'd better come off in the same boat. But what about your luggage? Where are you staying?"

"I haven't arranged to stay anywhere. I don't imagine there'll be much difficulty in finding a room in a boarding-house at this time of the year."

Carrington was now beginning to see the funny side of the situation, though what could have happened to Howard—or Mr. Hitchcock, if indeed there was such a person—he could not imagine. As the car turned the corner at the bottom of the hill he caught a glimpse of Gardner following close on their heels, and at once he was struck by a sudden whim. Quite clearly Gardner had already begun to suspect what he himself had suspected when he first saw the old lady. It would be amusing, he decided, to foster Gardner's illusion for as long as possible.

The driver was slowing down at the fish quay. "Shall I stop at the jetty, sir?"

"We're not sure yet. Can you suggest a boardinghouse

where the lady might find a room for the night?"

"Well, sir, the trouble is so many of them shut down altogether at the end of the season. But you might try the Bay View, which is run by a friend of my wife's. I did hear there was a room vacant a couple of days ago."

"Clean? Good food?"

"Oh yes, sir."

"Right, take us there first. And then perhaps you'd wait a minute or two and bring us back to the jetty to catch a boat."

"Very good, sir."

Carrington was beginning to enjoy himself.

"It's very good of you to take all this trouble on my behalf," said the old lady.

"Not at all, it's a pleasure," he said, with perfect truth. Gardner was still close behind them. Carrington put his face close to the rear window, assuming an anxious expression for Gardner's benefit.

The taxi pulled up at a gray-stone Victorian terraced house on the farther side of the harbor. Above the front door a fanlight window with a curving line of raised white letters identified the house as the Bay View. As they came to a halt Gardner's car passed them at slow speed, then accelerated and drove on toward the Berry Head hotel. A minute later he came past in the opposite direction and went on to the Anchor.

The taxi driver proved to be correct. The Bay View had a vacant room—on the first floor and overlooking the harbor. Carrington helped the driver in with the old lady's luggage, reminded her that the schooner's launch was due ashore in five minutes, and said he would wait for her in the car.

The driver turned the taxi so that it was facing back in the direction of the harbor. Looking out toward the schooner Carrington saw that the boat was already on its way toward the shore. He was in fact extremely anxious not to miss it. Now that Howard hadn't arrived on the train he was beginning to wonder again whether he hadn't perhaps been on board the schooner all the time. It would be interesting to have a look at those other two passengers.

His attention was caught by a movement at the front door of the Anchor, some hundred yards or so away. At the sight of Jane in her familiar green coat he experienced that unmistakable spurt of emotion, halfway between pain and delight, which tells a man he is in love. Then Gardner came out of the hotel immediately behind her, and they strolled together round the inner harbor toward the jetty.

The boat was now already halfway to the shore. Carrington glanced anxiously up at the windows of the Bay View, wishing the old lady would hurry up.

A small boy kicking a stone along the pavement offered a solution to his problem.

"Hey—sonny! Would you like to earn yourself a couple of bob?"

"Yes, sir."

"Well, look, here's a bob to start with. Run down to the jetty. You see that boat coming ashore from the schooner? Tell them, would they mind waiting a minute or two for Mr. Carrington, please. Mr. Carrington—got that?"

"Yes, sir."

"And there'll be another bob for you if the boat's still there when I arrive. Off you go—hurry!"

Fortunately Carrington had to wait only a minute or so longer. As the old lady appeared at the front door he hurried forward to help her down the steps and into the taxi. He was disappointed to see that she was not wearing her dark glasses and still had her veil fastened up on the rim of her hat.

"I see you don't wear your glasses all the time," he said diffidently as the taxi moved forward.

"Oh no," she said. "Only in the middle of the day when the light is a little bright for my poor old eyes. I'm not so young as I was, you know," archly placing her hand for a moment on his arm.

"If you don't mind my saying so," he said, smiling back at her, "I *am* rather afraid you may find the light rather strong out in the harbor. It's the reflection off the water, you know."

"Oh, do you think so? Well, if you think I should . . ." and she fumbled in her great black bag, found the glasses and put them on.

"It may be a little windy too," he continued. "I do think you would find it a little warmer with the veil. I hope you don't mind my making these suggestions, but I should hate you to catch a cold in your eye."

"No, I shall do as you say. It's very nice of you to look after me so well."

They were now arriving at the jetty. The schooner's launch was still waiting, with its engine ticking over. Gardner, Jane and the small boy were standing at the bottom of the steps, watching them as Carrington helped the old lady out of the taxi. Despite her protests he paid off the driver and then gave her his arm.

"These stone slabs can be a bit slippery sometimes," he said.

As they reached the top of the steps he could not help chuckling to himself at the situation. We must make a splendid picture, he thought. And there was Gardner, standing below him, staring intently at the old lady as she hobbled down the steps on her supporting stick.

The coxswain of the launch, a tall Jamaican in white jersey, dark-blue trousers and rope-soled shoes, leaned down to help her over the gunwale and guide her to a seat under the spray shield.

Carrington patted the small boy on the head, gave him his final shilling, and then turned to Jane. "Hullo," he said, taking her by the arm, "we'd better get aboard." They climbed in, followed by Gardner, and the three of them stood leaning their elbows on the curve of the spray shield.

But the coxswain, standing at the wheel behind them, was still waiting, looking expectantly toward the town front. Carrington looked round over his shoulder.

"We're all here, I think," he said.

"But . . . Mr. Hitchcock . . . he is not here yet."

Carrington looked at Gardner.

"Well, I don't think he will be coming. He wasn't on the afternoon train."

The coxswain looked a little anxious. "I was told he would be here," he said, surveying the fish quay and the harbor front. He waited another minute, looked at his watch and shrugged.

"All right, cast off," he said, putting the gear into reverse. The Creole seaman in the bow jerked his boat hook free and shoved the boat clear of the bottom step. A few seconds later they were slipping out of the inner harbor and swinging round to make a course for the schooner.

"So that's why you deserted me this afternoon," said Jane, speaking quietly into Carrington's ear, teasing him. "Meeting another woman, huh?"

He put his arm round her shoulder and smiled at her.

"Who is she anyway?" she said.

He put on a mock-mysterious expression. "Tell you all about it later," he murmured.

"Aren't you going to introduce us to your friend?" said Gardner in a low voice, leaning toward him on his other side.

"Presently," answered Carrington in the same tone. "Actually, she's a bit hard of hearing."

Gardner glanced angrily at him, decided to say nothing, and turned his head away, looking grimly ahead at the approaching schooner.

10

To Carrington, standing with the palm of his hand on Jane's shoulder—the second time that day it had rested there—the *Black Pearl* seemed almost to be gliding toward them over the steel-blue water. In this foreshortened, bows-on view of her the black hull appeared broad, squat, darkly menacing. The tall spars, gleaming with new varnish, stood militantly against the sky; the topmasts were like fixed bayonets, glinting in the orange light of the evening sun. And as the launch chugged steadily toward the *Black Pearl,* Carrington's unexpectedly sinister impression was reflected in a sharp change of mood.

He was beginning to feel a little worried.

He had been half prepared for the fifth passenger to turn out after all to be, not Bill Howard, but a genuine person called Hitchcock. What he had not expected was the nonappearance of any fifth passenger at all. Something surely had gone wrong. The *Black Pearl* was due to sail sometime that night. If Bill's plans included taking passage in her, the sands of his time were running out. But if Carrington's guess had been wrong, and the schooner had nothing to do with Bill, when *was* he going to turn up? How much longer did he expect Carrington to hang around in Brixham? The office would be expecting him back in a day or two. Not that he particularly wanted to leave Brixham so long as Jane was there. But even his indulgent uncle would begin to grow restive if he delayed his return much longer. Jane, after all, worked in London; he would be able to see her again.

At any rate, he thought, glancing sideways at Gardner's stony face, I'm not the only one who's baffled.

He decided that if he heard nothing from Bill by the following morning he would have to assume that his plans had gone astray and return to London.

They were abreast of the schooner's stem now, passing smoothly down the port side. The lines of the hull began to elongate into their true graceful beauty. A ship chandler's launch was tied up alongside, loading stores. A large net, hoisted on a derrick and bulging with massive joints of raw beef and lamb, swung in mid air; the deck was a shambles of packing cases and gear of all kinds. From somewhere aloft came an urgent noise of hammering.

Checking their speed with an abrupt jerk of the gear lever, the coxswain brought them in a tight sweep around the schooner's stern. Below the varnished taffrail, on the black upward curve of the short counter, the words BLACK PEARL, MONTEVIDEO proclaimed her name and port of registry in raised brass letters, reminding Carrington suddenly of seamy waterfronts in foreign ports, sunlit archipelagoes, the white haze of distant surf breaking silently on coral reefs.

Captain Gustavsen was waiting to welcome his guests, standing above them at the top of the short wooden gangway like a more-than-life-sized statue. He gazed down in astonishment at the unexpected sight of a heavily veiled old lady climbing with some difficulty out of the boat and hobbling up the steps toward him. Saluting politely, he greeted her with a stiff, formal bow.

"Good evening, madam, welcome aboard. I don't think I've had the pleasure . . ."

"Good evening!" She waved her stick in the general direction of the mainmast. "Are you the gentleman in charge of this ship?"

Gustavsen raised his eyebrows, uttered a polite cough and bowed again. "I have that honor. Captain Gustavsen at your service."

"I am Mrs. Butterfield. I have come to visit Mr. Van Krimpen, who is a passenger of yours, I understand."

"Mr. Van Krimpen—yes, indeed."

"I am his mother-in-law. He is not expecting me—I wanted it to be a surprise."

"Of course. I am sure he will be delighted to see you. Ah, good evening, Mrs. Day . . . gentlemen. Pleased to see you again."

Suddenly he made a dash to the rail and called loudly down to the coxswain of the boat.

"But what have you done with our passenger? Where is Mr. Hitchcock?"

"He did not come, sir."

"What!"

Carrington intervened: "He didn't arrive on the afternoon train, Captain. I happened to be at the station, and there was certainly no Mr. Hitchcock on that train."

"Damn the fellow! And he booked his passage by telephone only two days ago." Gustavsen turned his face toward the shore, as though by doing so he could conjure Mr. Hitchcock out of thin air. "Well, if he's late he's late. I shan't wait for him. We sail on the tide at two o'clock in the morning, Mr. Hitchcock or no Mr. Hitchcock."

He turned again to his guests. "We are in a horrible mess, as you can see," waving his great arm at the jumble of stores and equipment littering the deck. "But it is always like this before sailing. Somehow it all gets put away. . . ." And then, raising his powerful voice to the mate, who was standing over by the port rail trying to bring order out of the chaos: "Take care with that wine, Mr. Isaaksen!"

They all stood for a moment watching with amusement the scene of confusion, the crates of whisky, brandy and champagne standing cheek by jowl with cartons of cigars and cigarettes, boxes of tinned food and dried provisions, coils of new rope, carcasses of meat, engine-room spares, first-aid kit. . . . And in a rapidly diminishing space in the center of all this, a young purser, evidently new to the ship, was desperately trying to check the items before they were taken away for stowage. Growing flustered under the critical eye of the mate, he seemed to be fighting a losing battle.

"Come," said Gustavsen, laughing quietly, "let us go below and have a drink."

Giving his arm to Mrs. Butterfield, he led them across the white scrubbed deck to the companionway. Gardner, who had all this time been carefully watching every movement of the old lady, followed close on their heels, and for a moment Carrington and Jane found themselves standing alone together.

"What a wonderful ship!" she exclaimed, looking around her with pleasure.

"Yes." He was enchanted by her unaffected loveliness, and remembered how beautiful she had looked lying by his side earlier that afternoon. "Don't you wish you were sailing in her?"

"I don't know that I'd be a very good sailor," she said, smiling up at him.

"I'd look after you. . . . Come on, let's join the others."

But she pulled him back so that he had to stand still and look at her.

"Peter, what's going on?"

"What do you mean, what's going on?"

"You're up to some mischief, and I don't know what it's all about."

He hesitated. "Darling," he said, looking seriously into her eyes, "I can't tell you just yet. Later on, perhaps . . . Come on."

He led her by the hand to the top of the companionway. As he followed her down the steps he was assailed by the familiar sounds and smells of a ship's interior: the steady purring roar of the ventilation fans, the distant hum of the ship's generator, the pervading aroma of polished wood and clean blankets and diesel oil. He noted everything with nostalgic pleasure: to his left, behind curtains and halfway down the stairs, a chart table, with parallel rulers lying across an open chart of the Eastern Atlantic; to his right, a curtained bunk, presumably the captain's sleeping quarters at sea. At the foot of the stairs, a thickly carpeted passage, with two doors leading off on either side.

One of these doors was half open. Jane stopped momentarily to catch a rapid impression of a spacious cabin with a wide bunk, wash basin, mirrors, silk-shaded lights and all the appurtenances of luxury. A suitcase had been thrown carelessly on the bunk.

Carrington, with his hand on her waist, urged her gently forward along the passage and through the door into the saloon.

"Goodness!" exclaimed Jane. "What an enormous room!"

As they entered the saloon, which stretched the full width of the ship with porthole glimpses of the sea at either end, Gustavsen was announcing his guests.

"And for you, Mr. Van Krimpen, a special surprise. . . ."

Already Van Krimpen was struggling out of a deep armchair, one forefinger adjusting his rimless glasses on the bridge of his nose, his eyes blinking in astonishment.

"Good heavens!" he exclaimed, walking forward to the old lady and planting a kiss on her veiled cheek. "What on earth are you doing here, Mother? If I had known you were coming . . . Well, come and sit down. This is wonderful, wonderful!"

The other two occupants of the room had also risen to their feet, with the reluctant politeness of men who have been rudely disturbed from a peaceful afternoon. One of them was Carl Brünner, the bald, sallow Swiss lawyer whom Carrington had met with Van Krimpen in the pub the night before. The other was a gloomy-looking, round-shouldered individual with thick-lensed horn-rimmed glasses, pink skin, smooth black hair, thin black mustache and a rather feckless, rabbity expression about the mouth. The only really striking thing about him was that with his light-gray shantung suit he was wearing a black woolen tie and a black arm band. This, supposed Carrington, was the bereaved Englishman whom Brünner had mentioned to him the previous night.

All this Carrington took in at a glance. Meanwhile Gustavsen had got everybody sitting down in a wide circle round a low table at the starboard end of the saloon. The old lady, settled comfortably in an armchair and chatting loudly to her son-in-law, now began removing her veil and glasses.

Carrington was watching Gardner's face. As the simple truth about the old lady was revealed, Carrington fixed his eyes gravely on the heavy green-glass ash tray on the table in front of him and busied himself in extracting a packet of cigarettes from his pocket. Offering it first to Jane on his left (and wondering vaguely why she was looking so amused), and then to the gloomy Englishman on his right, he took one himself and struck a match. As he leaned sideways to light Jane's cigarette he observed Gardner regarding him intently with an expression of grudging admiration, like that of a man whose chess opponent has unexpectedly countered an apparently inescapable checkmate.

"*Touché!*" said Gardner quietly, thoughtfully rubbing his knuckles along his jaw.

Carrington put on an owlish air of puzzled innocence.

"Cigarette?" he said.

Gardner waved a negative reply, and then shifted his gaze to Gustavsen, sitting immediately on his right. The captain was at this moment speaking to a charming Jamaican stewardess in a white coat who had appeared from nowhere and was now standing attentively by his chair.

"Katie, my dear. Let's have some drinks. Go round to everybody and find out what they'll have. And bring the cigarette box—our guests must not smoke their own."

Gustavsen then leaned toward Jane on his right and began talking to her with the pompous gallantry he evidently affected when conversing with attractive women.

Carrington turned to his morose neighbor. "I'm sorry," he said, "I'm afraid I didn't catch your name."

"Ramsey." The man's voice was timid, soft and pedantic.

"You are one of the passengers?"

"Yes."

This is going to be hard work, thought Carrington, racking his brains for something else to say.

"There are four passengers altogether, I understand?"

"Five," said Ramsey. "Someone is arriving this afternoon, I believe."

"Well, I gather he's rather a doubtful starter. He should have come on the afternoon train, but he wasn't on it after all."

"Oh. He's running it rather fine, isn't he?"

"He certainly is," agreed Carrington, his attention wandering. He had suddenly realized that someone was missing.

"So there's yourself," he continued, "and Mr. Van Krimpen and Mr. Brünner. There's one other passenger, then, whom I don't think I have met."

Ramsey looked quickly round the room. "Yes, the Dutch doctor, Doctor Friedhof. He doesn't seem to be here at the moment."

"Ah, yes, Mr. Van Krimpen mentioned him last night."

The stewardess was bringing round the drinks. Carrington had asked for a gin and French. Ramsey, sipping a dry sherry, said, "The lady with you—is she your wife?"

"No, no," replied Carrington, with an unexpected twinge of pleasant emotion at the idea of it. "No, we met on the train coming down here."

"Are you spending a holiday in these parts?"

"No—Mrs. Day is, but I'm afraid I've come down to do some complicated work in peace and quiet."

"I see."

Their conversation seemed to be leading nowhere, and for a moment or two there was an embarrassed silence between them. Gustavsen was still talking to Jane. Gardner, alert to everything that was going on, appeared to be listening politely to Mrs. Butterfield's description of her daughter's home in Rotterdam. Van Krimpen and Brünner had lit cigars and were exchanging desultory remarks in German.

Carrington tried again. "Are you taking passage for the full trip?"

"I don't quite understand you. . . ."

"Are you going all the way to Antigua, or are you getting off at Tangier or somewhere?"

"No, no, the full trip."

"And will you be staying in the West Indies for long?"

Ramsey hesitated, clearing his throat.

"I don't know. I am a schoolmaster, you know—my headmaster has very kindly given me leave for a sabbatical term. I had a . . . a sort of nervous breakdown a few weeks ago. . . . You see . . ."

Carrington looked at him in alarm. The man's voice had suddenly become extremely emotional, and he was pulling a handkerchief from his breast pocket.

". . . the truth is, my wife . . . died a month ago, and I . . ."

The poor man was clearly near to tears. And a moment later he stumbled to his feet, muttered an apology and walked quickly out of the room.

There was an uncomfortable hiatus in the general conversation.

"I'm sorry," said Carrington. "I seem to have said the wrong thing."

Brünner moved over and sat next to him.

"No, Mr. Carrington," he said, putting his hand on his arm, "it's not your fault. Poor Mr. Ramsey still can't get over his wife's death, and the least thing is liable to remind him of it. He often gets upset like that, and we find it better to leave him alone as much as possible. He seems to prefer it that way at the moment."

"Yes, poor fellow," said Gustavsen, "his wife's death has upset him a good deal. She was quite young, I believe. . . . Katie, let's have another drink all round."

It did not take long for the conversation to regain its momentum. Gardner turned to Captain Gustavsen and began showing great interest in the details of the *Black Pearl*'s luxury cruises in the Caribbean. Released from the captain's tedious attentions, Jane moved across to the chair just vacated by Brünner and began talking to Van Krimpen and his mother-in-law. Carrington found himself involved in a long discussion with Brünner on the subject of capital punishment and the differences between Swiss and British law.

Presently the door opened and a man walked in whom Carrington had not seen before. He guessed his age at nearer sixty than fifty-five and his height at an inch or two under six feet. The handsome, neatly chiseled, clean-shaven face, the iron-gray hair brushed straight back from his forehead, the pince-nez balanced carelessly on his nose and attached to the lapel of his jacket by a black silk ribbon, the almost rigid uprightness of his posture—all combined to give the newcomer an impressive air of dignity. He was wearing a light-weight fawn-colored suit, with a soft white shirt and plain orange tie, but put him in a black coat, striped trousers and wing collar and he could not have been mistaken for anything but a highly respected professional man.

"Ah, Doctor Friedhof!" cried the captain, turning round in his chair and waving his arm. "Come and have a drink."

But the doctor seemed a little put out at finding the room so full of strangers. He remained standing by the open door, and made a pretense of looking at his watch.

"Thank you, but . . ." He hesitated. "I am trying to finish one or two letters. I really came in to inquire when the last mail will be leaving the ship."

His words came a little slowly, with a trace of guttural emphasis on consonants, but like most Dutchmen he spoke excellent colloquial English. Carrington watched him carefully, trying to imagine what his face would be like without the pince-nez and with the chin concealed by a ginger beard. The mere removal of a beard could be enough, he knew, to make a man well-nigh unrecognizable even to his friends. Was it conceivable that this was Bill Howard, brilliantly disguised?

A quick glance at Gardner showed that he, too, was scrutinizing the Dutchman's features with close interest.

"There will be a boat leaving in about half an hour to take our friends ashore," Gustavsen was saying. "That may be the last opportunity before we sail, but of course if you have anything important . . ."

"Thank you, that will just give me enough time," said the doctor, and excusing himself to the company with a smile and a little nod he left the room. By this time Carrington had decided, with a sense of disappointment, that Doctor Friedhof was genuine enough. Even with the greatest stretch of the imagination he could not see him as the man he was looking for.

Carrington took out his pipe and began poking tobacco into the bowl with thoughtful deliberation. He became aware that Gardner was looking at him; he was frowning, clearly puzzled and suspicious. Carrington lit his pipe, shook the match out with a flourish and returned Gardner's stare with a poker face.

At this moment the Swedish mate entered the saloon, smiling cheerfully as usual, threw his cap onto a small card table near the door, and sat down in the empty chair between

Carrington and the captain. The stewardess, standing by the wine cupboard, held up a bottle of Bols and flashed her teeth in a smile of interrogation. The mate nodded his head.

"Well, Jan," said Carrington, "you seem to be having a busy day."

"Ja, but . . . it will soon be finished. That new purser, he is a bit young, a bit slow, but he will learn."

The stewardess put his glass of Bols on the table.

"It looks as though you will have good weather—at any rate for the start of your voyage," said Carrington.

Isaaksen shook his head doubtfully. "Too little vind, and it is growing misty again. . . . Goot evening, Mrs. Day, nice to see you again!"

Carrington turned his head and looked out of one of the starboard portholes. The mate was right. The land had become noticeably less distinct during the last hour.

"Hullo, Mr. Isaaksen," said Jane. "I've completely fallen in love with your ship. You couldn't find room for an extra passenger, I suppose?"

"Ja, ja, plenty room. Come with us, and fall in love with me too!" And he roared with laughter.

"I don't think you've met Mr. Van Krimpen's mother-in-law," said Jane, smiling. "Mrs. Butterfield, this is Mr. Isaaksen."

The Swede stood up and shook hands with the old lady across the table.

The conversation now became general. Carrington sat quietly puffing at his pipe, not saying much. His mind was occupied with his problem. There was no sign of Bill among the passengers, and he was at last forced to the conclusion that his former commanding officer had, both literally and metaphorically, missed the boat. In due course, he supposed, he would hear from Bill and learn what had happened. Meanwhile, it would seem, he himself would have spent three days away from his office desk to no purpose. On the other hand, if it hadn't been for Bill's phone call he would never have met Jane.

He looked across at her; she was listening with amusement to something Van Krimpen was saying to her. Her lips were slightly parted—those same lips that had kissed his own so passionately, was it only two hours or so ago? She had twisted sideways in her chair, and her coat had fallen open to reveal the full-bosomed curves of her light-gray jersey outlined against the dark shadows of the lining. He leaned forward and knocked his pipe out in the ashtray, sensing a rising excitement within him as he remembered their dinner date for tonight. Tomorrow he must go back to London. But meanwhile the evening was, he felt, full of promise.

He bent his head toward Brünner, who had turned toward him and was about to make some remark.

When they finally came up on deck the day's brightness had begun to fade. With the sun's departure the cool air drifting in over the warm sea had been condensing its vapor in finespun wisps of grayness that curled up from the surface of the water. The *Black Pearl* had quietly swung round on her anchor cable, pointing her bowsprit toward the sea's horizon. The Brixham waterfront, which Carrington had expected to see by looking forward along the deck, was now lying beyond the schooner's stern. The outlines of the houses were blurred by the returning mist.

The captain, the mate and Mr. Brünner had come to the head of the gangway to see the guests off the ship. Van Krimpen was going ashore in the boat to escort his mother-in-law to her boardinghouse, returning by the same boat. There was no sign of Doctor Friedhof or Mr. Ramsey, neither of whom had made a further appearance in the saloon.

Thanks, farewells, wishes for a good voyage . . . and then Carrington was going ahead of the old lady down the gangway to the waiting launch, keeping one step ahead of her to give her support with his arm.

Van Krimpen and Mrs. Butterfield sat down under the spray shield; Carrington and Gardner, with Jane between them, resumed the standing positions they had occupied on the outward trip.

The launch was about to push off when Carrington saw the Jamaican stewardess appear at the top of the companionway. Running long the deck, she spoke rapidly to the mate and pointed downward toward the launch. The mate came to the head of the gangway and called out, "Wait a moment!"

The stewardess hurried down the steps.

"Mr. Carrington? I think you left your cigarettes behind." She was holding out a packet of Players Number 3.

"No, I don't think so," said Carrington, feeling in his right-hand pocket. But the packet he expected to find was not there. "Oh, perhaps it is, after all. Thank you very much!"

With a last farewell wave to their hosts they were off. As the launch swung round toward the shore, Carrington absent-mindedly opened the packet of cigarettes that had just been handed to him. He was about to offer a cigarette to Jane when he noticed something he had not expected to see.

A torn scrap of blue note paper had been slipped inside the front of the packet. It had been placed in such a way that the short penciled message scrawled across the top of it in capital letters was clearly visible.

The message read:

BOAT YARD 7:30 TONIGHT

The words sprang out at Carrington with the shock of a cold shower. Suddenly the whole situation was changed.

11

He was so taken by surprise that he hesitated for a moment with the packet of cigarettes in his hand. Then, recovering himself, he thrust it abruptly into his pocket.

But he had hesitated just too long. Gardner was alert with suspicion.

"Can I beg a cigarette of you, Carrington? I seem to have finished mine."

Damn the fellow, thought Carrington. But instead of handing the packet over to Gardner he extracted two cigarettes and held them out in his fingers.

"Jane—cigarette?"

"Not just now, thank you."

He passed one of the cigarettes across to Gardner and put the other between his own lips, returning the packet to his right-hand pocket with deliberate slowness. He struck a match and lit his cigarette, and then observed that Gardner was having difficulty with his lighter because of the movement of the air.

"Try one of these," said Carrington, tossing his box of

matches across the curving top of the spray shield. Gardner took the matches, lit his cigarette and returned the box with a gesture of irritation.

My round, I think, said Carrington to himself.

Meanwhile he had some quick thinking to do. He had no doubt in his mind that the message was from Bill Howard. Clearly Bill was aboard the schooner after all—but how was it, wondered Carrington, that he had noticed no evidence of his presence? He had seen all four of the passengers; they seemed bona fide enough. And the fifth passenger had not arrived. Bill could hardly pass off as a member of the crew without arousing the suspicions of the rest of them, and in so small a ship he could not hide as a stowaway for long without the knowledge and connivance of the captain and the mate at least.

The launch had nearly reached the landing steps. Carrington looked stealthily at his watch and saw that it was already nearly ten past seven. He had twenty minutes to elude Gardner and get to the boat yard. And what about his date with Jane? Dinner at the hotel was at eight o'clock. Provided Bill did not keep him long he could just make it in time. But it was going to be a near thing.

Now they were alongside, and helping the old lady out of the boat.

"You will wait for me?" said Van Krimpen to the coxswain. "I won't be more than ten minutes at the most."

They mounted the uneven steps, moved slowly on account of the old lady. To Carrington it seemed an age as they walked round the fish quay toward the Anchor. At the door of the hotel they stopped to say good-bye to Van Krimpen and his mother-in-law.

"Good-bye, young man," boomed the old lady from behind her veil, holding out her hand to Carrington. "Thank you for being so helpful to me when I arrived. If you ever find yourself in Norwich you must come and look me up."

"Thank you, Mrs. Butterfield, I will," said Carrington, now almost beside himself with impatience.

"Shan't we see you tomorrow?" asked Jane.

"No, my dear, I must get away as early as possible. . . . Well, good-bye everybody . . ."

"*Bon voyage,* Mr. Van Krimpen," said Carrington, holding the door open for Jane . . . and at last they were inside the hotel.

"What about a drink?" said Gardner.

"I've got to disappear upstairs for five minutes," said Jane.

"Join you in a moment, Gardner." Carrington moved toward the "Gentlemen" sign at the end of the passage. As he reached the door he looked back. Gardner was entering the cocktail bar.

"Mine's a gin and French," called Carrington as he disappeared into the lavatory.

Inside, he stood for a moment, leaning against the doorpost. Then he opened it a crack, looking along the passage. The coast was clear. He walked rapidly toward the hotel entrance and came out into the street, unaware that the door of the cocktail bar had opened slightly as he passed. He turned to his right and began striding at a smart pace along the road leading toward the boat yard. He had six minutes in hand.

With the approach of dusk the mist was closing in fast. Already the schooner was hidden from the shore. On some impulse he looked back toward the hotel. Was that a man's figure, that shadow of darker gray against the gray-white background of mist? He could have sworn it had been moving when he first turned his head, that it had immediately frozen into immobility like a suddenly arrested film. Gardner? Or some trick of light in the murky halfway stage between dusk and dark?

He had nearly reached the corner of a street coming down at right angles to the harbor front. He walked quickly on, turned the corner with a sudden dart to his right, and looked for a hiding place. Two doors up from the corner was a men's outfitters; it had one of those shop fronts where the entrance door is set well back from the pavement and the public can walk not only between but also behind the window displays. The shop was in darkness. Carrington dived into the shadows and stood stock still, watching the corner of the road over the shoulders of the stiffly tailored dummies.

A moment or two later, and so soon that he must have covered the remaining distance at a run, Gardner appeared on the corner, pulling himself up suddenly as he found himself confronted by alternative avenues of pursuit. After a brief hesitation he took a few steps up the street toward Carrington, peering cursorily into the shadows of doorways. At one moment he seemed to be looking directly at Carrington, but it did not occur to him to examine every one of the faces grinning inanely into middle distance.

He continued on past the gentlemen's outfitters, moving away from the harbor front. And then suddenly, to Carrington's disappointment, he turned round, sprinted back on his tracks and disappeared round the corner to the right.

The road he had now taken was the road leading toward the boat yard.

"Bugger it!" said Carrington, emerging from the shadows of his hiding place. Gardner was now between him and his objective.

He went to the corner and stood listening. Gardner had already vanished in the mist. At first he could hear the diminishing sound of his footsteps hurrying along the road ahead of him, but presently they died away altogether.

What the hell was he going to do now? He dared not follow Gardner. At some point or other the fellow was bound to turn back when he could find no sign of his quarry, and then Carrington might be trapped in the vicinity of the boat yard. That would be a disaster, not only making it impossible for him to keep the rendezvous but possibly also leading to the discovery of Bill himself.

He stood irresolutely on the corner, desperately seeking inspiration.

And suddenly, miraculously out of the blue, it came.

A motorcycle was coming slowly down the street toward the harbor. The engine was sputtering unevenly, alternately revving up and idling. The rider was an anonymous figure in goggles and white crash helmet. He came to a stop when he saw Carrington.

"This *is* Brixham, mate, isn't it?" said the voice of a young man.

"Yes."

"Can you tell me where I find the Berry Head hotel?"

Carrington at once saw that here was the solution to his problem.

"I happen to be going there myself," he said, grinning cheerfully at the face under the goggles. "If you would like to give me a lift on the back I'll take you right there."

"Good-oh! Hop on and hold tight."

They set off with a roar. "If I were you," yelled Carrington, "I'd have my headlights on. It's a dark road. . . . Bear left now and follow the road along."

Over the driver's shoulder Carrington watched the trembling beam of the headlight swinging round the curve of the wall. They had gone some way past Uphams' boat yard before he saw Gardner. He had already turned back on his tracks and was walking slowly toward them at the side of the road. As they flashed past him, safely invisible behind the dazzle of the headlight, Carrington had a clear view of him screwing up his eyes against the glare.

A hundred yards or so beyond, Carrington tapped the driver on the shoulder. "Can you drop me here?"

"Okey-dokey." He slowed down and pulled in to the side of the road.

"Straight on will bring you to the Berry Head hotel any minute now."

"Right-oh. Thanks. I'll say cheerio, then."

Carrington stood perfectly still as the motorcycle drove on. When the noise of it began to fade he thought he could hear Gardner's footsteps echoing against the road wall, still going back toward the harbor. He half walked, half ran on tiptoe, pausing from time to time to make sure he could still hear Gardner on the move. Presently he stopped dead. He had just caught sight of Gardner's silhouette thrown up by the yellow beam of a street lamp; he was still walking, and still a few yards short of the boat yard.

Carrington quietly crossed the road to get away from the lamplight. Walking on the soles of his feet he began shadowing Gardner. He was so intent on keeping him under observation that he failed to avoid a stone lying in his path. It was a small stone, but as it rattled forward along the road from the impact of his toe it made enough noise to attract Gardner's attention. Carrington stopped in his tracks a second before Gardner wheeled round and peered suspiciously in his direction.

He's got the light from the street lamp in his eyes, thought Carrington. In this misty half-light he won't be able to see more than a few yards beyond it. If I stay absolutely still he won't spot me.

And a moment later Gardner turned away and continued walking past the boat-yard entrance. Carrington waited until he had disappeared into the mist, then recrossed the road and stood facing the high wooden double doors. They looked firmly shut.

He looked at his watch. It was 7:35. Thanks to Gardner he was already five minutes adrift. At this rate he was also going to be late for his dinner with Jane.

Somehow he had to get past those doors.

In fact it proved to be easy. Built into the left-hand door was a smaller door of ordinary size. He tried the handle, and to his surprise it opened. He slipped quickly inside, shutting the door behind him. As he did so he bumped into a dustbin, and the lid fell to the ground with an appalling clatter.

There was a light burning in a hut at the far end of the entrance yard. A man came out and stood at the hut door for a moment, listening and looking into the misty shadows, but almost immediately turned and went back into the hut.

But already Carrington's ears had picked up the sound of Gardner's footsteps running back along the road. To his dismay they slowed and came to a halt on the other side of the door he was leaning against. He swore in silence. Damn the f——ing dustbin! Turning his head he found his eye near to a crack between the planks of the door—a crack wide enough to give him a startlingly close view of the back of Gardner's head. He needs a haircut, he thought irrelevantly.

Gardner was breathing heavily, turning his head to look up and down the road.

Suddenly Carrington felt a cold tingle creeping up his spine: something soft was rubbing against his ankles. He looked down and saw that it was a mangy black cat with malevolent green eyes. And then the thing began to mew. Carrington bent down and tried silently to shoo it away with his hands. But the cat seemed determined at all costs to be friendly. It went on mewing.

Carrington began to sweat. At any moment Gardner might take it into his head to try the door.

Looking to his left along the door he saw a bolt just within reach of his hand. But it was unlikely that he could push it home without making a noise. With a desperate movement he picked up the cat and hurled it over his shoulder to the top of the gate. The cat gave a blood-curdling yowl and jumped down on the other side as Carrington pushed the bolt across. Looking quickly through the crack in the door he saw a startled Gardner brushing his shoulder with his hand. With a muttered "Bloody cat!" Gardner turned on his heel and started walking rapidly away in the direction of the harbor.

For perhaps a quarter of a minute Carrington listened to the fading sound of his footsteps. Then he began making his way stealthily across the yard and down a series of steps toward the boat shed.

He was now ten minutes late for the rendezvous.

Under its great corrugated roof the boat shed was a cavern of twilight grayness. In that vast space, with its concrete floor sloping gently down to the water's edge, Carrington could make out the mist-blurred forms of twenty or so boats chocked up on the slipways in various stages of repair or construction. One of them, little else yet but keel and ribs, might have been the skeleton of some great sea monster, thrown up on the beach and picked clean by gulls.

The slip rails led straight down to the water. Ropes, chains, an anchor or two, rigging blocks and other miscellaneous nautical gear lay about the floor in orderly confusion. There was a smell of newly sawn wood, varnish, paint, tarred hemp and seaweed.

But there was no sign of Bill Howard.

Had he gone already? Surely he would have waited.

By Carrington's watch it was nearly a quarter to eight. He sat down on a massive balk of timber and set himself to wait. His eyes were beginning to get used to the half light. Under the keels of the boats he commanded a view of most of the shed, and he could hear the water lapping and surging on the narrow edge of shingle between the concrete and the sea.

Presently he became aware of a new set of sounds: the rhythmic bump of oars against rowlocks, the quiet dip of blades in water. The sounds were muffled, as though the oarsman was trying to make as little noise as possible. A moment later he could just distinguish the black shape of a small boat, something like a ten-foot dinghy, gliding in toward the shingle; then the blob of a man's head and shoulders, and the regular rise and fall of the oars. Close to the shore now, the oarsman turned his head, ceased rowing and silently swung the oars into the boat. There was a soft bumping and grating, followed by a gentle crunch as the man vaulted over onto the shingle. He pulled the boat up a yard or so and secured the painter to one of the slip rails.

So far the man was an anonymous silhouette in the misty grayness. Carrington's heart was thumping against his ribs. He watched the man as he walked softly up the shingle, moving purposefully toward the boat shed. He lost sight of him for a moment: he had disappeared behind the hull of one of the boats. When he appeared again he could not see the upper half of his body at all. The man was wearing rubber shoes, and as he came up the concrete slope, zigzagging between the boats, he made no sound at all. All Carrington could see was a pair of trousered legs, moving stealthily, stopping now and then as their owner paused to listen, but all the time coming steadily nearer.

Carrington stayed rigid in his crouching position, waiting for a sign from Howard.

Now the legs were only two boat-widths away. A moment later they had moved so that they were standing within ten yards of him. There was now only one boat between Carrington and the mysterious figure.

Then, a voice from the other side of the boat:

"Mr. Carrington?"

Carrington frowned. There was something vaguely familiar about the voice, but he could not be absolutely sure that it was the voice of Howard. And why this "Mister"?

There was no point in further concealment. He got up and walked along the side of the boat's hull toward the bow.

Coming round the bulging curve of the bow he found himself looking into the barrel of a small automatic.

And the man behind the gun was not the man Carrington had been expecting to see.

12

For years Carrington had suffered from a recurrent nightmare. The details of the dream might change, but the end of it was always the same. A faceless man would be showing him round an office. The man would open a door, standing obsequiously aside to let him pass, and Carrington would move forward in the confident belief that he was entering another room. Instead, he found himself in mid-air, falling from a skyscraper, with the traffic moving like beetles below him. He would wake up in a running sweat with a terrible feeling in the pit of his stomach.

Now, in the first shock of his surprise, he experienced that same sickening lunge in his stomach. Yet what shook him to the core of his being was not so much the jolt of being confronted with the business end of a gun as the total unexpectedness of the face beyond it. It was certainly not the face of Bill Howard; it was the face of a man he had met for the first time only an hour or so ago: a solemn man with thick horn-rimmed glasses, dark hair brushed smooth and flat, a narrow line of black mustache, and with chin and lower lip receding a little behind the protruding upper teeth. A light gray suit, a black tie and a black arm band completed the picture of the grief-stricken schoolmaster who had been sitting next to him in the *Black Pearl*'s saloon.

"Mr. Ramsey! . . . What the devil . . . ?"

The schoolmaster lowered the gun and put it into his jacket pocket. Then, leaning against the hull of the boat behind him, he began to laugh, slowly and quietly, with a gentle shaking of his shoulders. The frosty blue eyes behind the horn-rimmed glasses no longer wore their habitual look of stony misery; unexpected lines of humor creased the pink skin of his cheeks. And as his chin relaxed forward, his mouth, by some imperceptible metamorphosis, seemed suddenly to have lost its rabbity expression.

"All right, Pedro," he said presently, in a voice quite unlike that of the pedantic, soft-spoken schoolmaster. "Take it easy."

Carrington stood rigid, staring at him, unable to credit the transformation scene taking place before him. The voice that had addressed him by the old familiar nickname—that certainly was the voice of Bill Howard. But still, the face . . . He took a step nearer, trying to fit the face into an imaginary framework of ginger beard and hair. It seemed incredible, but—

"Is that better?" said the man, whipping off his glasses and looking at Carrington with an expression that was half serious, half smiling.

"Bill!" exclaimed Carrington. "Well, my God, you had me absolutely fooled!"

"Sorry about the gangster dramatics just now," said Howard, putting the glasses away in his breast pocket, "but I can't afford to take chances. Yes, it's amazing what you can do by dyeing your hair and taking off a beard you've worn for years."

"But what's all this mourning in aid of—this arm band and so on? You haven't really just lost your wife, have you?"

"Good Lord, no. Haven't you noticed how people never like to look too closely at a man who's just been bereaved? It embarrasses them, I suppose—some kind of inverted guilt complex. Besides, I find it a useful gag to get me out of awkward situations. I used it on board the schooner just now when I felt you were beginning to ask too many awkward questions. The one I was worrying about was Tony Gardner—he was sitting opposite me, and he's known me for a good many years. What is he doing here—do you know?"

"No, I was hoping you'd be able to tell *me*," said Carrington. "I wish you'd warned me about him."

"My dear Pedro, I'd no idea he was going to be here. How the devil he got onto the fact that I was going to Brixham I don't know. Has he any idea that you've been waiting to see me?"

"Well, he's no fool. He remembered who I was, unfortunately, and it can't have taken him much thought to put two and two together. He was very suspicious this evening, and I had a hell of a job getting rid of him before coming to meet you."

"Oh. That's not so good. . . . And who's the girl?"

"Jane Day? We met coming down on the train yesterday."

"What is she doing in Brixham?"

"Just taking a few days' holiday, that's all."

"Does she know Gardner?"

"She didn't until I introduced them to each other last night. But why all these questions about Jane?"

"I just don't trust anybody at the moment. How much does she know about what's going on?"

"Nothing that I've told her; not that I could have told her much anyway. Of course, Gardner's been hanging on to me like a leech, so she could hardly help realizing something was up. But I've told her nothing."

"Well, she's probably perfectly all right, but I'd prefer you not to tell her anything about me, if you don't mind. Women love to talk."

"O.K. . . . But when am *I* going to be let in on the secret? What *is* this all about?"

Howard looked hard at Carrington, and then began pacing

up and down, with his hands in his pockets, his rubber shoes making scarcely a sound on the concrete floor. Carrington thought how much older his former captain was looking since they had last met. Most men look younger clean-shaven, but with Howard the removal of his beard had in some way emphasized the bitter lines at the sides of his mouth. He looked smaller, shrunken. He had the pinched look of a man who has been going through a long period of strain. Perhaps it had something to do with the fading light.

Presently Howard came to a halt in front of Carrington, not looking at him but facing down the slope toward the sea.

"If a man," he said, "after searching his conscience over a number of years, comes to the conclusion—a sincere conclusion—that he must take a particular course of action, in spite of . . . even though that course of action means going against all the accepted codes of loyalty and honor—codes to which he has been born and trained—what is that man to do? Should he conform to the accepted code and know himself for a moral coward for the rest of his life . . . or should he follow that course of action and risk losing the reputation, and the friends, of a lifetime?"

There were lines of suffering on his face; clearly he had been living with this dilemma for a long time. Carrington, moved by a feeling of compassion, considered the question for a moment in silence.

"Well, Bill," he said presently, "it's difficult to give a specific answer when the problem is put in such general terms. But I would say the right thing to do would be to make some sort of announcement of his intention and then go ahead and do it."

"But suppose the course of action, by its very nature, makes it impossible to advertise his intention."

"You mean, if it involves deception . . . betrayal . . . ?"

"Perhaps, though not by design."

"Or treason?"

The word hung on the damp air like a spreading stain.

Howard scratched his upper lip with the fingernails of his left hand. Carrington recognized the old nervous gesture.

"Treason?" echoed Howard, frowning. "Treason is a dirty word. It begs the whole question. Some might think that disloyalty to one's deepest convictions is treason. The world is changing, Peter. Nationalism is already out of date. The traitors of today will become the heroes of tomorrow's history books."

Carrington stared at him, incredulous. He suddenly felt an overwhelming sense of depression. There was a long silence.

"So," he said, looking gloomily at the floor, "where do I come in on all this?"

"Peter," said Howard, turning to look directly at him, "there isn't time to beat about the bush. What I have done is done. It was done, believe me, from honest conviction, not for gold. But now the boys are onto me, and I've got to get out. It is simply a question of my freedom, probably of my life."

"And you saved mine. . . . I know. I haven't forgotten."

"There was no one else I could turn to. All I want you to do for me, if you will, is to post two letters which for various reasons I can't post myself."

"Just post two letters? Is that all?"

"That's all. One is a letter to my wife, the other . . . a matter of business. They both have to be posted in London. You may wonder why I couldn't simply post them myself. The reason is that I particularly don't want them posted until after I have sailed, and if they had a Brixham postmark they might lead a trail right back to the schooner."

Carrington was hardly listening. He was staggered at Howard's revelation. That his admired hero, this submarine ace of World War II, should virtually admit to being a traitor to his country—this he found unbelievable. There was, of course, no doubt as to what he ought to do.

"Well, Peter, have you decided? Will you take the letters for me? Or are you going to turn me over to Gardner?"

For a moment or two Carrington remained silent. In his imagination he was suddenly back in the rubber dinghy on that unforgettable night off the scented coast of Malaya, rowing his guts out, with the Japanese searchlight sweeping the darkness.

"Damn you, Bill! This is moral blackmail. You've no right to ask my help in a thing like this. You know I can't refuse you."

"No right, perhaps. I'm just asking you."

"O.K., then. Give me the letters."

"In case we weren't able to arrange a meeting, I deposited both the letters, enclosed in an envelope addressed to you, to be called for, at the post office here in Brixham."

"Right."

"But there *is* one more thing I have to ask of you."

Carrington looked at him in silence, with eyes that were becoming a little weary with disillusion.

"If this mist doesn't get too thick," said Howard, "we sail tonight. As Gardner is being so inquisitive, I would be grateful if you could stay on in Brixham for another twenty-four hours after we sail, to distract his attention from the schooner. If you leave Brixham in the morning he will at once assume that the purpose of your visit here is over, guess that I am on board and send the Navy chasing after me. But if you stay on, he may well think you are still waiting for me to turn up. And it might be a good thing, too, if you didn't collect my letters from the post office until late in the afternoon."

"All right. I had, actually, planned to start back to London tomorrow morning, but I suppose I can ring my office and tell them I've been delayed. God knows what sort of a story I'm going to concoct for my uncle when I get back. . . . Well, Bill, I don't know—I don't want to know—what you've done, or what you're doing, and I'm sure I wouldn't like it if I did, but —all I can say is that I hope things will turn out all right for you."

The boat shed was now in almost complete darkness.

Howard dropped a hand on Carrington's shoulder.

"Thanks, Pedro. I don't suppose we shall ever meet again. Don't judge me too harshly. It was a hell of a decision to take, you know. One day the world will see these things differently. Well, thanks again, and good-bye."

And then, as Howard turned to walk down to his waiting boat, a sudden thought struck Carrington.

"By the way . . . who is the fifth passenger?"

Howard stopped and turned his head, smiling quizzically.

"I am the fifth passenger."

"But . . ."

"I always had to reckon with the possibility that Gardner— or somebody—might follow my trail down here. My passage in the guise of Ramsey was booked over a week ago—his character and, of course, his false passport have been in cold storage for some time, in readiness for just such an emergency as this. But at the last moment before leaving London, the day I rang you, I decided to telephone a booking for another passage—in the name of Hitchcock this time, saying I would arrive by train this afternoon. I hoped this might help to confuse the issue, to divert attention from Mr. Ramsey, who would already have been quietly on board for a couple of days."

"Dammit," exclaimed Carrington. "To think I actually went and met that train, hoping Mr. Hitchcock would turn out to be you."

"I'm sorry! I should have made my number with you earlier, but Brünner mentioned he had met you and thought you were coming aboard for drinks, and I thought the longer I kept out of the way on board the better."

"As it happened, Gardner met the train, too."

"Well, so the gag seems to have served its purpose. Let's hope he still suspects that Hitchcock and I are one and the same person, and that I've changed my plans and just haven't turned up after all. Your staying on tomorrow after the *Black Pearl* has sailed will help to foster the illusion. . . . Well, I must be off. They'll be wondering what has happened to their dinghy and the mad schoolmaster who borrowed it for a little rowing exercise. Once again, Pedro, good-bye."

"Good-bye, Bill. Look after yourself."

When Carrington let himself out of the boat-yard gate and looked at his watch in the light of a street lamp, he found to his dismay that it was already 8:35. He hurried back to the hotel, half running, half walking, wondering what sort of excuse he could possibly give Jane for ruining her birthday dinner. By the time he reached the hotel he was pretty breathless.

He went straight to the dining room. Jane and Gardner were sitting together at a table for two, drinking coffee. Two liqueur glasses were on the table.

Dinner was over.

As he entered the room he knew Jane had seen him out of the corner of her eye. Without looking up she said something to Gardner, who then slowly turned his head toward Carrington.

"Ah, the wanderer returns!" he said, with an irritating inflection of mockery in his voice. "Mrs. Day seemed a little lonely, so I came over to keep her company for coffee. Don't let me keep you from your dinner." And with a little bow to Jane he picked up his glass and went to his own table.

Carrington sat down opposite Jane. She was looking down at the table, stirring her coffee, and the expression on her face was ominously calm.

He was still breathless from running.

"Jane . . . I've ruined your birthday dinner. I just don't know how to begin to apologize."

The waitress was at his elbow.

"Were you wanting dinner, sir?" she said, looking pointedly at the clock over the mantelpiece.

"Well . . . I know I'm terribly late. Is it still possible?"

"I'll go and ask madam, sir."

He turned back to Jane. "Jane, I'm terribly sorry."

She raised her head and looked directly at him, without warmth. Her eyes were magnificent, and quite devastating.

"You needn't bother to apologize any more," she said in a flat voice. "I had a very pleasant dinner, thank you, and now I'm going to leave you to enjoy yours in peace. Good night."

She picked up her handbag and stood up. He half rose in his chair.

"But Jane—your coffee, your drink . . . Jane! Don't go!"

"Good night, Mr. Carrington."

She was gone. She might just as well have slapped his face. And instead of her, there was the waitress, bringing him a plate of smoked salmon.

"Mrs. Porter says to tell you, sir, she's kept the roast beef warming for you, but she's afraid it won't be very nice. Dinner's supposed to be at eight, you see, sir."

"I'm sure it will be delicious all the same. Please tell Mrs. Porter I'm extremely sorry."

"Very good, sir."

He ate his smoked salmon in a moody abstraction. His spirits were at a low ebb. Bill, it seemed, was a traitor. He himself had become incriminated in helping him to escape from the country, even though in a minor way. And now the evening that had been so full of promise lay about him in ruins.

The roast beef, when it came, was hideous with congealed gravy, leathery roast potatoes and tepid sprouts. He was cutting into the beef with a sort of desperate anger when Gardner came over to the table and sat down in the chair Jane had been occupying.

"Mind if I join you for a moment?"

"No, go ahead."

"Where did you get to? I had a gin and French lined up for you in the bar."

"I'm sorry. I didn't feel well, needed some fresh air. Perhaps I drank too much on the schooner. I don't know."

"Do you mind if I smoke while you eat?"

"It can't make it taste any worse."

Gardner lit a cigarette, gave Carrington a long, considering look, and then, leaning forward with his elbows on the table, said, "Look here, Carrington, I don't know what game you're playing, but I just hope you know what you're doing."

With a mouth full of potato, Carrington said, "What the hell are you talking about?"

"When did you last see Bill Howard?" said Gardner, rapping out the words like a prosecuting counsel.

Carrington dropped his knife and fork on the plate in an angry gesture. "For crying out loud! I haven't seen him for three years at least. What the hell's the matter with you? For the last twenty-four hours you've done nothing but needle me and spy on me. I'm fed up to the teeth with the sight of your bloody face."

He wiped his mouth on his napkin, stood up, threw the napkin on the chair and stormed out of the room.

In a black rage he went out and walked round to the Dolphin. There was no one there from the schooner, and the bar was astonishingly quiet. He drank a couple of pints of beer by himself, but they only made him feel more depressed than ever. He decided to return to the hotel and go to bed.

As he drew the curtains across his bedroom window he noticed that the schooner's riding lights were just visible. The mist was thinning out a little.

He undressed and got into bed. For an hour he concentrated on the problems of the Dring Development Trust, making pencil notes in the margins of the draft articles. Then the arid legal phraseology began to lull him into a state of drowsiness. He got up, drew the curtains back, opened the windows and returned to his bed. Switching off the light he tried to go to sleep, but his brain was now maddeningly wide awake, tormenting him with an endless recapitulation of the day's events. He was filled by a deepening resentment against Howard: his hero had revealed feet of clay, had called in the long-standing debt by making him an accessory to his treason, and had on top of it all been the unwitting cause of the calamitous end to his affair with Jane.

He tossed and turned on his pillow, and eventually went off into an uneasy doze.

About two o'clock in the morning he woke up with a start, alerted by a slow clanking sound out on the water. The schooner was winching in her anchor cable. He got out of bed and went to the window. The mist had almost cleared and the visibility was definitely improving. He could make out the sounds of distant voices, the slow throbbing of diesels. The metallic clinking of the winch came to a stop, and presently he was aware that the masthead light was beginning to move. The *Black Pearl* was under way, bound for Tangier and the Caribbean.

He watched the light until the schooner had cleared the great breakwater and turned to starboard. Then he got back into bed. It must have been a good hour before he finally dropped off to sleep.

When he awoke it was broad daylight. The mist had entirely vanished, the sky was a pellucid blue and the sun was pouring onto his bed. For a moment he felt a great surge of well-being, but with the return of memory his despondency rolled back over him like an advancing tide.

His watch told him it was already past ten o'clock. He was too late for breakfast, his favorite meal of the day. He pushed the bedclothes aside and walked, yawning and stretching, over to the window. The outer harbor was empty. A trail of smoke drifting from the funnel of one of the trawlers alongside the fish quay showed that what little breeze there was had shifted into the northeast. The *Black Pearl* had a fair wind for her passage down Channel.

As he shaved, he wondered how he would spend the day.

13

Naked except for his pale-blue swimming trunks, he lay full length on the beach with his eyes shut. The waves lapped the wet edge of the sand, and the gulls' clamor echoed off the cliffs surrounding the bay. With his head pillowed on a rolled-up towel and the sun drawing out his festering ill-humor like a poultice, Carrington was beginning to feel a little more human. A coffee and a couple of toasted teacakes at the café had assuaged his hunger, for the present at any rate. He hadn't had a decent meal, he remembered, for over thirty-six hours. Yesterday's lunch had been his picnic with Jane, dinner he preferred not to think about, and he had missed this morning's breakfast altogether.

He had seen no sign of Gardner this morning—or of Jane. He wondered gloomily if, after last night's fiasco, she had now decided to go off to Torquay and visit those damned aunts of hers.

With a sigh he turned over onto his stomach, propped himself up on his elbows and pulled the Dring file in front of him. Flipping through the typescript pages he checked over his pencil notes of the night before. But he found it difficult to keep his mind on his work. He kept thinking of Howard—and of the *Black Pearl* now presumably somewhere off Start Point and trickling along with a light following breeze and all sails set. It was a pity she had had to make her departure at night; he would like to have seen her under sail.

A sudden shadow on the page, a soft footfall in the sand close beside him—and then Jane's voice, warm with laughter.

"Hullo!" she said. "Working hard?"

"Good God!" he exclaimed, sitting up and screwing his face against the sunlight. She was wearing orange slacks, a white shirt, white sandals and dark glasses, and she was carrying a bathrobe and towel. She flopped down in the warm sand.

He said, "I thought you were never going to speak to me again."

She stroked his elbow with an outstretched forefinger. "I was beastly to you last night," she said.

"No, you were quite right. I mucked up your evening."

"I'm sure you didn't mean to. Let's forget about last night. It's *such* a marvelous morning! Are you going to swim?"

"I thought I would, when I'd got nicely cooked on both sides. Are you?"

"I saw you leaving the hotel carrying a towel, so I guessed you were going to bathe and decided to come and join you."

Still sitting, she peeled off her shirt and slacks and revealed herself in a superb one-piece costume that was the color of gold brocade. With her legs straight out in front of her, she crossed her ankles and leaned forward from the hips with the palms of her hands stroking her knees and her head arched back a little on her neck. As she swayed forward her smooth shoulders pressed inward, deepening the cleft in the creamy flesh above her breasts. Carrington could not tell whether, behind those dark glasses, she was looking at him or not.

"Well," she said, after a little silence, "do you like me?"

The frankness of her question took him off his guard, and

he paused a moment to shape his answer. "It's a stunning costume," he said, "and it suits you down to the ground."

"That wasn't what I meant at all," she said, taking off her sunglasses and standing up. "Well, the sea looks so inviting I think I'll go straight in."

As she began walking down the sand he jumped to his feet and overtook her. He ran full tilt into the water and hurled himself into a shallow dive. The shock of the cold brought him quickly to the surface gasping for breath, but he struck out at once for deep water with a vigorous crawl. Presently, treading water, he turned and looked back at the shore. The hills were magnificent, clean as the first morning of creation. Jane was swimming out toward him. She was bareheaded, and she swam with a steady breast stroke, keeping her hair clear of the water. Her eyes were shut; she seemed to be in a trance.

He swam slowly toward her, thinking what an unpredictable girl she was. Twice now she had astonished him by her unexpectedly friendly mood.

When they were within a few yards of each other she opened her eyes.

"Hullo," she said, "isn't this wonderful!"

"Marvelous."

At the same moment he caught sight of a submerged patch of yellow rippling in front of her. She was holding something in her right hand, and it fluttered like a streamer as she moved her arms to the motion of her swimming. It was not until he saw the whole white shape of her body undulating in the limpid water that he realized, with something of a shock, that what she was holding in her hand was her swim suit.

"Do you always swim like that?" he said, laughing.

"Yes, when there's no one about."

The casual implication of intimacy pleased him absurdly. He gazed at her with frank admiration. Amid the shafts of sunlight playing wantonly about her pelvis, her pubic hair was a region of dark shadow. Her full breasts trembled a little on the outward swing of her arms.

"The water feels so delicious like this," she said. "Don't you ever swim with nothing on?"

"Sometimes, but not usually in broad daylight in mixed company."

"You don't need to be so stuffy with me. I don't mind."

He did not find it too easy, in deep water, to stay afloat and wriggle out of his trunks at the same time. Rolling, twisting, spluttering, he came to the surface, triumphantly holding them aloft. He swam away from her, using a powerful overarm side stroke, gripping his trunks in his right hand. The water ran coolly between his legs: he felt like a young god. He swam for several yards, reveling in the sheer physical pleasure of the embracing sea. Then he flipped into a sharp turn and flung himself backward into the cushioning water. Shutting his eyes against the sun he allowed himself to drift, floating in a dreamlike condition of weightlessness. The buoyancy of the sea thrust up at him from below. He surrendered himself to the primeval element, rolling over and over like a playful seal. The sunlit water trickling through his fingers was the color of dry white wine.

Finally he turned and came slowly back to her. They moved toward each other as though drawn by the mutual gravity of two asteroids lost in space. Gliding together they brushed mouths in a lapping confusion of cool lips and salt water. As they drifted apart he allowed his free hand to rest briefly on the hollow of her waist.

Presently she began swimming toward the shore.

"Going in already?"

"Yes, before I start to feel chilly."

They swam side by side. When they could stand on the bottom they stopped and wriggled into their swim suits.

"I expect you think I'm a brazen hussy," she said as they

swam the remaining few yards to the beach.

"On the contrary, I thought it was a charming thing to do. You're very beautiful, you know."

"Oh, rubbish!" she exclaimed, laughing at him. But she was pleased all the same.

Carrington looked up at the sky ahead of them. "Hullo! We were just in time. We're going to lose the sun before very long." Ominous banks of dark gray cloud were beginning to form on the skyline. "The wind's changed to the southwest, by the look of it. Well, let's enjoy the sun as long as it lasts."

They flung themselves on the sand beside their clothes. Invigorated by their swim, blissfully conscious of the sun burning into their backs, they lay face down with their chins propped on their folded arms. Carrington had not felt so happy for many years. He was completely captivated by this enchanting water nymph—and yet utterly baffled by her. What she had just done would, in any other woman, have seemed outrageously provocative; how was it that in her it had seemed the most natural thing in the world? And while they talked to each other with such ease about (it seemed) every subject under the sun, he was at the same time aware of some indefinable barrier beyond which he could not penetrate. It was as though she were deliberately excluding him from a whole section of her life. She would talk readily of the past, of her childhood, of foreign places, even of her long-ago marriage, but at every attempt of his to form some kind of picture of her present life —her job, her friends, or where she lived—he became aware (as he had become aware in the train two days earlier) of a cooling of the temperature, a tentative withdrawal of intimacy.

Engrossed in their conversation they had failed to observe the rapid deterioration in the weather. Within half an hour a gray blanket of cloud had swallowed up the sun and covered most of the sky. Dressing hurriedly, they walked the mile or so back to the hotel. After changing into warmer clothes they went along to the Dolphin for a pre-lunch drink. In the bar the fishermen's talk was all weather. There had been a brilliant red sunrise, the glass had been falling rapidly ever since, south cones were being hoisted all along the Channel coast, and the wireless had been announcing gale warnings for almost all areas. Dirty weather, it seemed, was on the way.

Back at the hotel they found Gardner already sitting in the dining room. He was looking depressed.

"Hullo," he said, "nice bathe? Are you two lovebirds going to join me for lunch or are you going to bill and coo in a corner by yourselves?"

"Oh, cheer up!" said Jane, taking a seat at the same table. "Of course we'll join you!"

Carrington was feeling so cheerful himself that he was prepared to be genial even with Gardner. For one thing, he was immensely encouraged by the fact that Gardner was looking so gloomy: it could mean that he was coming to the conclusion that he had been barking up the wrong tree all along. It was beginning to look as though Carrington's continued presence in Brixham was having the desired effect.

During the meal the rain began pattering on the window. The sky was full of sagging clouds with plenty of water in them, and it seemed that they were in for a typical seaside wet afternoon. And by two o'clock, when they had finished lunch, it was raining really hard. A blustery wind had got up and was hurtling the rain against windows and shimmering the surface of the water in the inner harbor. It was the kind of weather in which anybody who had to be out of doors walked fast and with hunched shoulders. The curtain of rain blurred the edges of the outer breakwater, and the sea was the color of lead.

Jane decided to go to bed and sleep for the afternoon. Carrington and Gardner sat themselves in the lounge in front of an electric fire. While Gardner fell asleep over a book, Carrington wrote a few letters and tried to do some more work on the Dring file. Presently Gardner woke up and suggested a game of chess. He seemed prepared to be more friendly.

"O.K.," said Carrington, "but I haven't played for quite a while."

"Never mind, I'm not a particularly good player. Do you object to playing on a pocket set? I'll nip upstairs and get it."

Carrington took a little while to get into the swing of the game. He soon realized that Gardner was employing a definite gamesmanship technique: he would make every move with a maddening air of confidence, as though it were part of a well-prepared plan which none of Carrington's maneuvers could hope to thwart; having made it, he would put on a smug expression and sit looking at Carrington as much as to say, Well, now, what are you going to do about *that?*—and Carrington would look anxiously about the board, convinced that his whole defense position was in jeopardy. When Carrington, for his part, made what he fondly believed to be a good attacking move, Gardner would smile knowingly and utter a sort of satisfied grunt which clearly intimated that this was the very move he had not only hoped but expected Carrington would make. And it was unfortunate for Carrington that after only twenty minutes' play Gardner was able to establish a clear moral advantage by allowing him to withdraw a foolish move: the elementary mistake of leaving his king and his queen in such positions that Gardner, in his next move, could have threatened both of them with the same knight.

Gradually, however, with a patient determination not to be ruffled by Gardner's tactics, Carrington fought back, and by the time Mrs. Porter brought in a tray of tea the antagonists were locked together in a tight and interesting situation in which it was difficult to decide where the advantage lay.

While they drank their tea they relaxed, discussing the opposing strategies of the game so far. They were more at ease with each other than at any time since they had met forty-eight hours earlier. When he had finished his tea Gardner stood up.

"Well, chum, it's your move. I'll leave you to think it over while I disappear for a moment. Shan't be long."

But five minutes later he had still not returned. Carrington went to the window and saw that the rain had stopped. He looked at his watch: it was just after half past four.

With Gardner out of the way, this would be a good opportunity, he thought, to nip out and collect the envelope which Bill Howard had left for him at the post office.

What he did not know was that Gardner was at this very moment in the post office, talking to the Admiralty from the telephone call box.

"Yes, a complete blank," Gardner was saying. "Did you check up on the schooner? . . . She's in the clear, is she? . . . Yes, I had a good look at everybody on board, passengers and crew, and I couldn't spot anything fishy going on. Passports? No, I didn't see them—I didn't have a warrant, of course, for making any kind of search. I gather the drill is that the captain hands in a list of passengers and passport numbers to the harbor-master, and that's that. I've checked with the harbor-master—our man wasn't on the list, of course. . . . No, no sign yet of this fifth passenger who never turned up. . . . What? Yes, Hitchcock, that's right. By the way, have you checked with Howard's wife? Nothing? Bit odd, isn't it? . . . No, Carrington's story seems genuine enough. He really is a solicitor and he really seems to be doing some genuine work—not very hard work, I admit, but still . . . It may be just one of those odd coincidences that do happen, though I certainly thought I was onto something when I ran into him. . . . Hullo, funnily enough, here he is, just coming into the post office here. Hold on a moment. . . ."

Gardner pushed the door of the telephone box slightly open with his foot. This served the double purpose of automatically switching off the light over his head and allowing him to hear what was going on. If Carrington happened to see him he would say he was trying to get through to Falmouth for news of his nonexistent boat.

Carrington, however, went straight to the counter and said: "I believe you have a letter for me. The name is Carrington."

"Mr. Carrington? Just a moment, sir." The girl turned to look at a rack of pigeonholes behind her and brought out a buff envelope, a trifle larger than the usual letter size.

"Do you have anything to identify you, please, sir? A driving license or something?"

Carrington pulled out a business card. "Will this do?"

Smiling, she handed the envelope to him.

"That's it," he said. Thank you very much. Good evening."

As soon as Carrington had left the shop, Gardner shut the door of the telephone box.

"Hullo, hullo . . . are you still there? Look here, something a little odd has happened. It may be nothing, but I'd better look into it. If it's of no significance I won't ring you again. Back tomorrow as planned in that case. If it leads anywhere I'll ring again on reverse charge later. Who's on duty tonight? . . . Fine. O.K. . . . be seeing you. Good-bye."

He came out of the call box and went over to the girl at the counter.

"Has the mail come in off the afternoon train yet?" he said. "I was rather expecting an urgent letter."

"No, sir, it hasn't come down yet."

"Oh . . . I just happened to see that gentleman collecting a letter, and I thought perhaps . . ."

"Oh no, sir, that letter was left here for the gentleman two or three days ago."

"I see . . . Well, thank you very much. Sorry to have troubled you."

"Not at all, sir. Good evening."

He walked back to the hotel with his mind racing. Two or three days ago, the girl had said. Perhaps, he thought, I'm onto something at last.

Carrington reached the hotel two minutes ahead of Gardner. He went straight to the lounge and resumed his study of the miniature chessboard. He had Howard's envelope, still un-opened, in his breast pocket. Wondering vaguely why Gardner was being such a long time, he took out his pipe and filled it. He was just lighting it when Gardner entered the room.

"Sorry I've been so long," said Gardner quietly. As he came across the room to his chair he was watching Carrington closely. "At any rate, you've had plenty of time to decide on your next move. Have you in fact moved yet?"

"No," said Carrington, surrounded by a blue haze of tobacco smoke. "I've got two or three possible lines of attack, and I can't make up my mind which one to take. However . . . let's see what happens if I do this." And he moved a pawn to threaten Gardner's only remaining rook and at the same time open up a line for his queen to put the king in check.

"Check," he said.

"Right!" said Gardner, sitting forward and studying the board with renewed concentration. Carrington glanced quickly at his face, surprised at the sudden grim hostility in the tone of that single exclamation.

The game now developed into an extraordinarily tense struggle. Up to this point Gardner still had his queen, two bishops, one rook and three pawns, whereas Carrington had his queen, two knights, one rook and four pawns. They thus still retained an equal number of major pieces, but Carrington was one pawn up. Their positions were closely interlocked, with both kings fairly near to the center of the board. Carrington was trying to keep the situation close and tight, to take advantage of his two knights; Gardner, on the other hand, aimed to loosen the game up to give greater scope to his free-ranging bishops. At this stage Carrington's extra pawn gave him a slight advantage.

Watching Gardner's face almost sweating with concentration, Carrington began to have a curious feeling that they were playing not one game but two—that superimposed on the game of chess was another and larger issue whose outcome depended on the result of the struggle between the opposing checkerboard armies. Will power, not skill alone, was going to be the deciding factor: it was a question of who was going to break first.

Twenty minutes later the game had opened up a little. They had each lost their remaining rooks, and Gardner had leveled up by capturing one of Carrington's pawns.

It was Carrington's move.

Gardner lit a cigarette, and then said, casually, "Has any mail arrived, do you know?"

"Not so far as I know," replied Carrington, frowning at the board. "Why, are you expecting something?"

"Not particularly, but I thought perhaps you were."

"I?" Carrington was startled, prickly with a sudden sense of danger. He forced himself not to look up at Gardner. What was the fellow getting at? "No, I don't think so," he said, keeping his voice quiet and moving his hand up to toy with his queen as though in contemplation of a move.

"Oh," continued Gardner. "I had an idea you said you were expecting a letter. Never mind."

"No, not so far as I know."

Carrington was very conscious of the bulge of Howard's envelope in his breast pocket. But he was certain Gardner couldn't possibly know anything about that. He decided he was bluffing, and continued the appearance of pondering his next move.

But his opponent's double-edged thrust of gamesmanship had fatally undermined his concentration. He saw an opening for a knight's threat against one of Gardner's bishops, and wondered why he had not spotted the opening before. So he moved his knight. To his surprise Gardner ignored the threat to his bishop, and instead swiftly moved a pawn to threaten Carrington's other knight. Too late Carrington realized that he had exposed the lynch-pin of his whole tactical position. Five moves later Gardner slowly pushed his queen across the full width of the board until she was poised at the head of a clear diagonal line leading directly to Carrington's king. And there was nothing Carrington could do about it.

"Check," said Gardner quietly . . . "and mate, I think."

With a deep sigh Carrington stood up and stretched his arms. "Well done," he said, "that was a good tight game."

Gardner was smiling at him in a rather curious way. "Yes," he said, "you had me very worried for a while." There was an odd coldness in his voice which made Carrington feel that his words held more than their face value. "Unfortunately for you Carrington, you made one careless mistake—and in this sort of game that's a thing you can't afford to do."

Carrington looked steadily at him, keeping a poker face and trying to guess what implications he should read into the seemingly innocent comment. Then he said:

"The mistake I made was to allow my concentration to be disturbed. But never mind—it was a thoroughly interesting game. I'd challenge you to a return match tomorrow, but unfortunately I'm going back to London first thing in the morning."

"Leaving so soon? But tomorrow's Friday. Why don't you stay down for the week end as well?"

"No, there's something at the office I have to attend to tomorrow afternoon—and besides," he continued, inventing a lie, "I have a dinner date in town in the evening. By the way, what about your boat from Falmouth? Surely she ought to have got here by now?"

Gardner looked out of the window, almost as though he expected to see the boat coming into the harbor there and then.

"Yes, I'm getting a bit anxious about her. With this gale springing up, though, I fully expect to get a phone call at any moment telling me she's put in at Plymouth or Dartmouth or somewhere."

"Well, I think I'll go up and have a wash and change into something a little more respectable. See you in the bar presently."

When he got to his room Carrington locked the door, sat down in a chair by the window and took Howard's envelope from his breast pocket. He slit the flap with a penknife and pulled out two white envelopes.

One of them was addressed in Bill's handwriting to Mrs. W. J. Howard at an address in Haslemere; the envelope was stamped. The other, to Carrington's surprise, was unstamped and bore not an address but the words *Urgent, to be delivered by hand*. Attached to this second envelope by a paper clip was a penciled note from Howard:

PEDRO,

Sorry about this. I'm afraid this letter can't be posted, as I don't know the address. I beg of you to carry out this one last assignment for me. It will not involve you in any way. All you have to do is this: As soon as you get back to London ring Paddington 2354. Simply say you have "a present from Angela." You will then be given delivery instructions. After that, you can wash your hands of me. I doubt if you will ever hear from me again. Don't think too unkindly of me.

Yours,

BILL

P.S. *Burn this note as soon as you have memorized its contents. God bless, and thanks for everything.*

Carrington read the note through three times, and then sat looking out of the window. This was something he had not expected. Surely Bill had said both letters were to be posted. He had thought all he had to do on reaching London was to drop them into the nearest letter box, and that would be that. But this was something quite different. And Bill had already written this note before their meeting in the boat yard: he knew *then* that one of the letters had to be delivered by hand. Bill had lied to him, lied because he was afraid he would refuse to take the letters. What sort of message was this that could not be entrusted to the post? It all had a sinister, underhand ring about it, and Carrington didn't like it one little bit. I suppose I shall have to do it, he thought—because of what Bill did for me, because I'm too involved already, because I can't let him down at this stage.

He sighed heavily, more than a little embittered toward Howard for having deceived him into this predicament. It was not quite playing the game.

"Blast!" he said aloud.

He read through the note again. Then he took out his pocket diary and turned to the section headed "Telephone Numbers." After the last name (it was "Julie" with a Sloane number) he now added in pencil the words "Angela, Paddington 2354." He went to the wastepaper basket beside the dressing table and picked out an empty two-ounce tobacco tin he had thrown into it that morning. He tore Howard's penciled note and the outer envelope into small pieces, put them in the open base of the tobacco tin and set light to them. When they were fully burned he stirred the ashes with his penknife, took the tin to the window and shook it into the air. The wind scattered the ashes into a fine and irrevocable dust.

The two envelopes he put carefully into the back pocket of his wallet.

Then he undressed and washed himself at the hand basin, thinking over the things he had to do: tell Mrs. Porter he was leaving, pay his bill tonight to save time in the morning, organize a taxi to catch the 8:40 train from Churston, and arrange for an early call. Breakfast he would have on the train. He would pack his bag tonight before getting into bed.

He stood in front of the mirror, brushing his hair. His face looked sullenly back at him: it had a worried frown between the eyebrows, and the mouth had a rather disagreeable expression of petulance. He bared his teeth in a ferocious scowl and then relaxed his whole face, trying to adopt a calmer and more cheerful appearance.

He put on a clean shirt and the light suit he had worn coming down in the train. Slipping on his jacket he wondered what sort of evening lay ahead—his last evening with Jane. That damned fellow Gardner, with his supercilious manner—if only he weren't around all the time. . . . He put his wallet in his breast pocket, took a clean handkerchief out of a drawer, adjusted his tie in the mirror, unlocked the door and went downstairs to the cocktail bar.

"This is a beautiful wine, Peter."

It was some three hours later, and they were alone in the dining room. The room was in darkness except for the intimate spotlight thrown on the cloth by the table lamp and reflected softly upward into Jane's hair. She had pushed back her plate of cheese and biscuits, and with her elbows on the table she was looking at Carrington over the top of her wineglass.

"Yes," he said, "it's the Château Latour we were supposed to have had last night. It's not too bad considering it was decanted twenty-four hours ago."

"Well, I think it's delicious."

"I must say it was very noble of the commander to take himself off to the pictures on a night like this, just to leave us on our own—all the way to Torquay, too."

"Yes, he's not so bad as you think, you know."

"I know. I've been rather beastly about him, I suppose. It's just that . . . "

"Just that what?"

"Oh, I don't know. Never mind, let's enjoy our wine. . . . What happened to the honeymoon couple, by the way?"

"I believe they left sometime this morning. They seemed very happy with each other," she said, looking dreamily over Carrington's shoulder. "I felt very warmly toward them. I suppose it's true, really, the old saying that all the world loves a lover."

"Was that why Mrs. Porter tactfully turned out the room lights a little while ago, do you think?"

Jane took a sip of her wine, and looked gravely at him.

"Are we lovers?" she asked.

He picked up the decanter and poured a little wine into each of their glasses.

"*I* am," he said, very quietly, warming his glass in the palm of his hand and looking down into the wine. Then he raised his head and looked at her. His face had gone deadly serious. "I'm in love with you, Jane."

She stared at him, turning a little pale. Her forehead wrinkled and her eyes had an expression of sadness which struck him so forcibly that he had to swallow a little wine to conceal his emotion.

"My dear Peter," she said, moving her left hand across the tablecloth toward him. He put out his own hand and held hers in a tight grip.

"This is a proposal, Jane. I want to marry you."

She shook her head slowly, biting her lower lip.

"It can never be, Peter."

He fixed his eyes on a wine stain on the tablecloth. "Could I be allowed to know why?" he asked.

"Peter . . ." she began, and then hesitated. She seemed to be looking for the right words to say something that was not easy to say. "This may sound a bit dramatic, but the truth is . . . there are things about myself I can never tell you. I can't marry you, Peter, but bless your darling heart for asking me. I shall never forgive myself for the way I've behaved to you these last two days. . . . Can you lend me a handkerchief?"

"Here," he said, passing his handkerchief across the table. She dabbed at her face. "I'm sorry. I'm so sorry."

"Do you love *me*, Jane?"

She looked at him wildly. "Don't ask me that, please," she said, and moved to stand up. But he held on to her hand and pulled her gently back into her chair.

"Forgive me," he said. "I'm upsetting you. Come, let's finish the wine."

He poured out the last of the decanter, sharing it equally between them. He held up his glass, and with an odd little crooked smile she clinked her own against it. He felt a tremendous tenderness toward her.

"To us," he said, raising his glass to his lips, and holding her eyes with his. She said nothing, but drained her glass to the last drop as though she was dying of thirst.

She opened her handbag and looked at her face in her mirror. "I must look awful. Do you mind if I do a few running repairs?"

"You look beautiful, but go ahead."

She began dabbing at her cheeks with her powderpuff, and he watched her in silence. Presently he said:

"Jane, I have to go back to London in the morning, you know."

"Yes, I know."

"Would you let me telephone you someday?"

"Peter, my dear Peter . . . we must never meet again."

He felt a sudden rage against this absurd wall of mystery between them. He wanted to shake her by the shoulders and cry: Why, why, why? But he held on to himself, and finished his glass of wine, drinking it slowly, savoring it to the end. Then he took out his wallet and extracted one of his business cards. Leaning forward, he dropped it into her open handbag.

"At least let me give you *my* phone number. In case you should ever change your mind."

"All right, Peter," she said, and without looking at it slipped it into one of the inner pockets, smiling sadly at him. She shut the bag, placed it before her on the table and rested her hands on it.

"Well, Peter, it was a lovely dinner. . . ." He knew at once from the way she spoke that this was the beginning of their good-bye. The evening was crumbling apart, and there was nothing more he could do to hold it together. His memory flashed back to the train journey on which they had met; their first meal together had ended rather like this. One moment he was riding high; in the next, without knowing why, he suddenly found he had trespassed beyond some invisible boundary, and the magic spell was broken.

He looked miserably at her. "You are leaving me?"

"Yes. I think I'll go to bed early. You ought to do the same if you've got to catch that early train." She was standing up.

"You can't say good-bye to me like this," he said, rising to his feet. "Not like this, for God's sake!"

She slipped the strap of her handbag over her arm and, moving quickly toward him, took his head in both her hands and kissed him with a desperate passion. "Don't make it more difficult for me, my darling," she said, murmuring the words into his lips. He could feel her tears flowing wet on his cheeks.

Then she broke away from him and went, almost running, to the door.

After she had gone he stood there for several minutes. Presently he sank back into his chair at the table. On the floor to his right, close to the table, he saw something small and white. He picked it up. It was her handkerchief. He held it in his left hand and pressed his face against it, breathing her perfume. Suddenly he remembered how, on the afternoon of the previous day—a whole age ago, it seemed—that same hand had held her sun-warmed breast; her nipple had been firm in the hollow of his palm. He groaned aloud, and at the same moment was aware that the door of the room had opened.

It was Mrs. Porter.

"Oh, is that you, Mr. Carrington?"

He pulled himself together. "Oh, hullo, Mrs. Porter. Yes, we've finished our dinner. I was just finishing the last of the wine." He slipped the handkerchief into his pocket.

She came up to the table. "I hope everything was all right?"

"Yes, marvelous, thank you. That's a very good wine."

"I'm glad you enjoyed it, sir. I hope Mrs. Day enjoyed it too. Are you feeling all right, sir? You look a bit . . ."

"Yes, I'm quite all right, thank you, Mrs. Porter. I'll tell you what, though, I wouldn't mind a nice large brandy."

"I've got Hennessy Three Star—is that all right?"

"Yes, fine, fine."

When she came back with the brandy she said, "I've made out your bill as you asked, Mr. Carrington, and your taxi is all arranged. And I'll get the girl to call you at half past seven with a cup of tea. Would you rather pay the bill now or later? Whichever you like, sir."

"I'll pay now, thank you. You added the brandy, did you?" He counted out the notes.

"Thank you, sir. . . . Well, I hope you enjoyed your stay. Perhaps you'll come again one day."

"Thank you, Mrs. Porter. Yes, I certainly will."

"Well, I'll leave you to enjoy your brandy. Good night, sir."

"Good night, and thanks for everything."

He sat at the table for perhaps half an hour, growing more and more depressed. Finally he knocked back the last of the brandy and said aloud, "Curse the whole bloody lot of them."

He got to his feet and went upstairs. In the corridor outside Jane's room he hesitated, longing to knock at the door on any wild pretext merely to see her once more. But he resisted the temptation and went along to his own room.

He undressed, got into his pajamas and then packed his suitcase, leaving out the clothes he was going to wear in the morning. He opened his wallet and extracted Howard's two letters. These he placed very carefully inside the front cover of his Dring Development file, slipped the file under his clothes at the bottom of the suitcase, locked the suitcase and put it into the wardrobe cupboard.

He was just getting into bed when he heard the sound of a car drawing up in the street below his window. He looked out and saw that it was Gardner's convertible. Then he got into bed, turned out the light and tried to get to sleep.

But sleep would not come. His brain was in a turmoil of bitterness and anxiety. He switched on the light and tried to lose himself in the Graham Greene novel he had brought with him.

Half an hour later he suddenly heard a soft knocking on his door.

"Hullo!" he called, a little startled. "Who's there?"

There was no reply, but almost at once he saw that a piece of paper had been slipped under the door. He jumped out of bed and picked it up. On it was written:

"I must see you. Jane."

14

He stared at the note for a whole minute. Then, crushing it into his pajama pocket, he went to the mirror and began combing his hair. There was a gray-blue shadow along the edge of his jaw; he brushed it with his fingertips and it felt like sandpaper. With deft movements he inserted a new blade in his safety razor, lathered his face and gave himself a quick shave. His heart was beating a little faster than usual as he toweled himself dry and slipped into his dressing gown. Shutting the door softly behind him, he walked casually along the corridor. Her door was ajar: he went in without knocking and found the room in darkness except for the glow of the gas fire. She was in an apricot dressing gown of light wool and kneeling in front of the fire with her back propped against a small armchair. She did not look up as he entered the room. The fire, striking upward like dimmed footlights, cast slanting shadows above her cheeks and through the shower of hair which had fallen forward over her brow; an enlarged silhouette of her head and shoulders hovered on the ceiling above the bed on the opposite side of the room. Outside, the storm rattled on the window panes. For a while he remained leaning against the door with his hands in his dressing-gown pockets. As he gazed at the girl on the floor, a surge of happiness rose within him, obliterating his recent mood like a spring tide flowing in over the mud flats of an estuary.

After a long silence she said, "I was terribly afraid you would decide not to come."

He went across and sat himself in the armchair behind her, cradling her shoulders between his knees. He kissed the top of her head and began to caress the lobes of her ears.

"Why should you think I mightn't?"

"You must think me a strange sort of person."

"Strange? Yes, I've never met a girl like you before. But I love you."

She looked up at him with an expression of almost maternal concern. "We had such an unhappy good-bye downstairs," she said. "I couldn't bear it to end like that."

"Must it end at all?"

"Don't let's talk about that, not just now. Were you asleep? Did I wake you up?"

"No, I couldn't have slept, anyway."

"You seemed such a long time coming."

"I was shaving."

She reached up and stroked his face with the palm of her hand. "Why did you shave?" she asked. His only answer was to lower his head and rub the side of his jaw against the warm curve of her cheek. She turned toward him, and as she did so her shoulder moved disturbingly against him. Overwhelmed by a sudden hardening of desire he dropped his hand onto her body and stroked it hungrily through the rough wool of her dressing gown. Sliding his thumb under the belt, he ripped it open. The hills and valleys of her nakedness glowed in the light of the purring fire, a landscape of wind-smooth sand dunes under a flaming sky.

"Be sweet to me," she said softly, offering her mouth to him and undoing the top button of his pajama coat.

The pleasure of their love-making on the cushioned floor was beyond anything in Carrington's experience. In her uninhibited responses to the promptings of his exploring hand he discovered an endearing blend of innocence and sophistication. An unexpectedly strong element of tenderness mingled with his sensuality, uplifting his physical sensations to a plane of hitherto unimagined ecstasy. His experienced seductive skill became, for once, entirely subconscious, submerged in the ardent expression of a genuine affection and love. The gentle deliberation of his entry, in a lyrical confusion of arms and thighs, stirred her to the innermost center of her being. For a while he checked the mounting rhythm of their passion, holding her perfectly still beneath him, breathing against her throat, exquisitely aware of her perfumed skin, of the rise and fall of her breasts against him, and of his maleness throbbing within its haven of warmth and moisture. Raising himself on his arms he looked down at her upturned face, her hair in disarray on the dark cushion, her eyes shining softly from the depths of his shadow, her body classic in its flowing beauty. Profoundly moved by her loveliness he blurted out her name, but she lifted her hand to his mouth to silence him. At the same moment he saw that her eyes had filled with tears. To his surprise she turned her head aside on the cushion and burst into a spasm of uncontrolled sobbing. Her whole body, pinned to the floor beneath him, began to tremble. Carrington was shattered. With the sudden ebbing of passion's tide his emotions were an agonizing tangle of astonishment, hurt pride and loving concern.

"Darling, whatever's the matter?"

She shook her head and turned her face into the cushion, unable to stem the flow of weeping. Utterly baffled, he lay beside her, stroking her hair and murmuring meaningless words of comfort.

Presently, raising himself on one knee, he gathered her into his arms and carried her, still sobbing, across to the bed, easing her gently between the sheets. In her distress her face had become swollen, ugly almost; she buried it in the pillow, biting on the knuckle of a forefinger and whispering, "So sorry, so sorry," over and over again.

He seemed powerless to soothe her. Frustrated, mortified, even a little angry, he dressed himself in his pajamas. Then he sat on the edge of the bed with his hand on her shoulder, leaned over her and kissed the back of her head.

"Perhaps you are right," he said, "and we ought not to see each other again. There's something between us that I don't seem able to understand. I'm sorry it had to end like this. I shall never forget you."

He left her then, put his dressing gown on and went toward the door. But at her cry of anguish he turned. She had flung the bedclothes aside and was standing, one foot on the floor and her left knee still resting on the bed, a magnificent young Amazon. Her eyes were a little wild, and her voice was husky with agitation.

"Peter, for God's sake, you mustn't leave me. I know I'm being an awful bitch to you, but please, please, don't go away. I promise you I'm all right now. I'll be good to you. I'll do anything you want me to."

She moved swiftly over to him and with desperate haste began pulling at his clothes, opening his dressing gown, ripping at his buttons, ravishing him with her hands, inciting him with every means of sensuality at her command. Carrington, who thought he had come to the end of being surprised by this unpredictable girl, found himself responding almost viciously to her onslaught. Their passion was brief, erotic, savage, and when the shuddering climax was past they lay exhausted across the bed in an abandoned tangle of limbs.

The first glimmering of dawn was beginning to show at the edges of the curtains when she roused him quietly from his profound sleep.

"Peter," she said, stroking his cheek with the back of her hand. "Darling, it's beginning to get light. Hadn't you better be getting back to your room?"

He grunted, and moved his hand drowsily on her body. Without opening his eyes he began to make love to her again, gently, affectionately, lazily almost. This time there was no breathless race to a toppling pinnacle, but rather a slowly rising flood of tenderness which finally brimmed over into a hinterland of overwhelming peace. Presently she sighed, a sigh so deep that he lifted his head and opened his eyes.

"Hullo," he said, smiling at her, "good morning!"

"Darling," she said, toying with a curl of dark hair on his temple, "you really must go, you know. It's getting light. And you've got a train to catch."

Groaning, he forced himself out of the bed and got into his pajamas and dressing gown. When he was ready to go he came and stood by the bed, looking down at her.

"Jane . . ." he began, but she reached up and pulled his head down for a kiss.

"I know what you're going to say. Don't spoil it. It's been wonderful, Peter, but please just go now—and remember me sometimes. Good-bye, darling."

With one hand on her breast he kissed her for the last time, and then turned and went to the door. Slipping back the catch, he went out without looking back.

As he entered his own room and switched on the light he suddenly had an inexplicable feeling that something was wrong. He shut the door and stood for a moment looking around the room. Everything seemed to be in order, just as he had left it. Then he thought of Howard's letters. He flung open the wardrobe cupboard: the suitcase was there, looking innocent enough. He pulled it out, rested it on the bed and unlocked it. There was no sign of its having been disturbed. He felt down in the case for the Dring Development file. It was there all right. He lifted it out and opened it. Lying on the top, exactly where he had placed them, were the two letters. Sighing with relief, he put them back in the same place, relocked the suitcase and shoved it into the wardrobe. Then he got into bed—the sheets felt cold—and daydreamed about Jane until the maid knocked on the door and brought in his morning cup of tea.

An hour later he was on the train, speeding back to London.

15

Carrington had no reason to think there was anything suspicious about the fair-haired man in a light brown suit who was sitting in the corner seat diagonally opposite to his own. The man had boarded the train at Torquay, and after passing his compartment three times had come in and sat down and buried himself in *The Times*. Preoccupied with bittersweet memories of his night with Jane and his anxieties over Howard, Carrington was in no mood for idle conversation. Except for a few stereotyped comments on the continued stormy weather the two men exchanged hardly a dozen words all the way to London.

Nor did he think it odd when, on their arrival at Paddington at half past one, the man in the brown suit walked down the platform with him, chatting amiably about nothing in particular. Preceding him through the ticket barrier, Carrington did not see the almost imperceptible signal which passed between his erstwhile traveling companion and a nondescript man in a raincoat and a bowler hat who was standing beside the barrier.

Carrington, who had eaten an early lunch on the train, at once took a taxi to his flat in Campden Hill Square. Having no cause to suppose he was being followed, it did not occur to him to turn his head and look out of the rear window; had he done so he might have wondered about the second taxi which followed him all the way to Notting Hill and actually passed him as he was paying off his own taxi at his front door on the western side of the square. By the time Carrington had entered his ground-floor flat, taken off his coat and flipped through his four days' mail, the man in the bowler hat was making a call from a phone box on the opposite side of the main road. From this vantage point he had a good view up the steep slope of the square, and no one could have left the house without his being aware of it. After he had finished his phone call he crossed the road again and stood waiting on the corner of the square. Some fifteen minutes later an unobtrusive gray sedan, traveling fast from the direction of Marble Arch, and occupied by the driver and four burly men in plain clothes, pulled up alongside him for a brief word, and then drove into the square. It turned at the top and parked a few doors up the hill from the attractive Regency house in which Carrington had his flat.

Unaware of all this interest in his movements, Carrington settled down at the telephone in his sitting room to make one or two calls. First he took out his diary, looked up the number he had written down after reading Howard's note the evening before, and dialed Paddington 2354. The ring was answered almost at once by a man's voice, terse, flat, unemotional.

"Who is speaking?"

"I have a present from Angela," said Carrington.

"I see . . ." said the voice, hesitating a little. "Well, perhaps we could meet and hear all the latest news. What about somewhere in the West End this evening?"

"That's all right with me."

"Right, Charing Cross Underground station, on the north-bound platform of the Northern Line. Stand looking at the large Underground map under the train indicator board. At five-thirty exactly. How shall I know you, please?"

"I'm tallish . . . dark, rather curly hair. I'll be wearing a navy-blue overcoat, white shirt, no hat. . . ."

"I'm afraid that's all rather too vague. Have you a brightly colored tie you could wear?"

"I could wear a yellow tie if you like."

"Good. A yellow tie will be excellent. And I suggest that in your left hand—your *left* hand—you carry a pair of gloves, a copy of the *Evening Standard* and some magazine—what shall we say? . . ."

"Would *The New Yorker* do? I happen to have one with me."

"Yes, *The New Yorker*. Good. So—five-thirty this evening, in front of the map under the indicator board, on the north-bound platform of the Northern Line at Charing Cross. Don't be late, please. Don't be too early either. Don't look around, look as though you are studying the map. Good-bye."

Carrington put the receiver down and sat for a while looking out of the window at the wind-tossed trees in the square. He couldn't help feeling the whole thing was a bit childish; it was the sort of nonsense you read about in cheap spy thrillers. But he ran his mind over the details of the instructions, memorizing them carefully.

Then he picked up the telephone again and dialed his office.

"Good afternoon. Prebble, Smith and Carrington."

"Oh, hullo, Mrs. Wharton. Peter Carrington here. How's everything?"

"Much as usual, sir. Nothing special to report."

"Anyone been chasing me?"

"Miss Henderson has telephoned several times—twice this morning as a matter of fact."

Miss Henderson was Julie, his current girl friend.

"Oh. Any message?"

"No, but she seems very anxious for you to ring her."

"Oh dear . . . Right, I'll take care of her. Perhaps I could speak to my uncle if he's free."

"I'll put you through, sir. Just a moment."

His uncle's precise voice came on the line. "Hullo, Peter. Where are you speaking from?"

"I'm in my flat, only just got in. I can be in the office in half an hour."

"It's hardly worth your coming in, is it? It's Friday afternoon, and everything's under control. I suggest you take it easy and make a fresh start on Monday morning. How did you get on?"

"It was all rather unsatisfactory, really. It's not very easy to talk about it on the telephone. Perhaps you could spare me half an hour on Monday."

"Are you doing anything tonight?"

"I hadn't planned anything."

"Well, if you could bear to drag yourself up to Hampstead, why not come and have dinner with us? Then you can tell me all about it."

"Thank you, that would be very nice. What time?"

"Shall we say seven-thirty?"

"Right, I'll be there. Thank you very much."

Carrington now had nearly three hours to waste before it would be time to set off for his rendezvous at Charing Cross. He pottered miserably about the flat, unable to settle down to anything. Once he picked up the telephone to call Julie Henderson, but he put the receiver down before he had finished dialing the number. She could wait. Instead, he had a bath. He lay for half an hour luxuriating in the hot water, torturing himself with memories of Jane and the knowledge that, unless she changed her mind and telephoned *him,* he was never going to see her again.

When he had finished his bath he stayed in his dressing gown, made himself a pot of tea, wrote one or two letters, played the gramophone and generally mooched around. At half past four he began to dress, putting on a dark lounge suit. After he had met this fellow and handed over Howard's letter, he decided, he would walk back to the Reform Club and prop up the bar until it was time to go off to his uncle's. He wished now he had not suggested the yellow tie: it was not quite the thing for dining out in. He would have to take a soberer tie in his pocket and change it when he got to the club.

At five o'clock he thought it was about time to get going. He put on his overcoat, slipped Howard's letter to his wife into one of the outside pockets, and placed the other letter carefully in the breast pocket of his jacket. Picking up his gloves and an old copy of *The New Yorker*, he went out, turning down the hill toward Holland Park Avenue. The driver of the gray sedan waited until Carrington reached the corner before starting up the engine and cruising slowly in the same direction.

At the corner Carrington turned right up the hill toward Notting Hill Gate Underground station. The impatient week-end traffic exodus was already piling up in a minor jam that would obviously be worse later on. The late-afternoon sun was flashing incendiary orange reflections from the high windows of the new apartment skyscraper over the main shopping center. Just before the station Carrington slipped the letter to Mrs. Howard into a pillar box.

At the top of the subway steps he bought an *Evening Standard*. Then he went down into the station booking hall, took a ticket to Charing Cross and rapidly descended the two escalators to the Central Line. Two minutes later he boarded an eastbound train. It did not occur to him to take any notice of four well-built but perfectly ordinary-looking men who mingled with the passengers and sat or stood in various parts of the carriage; to all outward appearances they had no connection with one another.

At Oxford Circus Carrington changed onto the Bakerloo Line. The Waterloo train was outrageously full; the evening rush hour was at its height, and the passengers were packed so tight that for the whole of this part of the journey he was actually jammed shoulder-to-shoulder with two of his shadowers.

Three stations later the train pulled in to Charing Cross, and as the doors slid open he allowed himself to be swept out with the disgorged flood of homegoing passengers. Following the signs directing him to the Northern Line, he was hustled along by the human torrent up a short staircase and through a long corridor tunnel until, feeling rather like a balk of timber coming into smooth water after tumbling through rapids, he finally debouched onto the northbound platform of the Northern Line.

He looked at his watch: he had timed it nicely. He had three minutes in hand.

Overhead, and almost immediately to his left, was the electric indicator board showing the destinations of the next three trains. On the wall directly below it was one of the colored London Transport maps of the Underground system. Looking along the concave wall with its myriad posters, he made sure there were no other maps in the vicinity, and then, holding his gloves, his *Evening Standard* and *The New Yorker* in his left hand, took up position in front of the map and made a show of being absorbed in a study of its ramifications. He did not have to wait long.

He soon became aware of a man in a dirty fawn-colored raincoat standing alongside him and leaning forward to look at the map. He had just had time to take in his cadaverous complexion, the balding patch on the back of his head and the long, pointed nose, when, without turning his head, the man said:

"Follow me. Don't say a word until I speak to you."

The crowd was so thick that Carrington had some difficulty at first in keeping close to him as he left the platform and began climbing an escalator at a rapid pace. But twisting, dodging, side-stepping, he pushed his way through, and at the top of the escalator he was tight on the man's heels, breathing hard. Turning to his left, the man led him into the wide central concourse. Here the congestion was at its worst, for they were now at the confluence of several converging and criss-crossing streams of rush-hour travelers.

Suddenly the man turned his head quickly and fell back for a moment into step with Carrington. There was something unpleasantly ratlike about his face. Still walking rapidly, he held out his hand.

"You have something for me? Quickly, please."

Carrington fumbled in his breast pocket, pulled out Howard's envelope and handed it over. As the man snatched it from him, Carrington found his arms brutally pinned behind his back.

The events of the next few seconds were so confused that afterward Carrington found it difficult to remember exactly what happened. Four tough plain-clothes policemen seemed to have appeared from nowhere; two of them were holding Carrington in a grip that sent an agonizing pain through his left arm; the others were diving forward into the crowd. The rat-faced man in the fawn-colored raincoat had vanished.

The pain in Carrington's arm was becoming unbearable. "Ease up a bit," he grunted over his shoulder. "I'm not trying to get away. I don't know what this is all about, but you're going to break my arm if you're not bloody careful."

"No funny tricks, now," said one of the men behind him, "or you'll be sorry. All right, Harry, easy now, but watch him."

With the relaxing of the pain Carrington began to take stock of his embarrassing position. The three of them were causing a considerable bottleneck in the pressing flood of men and women hurrying to their trains. A little crowd was gathering about them, curious to see what was going on, increasing the congestion.

"Come along now," boomed one of Carrington's captors,

in the wearily sarcastic tone of a policeman who was used to this sort of thing. "No need to hang about, you're only holding up the traffic. Move along please."

Reluctantly the crowd of onlookers began to disperse.

Carrington said, "You needn't worry. I don't intend to make a run for it. Do you mind telling me what this is all about?"

"We're Scotland Yard, Special Branch, sir, and we're taking you in for questioning."

"Would I be allowed to know what for?"

"You'll find out soon enough, sir."

"Well, what are we waiting for?"

"Don't get impatient, now. All in good time."

At that moment the other two plain-clothes men could be seen weaving their way back through the crowd toward them. They looked crestfallen.

"Any luck, Shorty?"

"Not a smell of him. Got clean away. It's worse than trying to find a needle in a haystack in this mob. What about this fellow? Giving any trouble?"

"Let him try, that's all. Well, boys, we'd better take him in. Come along, Mr. Carrington, and don't try any funny business, please."

So they knew his name.

His mind was in a ferment as the five of them made their way up the final escalator to the station exit. He was no longer under violent physical restraint, but with two policemen ahead of him and two behind there would have been no hope of making a bolt for it even if he had wanted to. He felt utterly defeated, numbed, resigned, and full of a growing anger against Howard.

In the station entrance hall they waited while one of the policemen made a phone call. Soon afterward a police car arrived, and they all got into it. The car drove up Villiers Street, stopped for the lights at the top, and then turned left along the Strand, crossed the bottom of Trafalgar Square and over into the Mall. Immediately after passing through Admiralty Arch, the driver pulled in at the entrance to the Admiralty itself.

Three minutes later Carrington was being ushered into a large room on the first floor. In the center of the room was a large conference table, and sitting at the far end of it a group of about eight men, some in naval uniform, some in civilian clothes. In the far left-hand corner, standing with her back to the room, a Wren officer was stooping over a small desk, gathering up a sheaf of papers.

As Carrington entered, followed by the four Special Branch officers, the men at the table turned their heads toward him. Somehow he was not surprised when he recognized Commander Tony Gardner sitting nearest to him on the left-hand side of the table. Of the rest of the men in uniform none seemed to be below the rank of commander. In the center of the table lay a tape recorder.

The man at the head of the table, a rugged, stern-faced admiral with a large head and white hair cropped very short, waved a hand toward the lonely chair at the bottom end of the table.

"Sit down, Carrington," he said curtly.

As Carrington took his seat at the table, the Wren officer turned from the desk in the corner and moved across to place a batch of papers in front of the admiral.

Carrington sat transfixed with horror. For a moment, as she stood back behind the admiral's chair, their eyes met. He stared at her, incredulous. She dropped her eyes, and then immediately raised them again to his, wrinkling her forehead in the way he remembered so well; her glance made a mute appeal for forgiveness.

Turning away from him, she bent her head toward the admiral.

"Will you need me any more for the moment, sir?"

"No, Jane, not for the moment, thank you. But you'll be around if we need you? This may take some time."

"Yes, sir, I'll be in my office."

Carrington did not watch her as she walked round the table and out of the room. He had buried his head in his hands, unable to credit this last shattering blow to his crumbling world.

But almost at once he pulled himself together and prepared to face his interrogators. Someone switched on the tape recorder.

16

The admiral leaned forward, shuffled the papers in front of him and turned to the man sitting on his immediate left: a ruddy-complexioned man, sprucely dressed in a dark gray lounge suit, with a somewhat bulbous nose, tough chin, stern but kindly eyes and short, graying hair.

"I expect you'd like to shoot first, Detective Superintendent?"

"Thank you, Admiral . . . Mr. Carrington, what we'd like to know first of all, as a matter of some urgency, is the name of the man you have just met at Charing Cross."

"I've no idea who he is," said Carrington truthfully.

"Come, Mr. Carrington, you go to meet a man in the middle of the rush hour, at one of the busiest spots in London, and you have no idea who he is? How were you supposed to recognize him if you didn't know him?"

"I didn't. He found me."

"Had you ever met this man before?"

"No."

"Then someone must have put you in touch with him in the first place."

Carrington was silent. His brain was doing its best to cope with a bewildering situation, trying to guess at how much they knew.

"Let me put it another way, Mr. Carrington. How did he get in touch with you to arrange the meeting?"

"He didn't. I telephoned him."

"I see! you telephoned *him*. May we then be allowed to know the telephone number you rang?"

Carrington flicked his eyes round the table. The faces were stony, impassive, neutral.

The superintendent's voice cut in on his hesitation like a cold chisel. "The man with whom you had an assignation happens to be an agent for a foreign and potentially hostile power. . . . The number, Mr. Carrington?"

Carrington was feeling slightly sick.

"It was Paddington 2354," he said, clearing his throat.

The superintendent wrote the number down on the pad in front of him and beckoned one of the Special Branch men standing near the door.

"Burke, I want you to find out from the G.P.O. the name and address of the subscriber using this number. Get out a search warrant and go over the place with a fine-tooth comb. Break in if you have to. Bring in anyone you find, and we'll sort them out later. It may be a wild-goose chase. . . . I'm afraid you'll find the bird is flown by now. It's probably only an accommodation address anyway, but you never know. Take as many men as you think you'll need."

"Very good, sir."

When the four policemen had withdrawn, the superintendent clasped his hands on the table and thrust his jaw forward like a challenging bulldog.

"Now, Mr. Carrington, I'd like you to tell us where you got this telephone number from, and who gave you the envelope you handed over to this man?"

Carrington appealed to the admiral. "Do I have to answer that, sir?"

"I think, Superintendent," said the admiral, "that it might be a good thing at this juncture if I were to put one or two points to Carrington."

"By all means, sir."

"Look here, Carrington, you've caused us all—and Commander Gardner especially—a good deal of trouble this week. Would you be good enough to explain your reason for spending the last few days in Brixham?"

Still half stunned by the turn of events and his utterly unexpected meeting with Jane, Carrington was completely at sea. All he could do for the time being was to try to stick to his original story.

"I went ther, sir, to get away from the office and concentrate on a rather complicated piece of legal work."

"You may not be aware, Carrington," said the admiral, frowning, "that we know about a certain envelope which was left for you at Brixham post office and which you collected yesterday afternoon."

Carrington looked sharply up at the admiral.

"I thought that would surprise you. We have a few other surprises in store for you. For one thing, we know what that envelope contained. It contained two letters—didn't it, Carrington?—one addressed to Mrs. W. J. Howard, and one which you were to deliver to someone in London, which in fact you delivered to this man this evening. Do you know what those two letters were about?"

"No, sir, I have no idea." Carrington's voice was almost inaudible.

"I hope you are right, Carrington. It so happens that *we* have a very exact idea of their contents. Indeed, I have photostat copies of both of them in front of me now. Superintendent, have you any objections to my showing Carrington the copy of Howard's letter to his wife?"

"No objection, sir."

"I think you ought to read this, Carrington, even though

some of it is of a somewhat private nature," said the admiral, passing several sheets of thin photographic paper down the table. "It might affect your attitude considerably."

Carrington stared at the document. It was certainly in Bill's handwriting. It bore no address, but it was dated Tuesday, September 26, the day Carrington had traveled down to Brixham. Presumably it had been photographed either while it was waiting for him at the post office or . . . and suddenly he remembered the strong sense of premonition he had felt on returning to his room after leaving Jane—when was it?—good God, only just over twelve hours ago. So that was the meaning of her note under the door, of her desperate measures to prevent him from leaving her room. His blood ran hot at the memory. He had, it seemed, fallen for one of the oldest tricks in the world. What a fool he had made of himself!

As he began to read the letter he was filled with a growing sense of disillusion.

DEAR MARJORIE,

I am afraid this letter is going to be a bit of a shock to you. In the old days I would have opened my heart to you long ago—told you of my doubts and hesitations and tried to carry you along with me. But ever since that terrible day in 1944 when I surprised you by coming home unexpectedly on leave, things have turned sour between us.

The fault, no doubt, is as much mine as yours. I merely record the melancholy fact to explain why I have not been able to tell you before of something that has been taking place over a number of years—a radical change in my whole way of thinking about life.

I think I can date the beginning of my conversion—for that, as you will see, is what it really is—to a precise event during the war. I had torpedoed an Italian merchant ship in the Mediterranean. She sank in less than three minutes, but they managed to get a lifeboat away. I surfaced to see if I could discover some information about my target. There were five men in the boat. Two of them were horribly injured, and one in particular, a lad of about nineteen, had had the side of his face blown away. We gave them what medical aid we could spare—and then a German plane came down at us and we had to dive in a hurry. Even during the depth-charging that followed, the face of that boy haunted me. It was no good telling myself that this was one of the inevitable accidents of war: this was something I personally had done to a young man on the threshold of life, the only life he would ever have. It was my act in firing that torpedo that had done it. The beastliness of war began to obsess me, and from that time on I could never fire a torpedo without feeling quite sick.

After the war I brooded over the causes of war in general. I began to read history and economics, studied philosophy and comparative religion. Slowly I came to the conclusion that in the modern world recurrent war is the inevitable result of the cutthroat self-interest of the business world.

Then, when I was doing that NATO job, four years or so ago (you may remember), in the course of my duties I struck up an acquaintance with a most remarkable Russian, a naval officer like myself. We took a liking to each other, and we began to meet frequently, sometimes at my place, sometimes at his flat in East Berlin. He had a fascinating mind, spoke excellent English and had a world-wide range of interests. Gradually I came to see at first hand something of the Russian view of the world. To cut the story short, I became convinced—there was no question of "brain-washing"—that the Communist way of life, with all its present faults (and heaven knows there are many), offers the only hope for peace and the future of the human race.

So you will shortly learn that the husband you hate, the husband you once, for a short while, loved, has turned traitor to his country. All right, you will say, but why didn't you do the decent thing, resign your commission and emigrate to Russia?—for that at least would have been an honorable thing to do. But, my dear Marjorie, words like honor and treason mean different things in different contexts. It so happens that by virtue of my job I was in a position to know that "the West" is on the point of perfecting an underwater weapon which will so revolutionize submarine warfare that the possessor of it will be in a position of overwhelming superiority at sea. Now I strongly believe that a naval or military superiority of this order leads to a dangerous and tempting situation. I saw an opportunity to serve the greater cause of peace and the future of mankind by passing on to "the other side" everything I knew about this important research project—a project of which it so happened I was in charge in this country. I have been taking that opportunity.

It was inevitable, I suppose, that I should eventually come under suspicion. Things have begun to get too hot for me at last, and by the time you read this I shall be on my way to Russia, where I have no doubt at all that my specialist information and knowledge will be able to make a small contribution to the cause I have now espoused.

Treason? It depends on the point of view. In my view, in this day and age patriotism is not only not enough, it is a dangerous and outworn anachronism.

Goodbye, Marjorie—
BILL

When he had finished reading, Carrington dropped the pages wearily onto the table. He caught Gardner's eye, and was surprised at the oddly whimsical look of sympathy he saw on the face of this man who had been one of Howard's greatest friends.

"Not a very nice picture, is it?" said the admiral. "Incidentally, we think we know who this 'remarkable' Russian naval officer is. We have good grounds for believing he is one of Russia's most brilliant Secret Service agents, one of a picked group of men specially trained to undermine the loyalty of perhaps the most vulnerable type of individual—the cultured intellectual in a position of high confidence and trust. The ordinary method of brain-washing does not work with such individuals. They are too aware of its mechanics for it to be effective. Subtler methods have to be used, as they were used in the cases of Fuchs, George Blake and so on. But what is unique about the case of Howard, and what makes it rank as one of Russia's greatest *coups* to date, is that Howard is a serving officer of entirely British origin and with a brilliant record behind him of outstanding service to his country. You find his defection difficult to believe? So did we. Let me tell you now what was in the letter you passed over to Howard's contact at Charing Cross this evening.

"It was in fact a coded message. Fortunately for us, one of our counteragents was able recently to provide us with a key which has enabled our cipher experts to decode this message. Briefly, the note informs Howard's contact that he had become aware he was under suspicion, that he had been unable to get a warning through to him because of a telephone breakdown on the crucial day, and that he had now taken passage in the schooner *Black Pearl*. Now here comes the really vital part of the message. *He has with him,* it says, *microfilms of the final engineering drawings of the secret underwater weapon.* He gives the approximate E.T.A. at Tangier, where he proposes to disembark and make for the Russian consulate. But, he suggests, to make doubly sure, it would be preferable if a Russian submarine, supposing one to be available in the Eastern Atlantic, could intercept the schooner and take him off.

"Now, Carrington, perhaps all this will make you understand what a dangerous situation you've got yourself into. We have been looking up your war record, and we realize that you may, perhaps unwittingly, have become involved in a certain course of action out of an understandable sense of loyalty to your wartime commanding officer, whom you had, quite naturally, admired, and out of gratitude for a brave action which undoubtedly saved your life. But such considerations do not justify the aiding and abetting of the escape of a traitor or the conveying of a coded message to a Russian agent. You may help to make the situation less ugly if you are prepared to tell us frankly everything you know. Perhaps you would now like to reconsider your answer to my earlier question and give us an account of your three days in Brixham."

Carrington folded his arms and fixed his gaze on the tall window over the admiral's right shoulder. Heavy gray clouds were racing across it from the west.

He didn't think he would ever be able to forgive Howard for lying to him about that second letter.

He took a deep breath, and began telling them his story from the moment he received the telephone call from Howard. He told them how he had hung about in Brixham all that first day waiting for him to appear, how he had met the train in the mistaken belief that Howard would turn out to be the fifth passenger, and how he had looked vainly for him among the passengers on board the schooner. When he described the incident of the cigarette pack and his discovery of the note from Howard, he saw Gardner turn his face toward him with a wry grin.

He amused them with his description of the way he had eluded Gardner on his way to meet Howard in the boat yard, and when he reached the point at which the man who came to meet him there turned out to be the schoolmaster Ramsey, Gardner threw his head back, clapped his hand to his forehead and cried, "Good grief!"

"Do you mean to tell me," said the admiral, "that this fellow you took to be a schoolmaster was in fact Howard in disguise, and that both you and Commander Gardner had seen him at close quarters on board the schooner without recognizing him?"

"Yes, sir," said Carrington, "it was quite fantastic how utterly different he looked without his beard and wearing glasses. I could hardly believe it, but it was Captain Howard all right."

He gave a detailed account of everything he could remember about his conversation with Howard. Finally he told how he had stayed on in Brixham the extra day to divert Gardner's attention from the schooner.

But in all this he never once mentioned Jane.

When he had finished, the admiral made a note on the pad in front of him and leaned back in his chair, looking severely down the table at Carrington.

"Did it never occur to you, as a result of your meeting with Captain Howard, that what he was doing was a crime against the State, and that it was your duty to report the matter to the authorities? Instead of which you followed a line of behavior which actually impeded Commander Gardner in the execution of his duty."

Fixing his gaze on the slowly revolving spools of the tape recorder, Carrington said, "Looking back on it, and knowing what I know now, I do certainly agree that what I did was wrong. I can only say that at the time I had no idea exactly what Captain Howard had been up to, though it was obviously something pretty serious. I somehow assumed that whatever he had done was an accomplished fact, and that it was now simply a matter of his getting out of the country to escape arrest. In view of what he had done for me in the past, I felt I could not refuse my help. But I certainly did not know what job he had been doing in recent years, and it never occured to me that he was actually taking a secret document with him. Clearly he did not think I would have agreed to help him if I had known the full truth, otherwise he would not have lied to me about the second letter. He definitely told me that both the letters were of a personal nature, and that all I had to do was to post them in London. It was not until I collected the envelope from the post office and found the instructions attached to the second letter that I realized there must be something odd about it. But by that time the schooner had sailed, and I felt I could not then go back on my promise."

There was a long silence. Presently the admiral turned to Gardner.

"Perhaps, Gardner, you'd take Carrington along to your office while the rest of us talk this matter over for a few minutes. I'll give you a buzz when we want you back."

Gardner's office was three doors further down the same corridor. It was a smallish office, simply furnished with a bare table, swivel chair, visitor's armchair, a couple of filing cabinets and several shelves full of books and files. Almost the whole of one wall was taken up by a blown-up aerial photograph of what appeared to be a large land-locked stretch of water. Carrington stood in front of it, trying to identify it.

"U.2 shot of the Eastern Baltic, showing Russian naval installations in fantastic detail," said Gardner, lowering himself wearily into the swivel chair. "Impressive, isn't it? Well, sit down and have a cigarette."

Carrington sank heavily into the armchair. "What's going to happen, do you think? Do I spend the next few years in jail?"

"Can't tell yet," said Gardner, "but I'd say you got a pretty sympathetic reception on the whole. The old admiral can be a bit of a tartar if he likes, and you never know. But my guess is you may get off with a stern warning, as you've been fairly co-operative. I must say, though, you had me foxed for a long time down at Brixham. I still find it hard to believe that schoolmaster really was Bill. It was a damned good disguise."

"Tell me," said Carrington, "when did you first realize he had actually got away?"

Gardner was looking extremely tired. He had had no sleep the previous night, and he had just driven two hundred miles up from Devonshire. But at Carrington's question his lean face crinkled into an impish grin.

"Do you remember when we finished our chess game, and I told you that you'd made one careless mistake?"

"I remember. I realized you weren't referring to the chess."

"By a sheer fluke I happened to be in the post office when

you went in to pick up your envelope. I was in the phone box
—telephoning the Admiralty as a matter of fact. I was so
curious that after you'd left the shop I had a word with the
girl, and she told me the letter had been left there two or three
days before. I knew then that it couldn't be anything to do with
your office. Putting two and two together I guessed what had
happened. Anyway, I just had to get a look at what was in the
envelope. On the pretext of going to the cinema, as you may
remember, I drove into Torquay to see the local police and
persuade them to bring photographic equipment over to Brixham. Then I came back and made arrangements to get you
out of your room for some time. . . ."

"Yes, damn your eyes," said Carrington, nervously chewing
the skin at the side of one of his thumbnails, "and I fell for it,
hook, line and sinker."

"Sorry about that—it's a dirty game this, sometimes. But I
couldn't think of any other way to do it. Anyway, it gave me
enough time to search your room, find the two letters, get them
round to the local police station, steam them open, photograph
them, and get them back into your suitcase. The photographs
were then rushed to London by fast police car from Torquay.
We realized the second letter was a code message, though we
didn't yet know what it was all about, but we decided for the
time being to let you carry on back to London, hoping the
cipher boys would be able to unscramble the code before you
got there. By this time, of course, M.I.6, the Foreign Office,
Special Branch, the Prime Minister—the lot—were all agog.
You were trailed from Torquay onwards."

"That, I suppose would be the fellow who shared my compartment."

"I imagine so. Meanwhile, as soon as you had left the hotel
in Brixham, Jane and I hopped into my car and hared up to
London. What a fiendish drive that was!"

"Why didn't you have me picked up in Brixham last night?"

"I'm coming to that. By the time you reached London, the boys here had decoded the message. This confirmed that it was addressed to Bill's contact with the Russians. It was decided to take a chance and let you make the rendezvous, hoping to bag the contact as well. You were now being followed, of course, wherever you went. Did you know?"

"No, I never had a clue."

"Unfortunately, as you know, the plan misfired. Not only did we miss the bugger altogether, but the message got through as well. Complete balls-up! By now the Russians will know that Bill is on that schooner. Even if he didn't have those drawings with him, it would be a disaster for us if he got into their hands. He knows too much."

"Can't we do anything about it?"

"I fancy the admiral will be cooking up some sort of scheme, which we'll no doubt hear about shortly."

"Perhaps I shouldn't ask this," said Carrington, looking carefully at the toes of his shoes, "but where exactly did Jane come in on all this?"

"Jane?" said Gardner. He looked carefully at Carrington before replying. "Jane has worked with me in Naval Intelligence for several years now. She's quite a girl—but I imagine I don't have to tell you that. She and I have worked on several jobs like this together. A woman can often create a useful diversion. In your case, she made it possible, for instance, to have your movements covered most of the time—a job I couldn't possibly have done on my own, and certainly not so discreetly if it had been another man."

Carrington ran his hand through his hair. "God, she must have thought I was a fool!"

Gardner pushed a button on his desk. Carrington heard the buzzer in the adjoining room, and a moment later Jane came in through the communicating door. She stopped dead on seeing Carrington.

"Come in, Jane," said Gardner. "Look, I've got to slip in next door to have a look at a chart or two. Could you keep an eye on this arch-criminal until I come back?"

"How's everything going?" she said.

"Don't know yet, but now that our friend here knows what Howard has been playing at he's being very helpful. My hunch is he'll get let off with a caution." He came round the table, grinning at Carrington and gave him a gentle clap on the shoulder. "Cheer up, you never know your luck!"

At the door he turned. "I'm expecting the admiral to ring through at any minute to say he wants us back. Let me know when he does." He regarded them both with a mock-serious, avuncular expression, winked broadly and went out of the room.

For a while they stood in an awkward silence. She looked trim and efficient in her Wren officer's uniform, but there were dark shadows under her eyes.

"I must congratulate you, Mrs. Day"—his voice was cold and formal—"on your brilliant piece of Intelligence work."

"Don't be angry with me," she said. "You don't imagine I enjoyed this particular assignment!"

"I'm sorry it was so unpleasant for you."

"You're being very unkind."

"Should I say, then, that you never gave a more convincing performance?" Even as he said it, he knew he was being childish and boorish.

"You're deliberately misunderstanding me," she said angrily. "How do you think I felt when I had to go on deceiving you, pretending I found you attractive, inviting you to come to my bedroom, begging you on my hands and knees to make love to me? Do you think I liked having to do that?" Her voice was rough with agitation.

Suddenly the phone rang on Gardner's desk. She went over and put her hand on the receiver. Before lifting it she said, with blazing eyes, "Damn you, Peter Carrington, I fell in love with you. Now can't you understand?" And still looking at him she mastered her emotion and picked up the receiver.

"Commander Gardner's office . . . No, sir, he's in the next room. Shall I call him? . . . Yes, sir . . . I'll tell him."

She put the receiver down and went swiftly past him and out of the room, leaving the door ajar. Carrington stared after her, contrite, baffled, astounded.

Almost at once she was back, with Gardner hard on her heels. Without looking at Carrington, she went straight to the communicating door and disappeared into her office, slamming the door behind her. Gardner looked at Carrington with surprise, but all he said was, "Come on, the admiral wants us back in the conference room. Best of luck."

The detective superintendent and the other civilians had now left. The admiral was leaning forward with his hands on the table and looking down at a large chart of the Atlantic.

"Ah, come in, Gardner. Look here, Carrington, I hope you realize that you rendered yourself liable to be charged with a very serious offense. You've been very foolish. However, we believe your story, and in the circumstances we have decided to take no action in the matter."

"Thank you, sir."

"Now, gentlemen, we haven't got much time. The object of the exercise now is to find this damned schooner before the Russians do. Howard must be prevented from getting into Russian hands *at all costs*. The trouble is that we can only spare two ships in the west Channel ports for an immediate operation. There's the cruiser *Birkenhead* standing by in Plymouth, and there's a submarine in Gosport, the *Accolade,* ready to sail at midnight. Now, it's essential that whoever gets aboard the schooner to arrest Howard should know what he looks like in this schoolmaster disguise. We can't afford a slip-up. I propose to send you, Gardner, in the *Birkenhead*. Being faster than the submarine she seems more likely to find the schooner first. I've got a plane waiting at Northolt to fly you down, and she'll sail as soon as you arrive. The submarine will have to make do with a detailed description of Howard—and this is where you could be very helpful, Carrington, as you saw him at such close quarters."

"Could I make a suggestion, sir?" said Gardner. "Carrington is an old submariner, sir. Why not let him go in the *Accolade?*"

The admiral stared at Gardner for a moment, and then turned to Carrington.

"Well, Carrington, what would you say to a short sea trip?"

"I'd like to go very much, sir."

"What about your family and your business and all that? You might be away several days."

"I'm not married, sir, but I would have to telephone my uncle, who's one of my senior partners—and expecting me to dinner tonight, incidentally. I'd need a few clothes too, I suppose."

"Let's see, where do you live?—Notting Hill way, isn't it? No, you won't have time. . . . Gardner, find out when the next Portsmouth train leaves Waterloo. . . . I'll ring Admiral of Submarines at Gosport and get him to lay on a car to meet you at the station and a boat over to Gosport. And I'll tell him you need a change of clothes and some seagoing gear."

He turned back to the table and resumed his study of the chart.

"The difficulty is, we haven't a clue as to *Black Pearl*'s position. We've been trying to contact her by radio, but a sailing ship of this sort wouldn't keep a constant W/T watch. She'd probably only listen to the twice-daily weather forecasts from Land's End. We're putting a message asking for her position on tonight's routine, but I'm doubtful she'll get it. The weather's too bad at the moment to send out search planes—and in seas like that they'd never spot her anyway. So the *Birkenhead* and the *Accolade* will have to find her. With these gales we've been having—the worst for fifty years, by all accounts—she may have been blown miles off her course. God knows where she'll have got to by now."

He bent forward and smoothed his hand over the chart.

"Now this is the probable situation as I see it. . . ."

17

At first Carrington could not remember where he was. Lying with his eyes shut he wondered why his bed was at one moment heaving upward at him and at the next dropping away from him with a sickening, shuddering, sideways motion. A continuous throbbing roar pulled at his eardrums; the noise was strange, yet somehow familiar.

At once it all came flooding back to him. He opened his eyes.

The first thing he saw was a droplet of condensation seesawing back and forth along the underside of one of the half-dozen pipes within eighteen inches of his head. Short pale-blue curtains ran the full length of his bunk: he watched them swaying to the roll of the submarine—surely, he thought, the range of their swing was less pronounced than it had been? Perhaps the weather was abating at last.

Suddenly he smelled the sharp, salty aroma of bacon and eggs, and realized with a rush of pleasure that he felt hungry for the first time in over twenty-four hours.

It was over fifteen years since he had been inside a submarine. Yet as soon as he went aboard at Gosport and climbed down the forehatch into the torpedo room he had felt at home. Here were the familiar, intricate mazes of pipes and electric leads, the wheel valves, the junction boxes, the ventilation trunking . . . the cramped, cheerful messes, the corked bulkhead curving overhead like the roof of a subway tunnel, the same pervading smell of oil. Making his way aft from the torpedo room, past the P.O.s' mess and the gallery, past the wardroom with its compactly fitted mahogany cupboards and bunks, and through the tough steel bulkhead doors toward the control room in the center of the boat, he was aware of a deep nostalgic excitement.

As the submarine maneuvered out of Portsmouth harbor, five minutes after midnight, he kept out of the way, sitting at the wardroom table, listening to the captain's orders coming down the voicepipe from the bridge to the control room. He was annoyed to find that he was already feeling the same sick apprehension he had felt in the old days every time he went out on patrol—a feeling which had always evaporated as soon as the submarine had settled down to her surface passage routine. But this time, as soon as the *Accolade* stuck her nose outside the Needles channel and met the full violence of the Force 10 gale, the unaccustomed motion of the boat had turned his stomach. Ashamed of his weakness, but thankful that on this occasion he was only a passenger, and did not have to endure the purgatory of bridge watchkeeping in such weather, he had retired to his bunk and slept as best he could.

Sleep came fitfully and uneasily. The ship, running westward on the surface into the teeth of the gale, was bucking like a frightened horse. Carrington's bunk was alongside the gangway, opposite the wardroom, and every seaman passing forward or aft leaned heavily on the bunk's leeboard to steady himself against the roll. As the stern came up out of the water the propellers thrashed the air like demented windmills and sent shuddering vibrations through the whole length of the hull. Seas breaking thunderously over the bridge sent water tumbling down the conning tower and cascading onto the control room deck. Carrington found it a disturbing and depressing sound. Sometimes an unusually mountainous wave, catching the bridge at an unlucky angle, would send the ship rolling over almost on her beam ends, holding her down interminably at an alarming angle; then Carrington had to brace himself against the bunk's leeboards to prevent himself from being thrown out on the deck.

Down below, with no visible portent of day or night, it was not easy to keep track of time. Not that Carrington was in a state to care very much. From time to time the wardroom steward brought him a cup of tea or soup, but he felt no desire for solid food. At last, overcome by weariness, he had fallen into a deep sleep.

. . . He pulled the bunk curtains aside and raised himself on one elbow. Two officers were eating breakfast at the wardroom table. One of them, wearing a frayed uniform jacket with the two-and-a-half stripes of a lieutenant commander on his sleeve, was the captain of the submarine, a well-built young man with deceptively lazy eyes, straw-colored hair and a firm, humorous mouth; the other was younger still, a lanky, angular boy with straight dark-brown hair and a laconic, bony face—the navigating officer, or "pilot." How young they all are, thought Carrington; they think of *me*, I suppose, as an old leftover from a prehistoric war.

"Good morning," he said. "Something smells good!"

They both looked up as he spoke.

"Hullo!" said the captain. "Feeling better?"

Rolling out of his bunk, Carrington stood on the deck and stretched his arms, combing the dark curls of his hair with his fingers, flexing his thigh muscles to balance himself against the roll of the ship. He was wearing a borrowed navy-blue overall type of suit and a pair of long gray woolen socks.

"Yes, I feel O.K. now, thank you. Sorry I've been such a miserable landlubberly passenger. It doesn't do to stay ashore too long."

"Don't worry, you're not the only one. Come and have some breakfast."

Carrington slipped his feet into a pair of short rubber boots and sat down at the table.

"Well, it's the roughest weather I've seen yet," said the young navigating officer, trying unsuccessfully to conceal his pride at having come through the experience without being seasick. "Several of the crew have been flaked out, and I don't think the chief has stirred from his bunk since we left harbor." He bent down to his right and pulled aside the curtains of the lower bunk behind him. "Hey, Chief!" he called. "Stir your stumps! Breakfast's up." But the engineer officer only groaned and turned his face to the ship's side. The pilot grinned. "See what I mean, sir?"

The wardroom flunky appeared with a plate of sizzling bacon and eggs which he put in front of Carrington.

"Tea or coffee, sir?"

"Monckton makes a good cup of coffee, you'll find," said the captain.

"Coffee, then, please."

Twelve hours earlier Carrington couldn't have looked at a plateful like the one he was now tucking into. He was beginning to feel really good.

"What's the weather doing?" he asked between mouthfuls. "It doesn't seem so bad now."

"No," said the captain, "the wind's eased off a good deal during the night. It's gone round into the northwest and is only blowing about Force 4. We actually saw the sun for half a minute just after dawn. But there's still a bloody great swell."

"I've even lost count of how long we've been at sea," said Carrington.

The captain laughed. "We've been chugging into this for

two nights and a day. Let's see—we left Gosport at midnight on Friday and it's now—what?—about eight-thirty on Sunday morning, so we've been steaming for just over thirty-two hours. We'll have a look at the chart presently and bring you up to date on the situation."

"No news of *Black Pearl* yet, I suppose?"

"Not a sausage. But we did have a message from the Admiralty during the night saying that if the improvement in the weather continues they hope to get search planes out this morning."

"What about the *Birkenhead*? A cruiser of her speed ought to have got well down into the Bay by now."

"Yes, she came up on the air about two hours ago with a signal to say she'd reached a position roughly level with Cape Finisterre and was turning north again to carry out a zigzag search along the reverse of the *Black Pearl's* probable track. But of course, after this fiendish spell of weather it's anybody's guess where the schooner is now, and I have a strong hunch we might be lucky enough to find her first yet."

When they had finished their breakfast the captain pressed the bell for the steward.

"Let's have the table cleared, Monckton, please. . . . Now, Pilot, it you'll mark our present position on the Eastern Atlantic chart and bring it over here I can show Mr. Carrington what's going on."

For a moment Carrington was alone with the captain.

"If your hunch is right," he said, "and we do find the schooner first, what's the plan of action?"

The captain lit a cigarette before replying. The smoke drifted across the table, shuddering in the vibrating air to the insistent throbbing of the diesels.

"A lot will depend on the state of the sea and the co-operation of the *Black Pearl's* skipper," he said. "We can't expect him to heave to for us in a big swell. He'll have to keep her sailing to keep way on, or she'd roll too much. If the swell isn't too bad I'll try to get our bow alongside her for a second or two and you'll have to jump for it. I propose to send my third hand with you. He's gunnery officer and a useful chap if there's any trouble."

"What about getting back to you with our prisoner?"

"I shan't be able to stay alongside or I'd bash her side in. I'll have to lie off and come in again when you signal you're ready—and you'll all have to jump again. It'll be a bit dicey, I'm afraid, but we'll put heaving lines on you so we can fish you out if you fall in the drink."

"Thanks!" said Carrington, smiling grimly. "It sounds as if it's going to be a very jolly party altogether!"

"You were one of Captain Howard's officers during the war, I gather?"

"Yes, I spent a year with him in Far Eastern waters."

"This can't be a pleasant assignment for you, exactly."

The navigating officer returned with the chart.

"Now then," said the captain, spreading it out on the wardroom table. He put an ashtray on one corner and stubbed his cigarette out. "Give me a pair of dividers, Pilot. . . . Well, here's our track since leaving Gosport—first leg to Start Point, then to Lizard, then to the south of the Scillies on a course roughly west by south. We passed Bishop Rock light about midnight. In this heavy sea we've only made good an average of eight and a half knots, so now here we are," and he tapped the position on the chart, "just west of eight degrees west, roughly 120 miles due south of Cork. Down here, about level with the northwest tip of Spain and some 450 miles to the south of us, is the *Birkenhead*, zigzagging slowly northward toward us. Problem—where is the *Black Pearl*? Her normal course would have taken her well clear of Ushant and then down onto a southwesterly course to clear Cape Finisterre. The *Birkenhead* has gone to the farthest point south that the schooner could conceivably have got to, and is now working backward.

"But I reckon the *Black Pearl* will have been blown well to the north. At the height of the storm, when she may have been facing winds of anything up to hurricane force, she'll have been carrying hardly any sails at all—a couple of trys'ls at most, and probably bare poles in the worst of it. With the gale heading her from the southwest she'd hardly choose to risk being blown down onto Ushant. She'd take the north-westerly tack to give herself plenty of sea room."

"But now the wind's changed to the northwest," said Carrington, "she'll surely have come round to a more southerly course?"

"Yes, she undoubtedly will. What I propose to do is to stick to our present course until we get to ten degrees west—that should take us until . . ." and he pricked off the distance with the dividers and measured it against the scale at the side of the chart . . . "let's say about four o'clock this afternoon. We'll then be pretty well on the edge of the hundred-fathom line and the deeper water should give us a longer swell—much more comfortable. Having reached that longitude we'll turn south. There's no point in *us* carrying out a zig because we'd be falling behind her all the time. But every half hour we'll stop engines, stick the periscope up and search the horizon carefully. That will give us a height-of-eye of about thirty feet. The visibility is extremely good at the moment, and if it stays like that I guess we ought to sight the tops of a schooner's masts a good fifteen miles away."

"That would mean we'd be searching a lane thirty miles wide," said the navigating officer.

"Yes, but only until dark, of course. It would be a wonderful stroke of luck if we did actually sight her ourselves, but at any rate, if we *should* get an aircraft sighting report, I reckon we ought to be in a good position to chase after her and get to her pretty quickly. Or the Admiralty may still manage to get through to her and ask her to report her position. Well, I don't know about you fellows, but I'm going to get a spot of shut-eye."

"It's all right, I take it, if I go up on the bridge for a breath of fresh air?" said Carrington.

"Of course. Pilot will lend you his duffel coat, I'm sure. It's more or less dry up top now, so I don't think you'll get very wet."

Carrington pulled on the duffel coat and went through into the control room. He paused for a moment to take in the old familiar scene. With the submarine on surface passage, and the thundering diesels greedily sucking the air down through the conning tower, it was a drafty place. The two periscopes were down in their housed position, smooth greased-metal columns growing up from deep wells in the deck and through the massive pressure-tight glands in the hull overhead. The long sensitive needles on the two large depth gauges on the port side were hovering between the figures 0 and 5 as the submarine rose and dipped in the swell. Below them the hydroplane levers, which controlled the submarine's depth when dived, were deserted. On the starboard side, guarded by the duty engine-room artificer, stood the gleaming battery of levers and wheel valves which operated the main vents and compressed-air supply to the external ballast tanks. To the untechnical stranger, a grim place, the control room of a submarine: here was the heart and nerve center of the vessel when submerged, a heart of cold steel and brass and baffling instruments, pumping its bloodstreams of water and compressed air through its arteries of pipes to the extremities of the ship's body, a nerve center flashing its operative instructions by electrical impulses and telemotor oil pressure. To an old submariner like Carrington, a place of technical fascination, triggering composite memories of sharp excitement, chill fear and peaceful monotony.

In the center of the compartment a steel ladder sloped up to the lower hatch of the conning tower. As the submarine rolled and pitched with a relentless corkscrew motion, a pool of daylight swayed on the deck like a questing searchlight. Carrington put a hand on the ladder and looked up. The gray-and-white bowl of the sky rocked and staggered across the open hatch at the top of the tower, and for a moment it was as if the submarine had become the still center of a drunken universe.

Carrington turned to the helmsman, who sat facing the forward bulkhead, watching the pointer on the clicking face of the gyrocompass repeater and slowly moving the spokes of the wheel from side to side.

"Would you ask the officer of the watch for permission for Mr. Carrington to go on the bridge, please."

The helmsman called up the voicepipe, turning his mouth close to the trumpet ear which curved toward him.

"Bridge! . . . Permission for Mr. Carrington on the bridge, please, sir."

A distant voice echoed faintly in the voicepipe.

"Permission granted, sir," said the helmsman.

Carrington climbed the ladder against the down-gale of wind. In the circular tower his feet rang hollowly on the steel rungs. At the top he heaved himself out of the hatch and took a step to the front of the bridge alongside the officer of the watch. All around him was the heaving panorama of the sea. The periscope standards towered massively above his head, and behind him two seamen lookouts stood motionless at the after end of the bridge.

The officer of the watch, muffled in his hooded waterproof suit, was searching the starboard horizon through his binoculars, his chubby, boyish face screwed up against the wind. Carrington recognized him as the third hand, the most junior officer in the ship.

"How's it going?" said Carrington quietly.

The third hand dropped his binoculars and let them hang in front of his chest. "Oh, hullo, sir. How are you feeling now?"

"I'm fine now, thanks. I imagine it's been pretty bloody up here."

"The first night was the worst. I really thought I'd had it when one very nasty sea came over. I'm sure we were com-

pletely submerged in solid water for a quarter of a minute or
so, but somehow we all managed to hang on. We eased the
revs down a bit after that!"

"I remember a night like that one winter during the war, on
the way to North Russia."

"God, that must have been bloody cold, too, sir."

"It was!"

"The wind's dropping all the time now. I think we ought
to be able to increase our speed before long."

"The sun looks as though it's trying to break through, too.
. . . By the way, I gather I may be having the pleasure of your
company if we find the schooner."

"Yes, sir," said the third hand, turning to face Carrington.
"It would be terrific to do an exciting, real job for once. Do
you think there's any chance of finding her before the *Birkenhead* does?"

"Your captain seems to think so, and he may well be right.
I only hope one of us finds her."

"Who exactly is this mysterious man we're going to arrest?"

"I don't think I'm allowed to say, at the moment," said
Carrington, smiling at the third hand's eager face. "The whole
thing's still on a very hush-hush top-secret level. All I can tell
you is that it will be a very serious thing if we don't find him.
We've got to get him—'at all costs' was the phrase the admiral
used."

They stood in silence for a while. The third hand raised his
binoculars and resumed his patient search of the tumbling
horizon. Carrington looked down at the fore part of the submarine rearing and plunging against the interminable swell
rolling in from mid-Atlantic. The slim bow drove into the
boiling ocean like a snorting whale; the sea, forcing itself
under the free-flood casing which formed the deck over the
pressure hull, fountained up through the air holes in the deck
in a rapid succession of little waterspouts like a spurting line
of machine-gun bullets. And as the submarine heaved its

tubular bulk out of the valley toward the next wave crest, draining the sea from the deck casing, a torrent of foam sluiced out over the black curve of the hull. The sea was a dirty gray-green, with streaks of mottled white streaming down wind like mucus. The snotgreen sea, quoted Carrington to himself, thinking: Joyce knew his northern sea as Homer knew his wine-dark Mediterranean.

Presently Carrington heard someone climbing the conning tower. The pale hair of the captain appeared in the hatch. Hauling himself out, he stood blinking in the bright daylight like someone who has been wakened out of a deep sleep. He looked quickly round at the sky and sea, and then leaned over the bridge alongside Carrington.

"Just had a signal from Admiralty which you'll be interested in," he said. "They've D/F'd two separate lots of transmissions on the Russian submarine W/T frequency—one from some-where south of the Azores and the other from a position about 350 miles due west of where we are now. Both the Russians appear to be closing in toward the European coast. Pilot's got them plotted on the chart, and it would seem that the second one, the more northerly one, could probably get to our area by dawn tomorrow."

"Blimey!" exclaimed Carrington. "That *is* interesting!"

All day the weather continued to ease, and by the time the *Accolade* had reached longitude 10 degrees west and turned onto her southward course the sea had lengthened to a gentle rolling swell. It was not until just before midnight that the Admiralty were able to send out the following coded signal addressed to H.M.S. *Birkenhead*, H.M.S/M. *Accolade* and all relevant authorities:

> *W/T contact with schooner Black Pearl now established. Approximate position, course and speed at 2300: 48°05'N 09°52'W 205° eight knots. Master has been informed of situation and agreed to co-operate. Accolade proceed at best*

speed to intercept and act in accordance with previous instructions, reporting position on sighting. Birkenhead close position along reverse of schooner's estimated track in event of Accolade failing to contact. Soviet submarine believed heading for area from the west. Use all measures short of actual hostilities to prevent Russians from approaching schooner.

Although *Accolade* had, it seemed, overshot the mark, having gone too far to the north and west of the schooner, she was nevertheless in a fairly good position to make the interception. The *Black Pearl* was now some seventy miles to the east of her and sailing southwest. The captain of the *Accolade* immediately ordered an alteration of course to the southeast and maximum revolutions from the engine room. Radar and asdic were fully manned, and extra lookouts were posted on the bridge.

Anticipation ran high throughout the submarine. Only Carrington did not share in the common excitement. With at least four hours to go before there could be any possibility of sighting the schooner, he decided to occupy his mind by writing a letter to Jane.

Shortly before three o'clock in the morning the radar operator reported an unexpected echo to the west of them. The captain altered course to investigate, but within two minutes the echo had faded out and disappeared from the screen. He dismissed it as one of those "false" echoes in which radar abounds, and brought the submarine back onto her southeasterly course. But they were to remember the incident later in the light of subsequent events.

18

It was still dark when the *Accolade* quietly submerged to a depth of one hundred feet to await the coming of morning light. There was no moon, and the horizon was woolly and murky. They had not yet sighted the schooner, but half an hour earlier they had picked her up on radar, at a range of ten miles and about two miles farther east than they had expected. After plotting her course and speed they had dived some seven or eight miles ahead of her. The captain wanted at least a glimmer of daylight for the coming boarding operation; but he did not think it advisable to sit about on the surface and advertise his presence to any Russian submarine that might be in the neighborhood.

Carrington, standing at the after end of the control room, had almost forgotten how peaceful it was to be underwater: the boat steady, no roar of air down the conning tower, no pounding throb from the diesels; just the faintest hum from the distant motor room and the occasional purr of the pumping motor under the deck. The first lieutenant, a tall young man with a florid complexion and fair wavy hair that was a shade too long over his ears, stood on the port side between the two seated hydroplane operators, watching the needles on the depth gauges, the angles of the hydroplane "tell-tale" repeaters and the level-bubble in its arc of pale-green liquid. From time to time he made minor adjustments to the submarine's trim by reaching up his hand and flicking the switch on the pump indicator, or by giving an order in his quiet, drawling voice. The captain brooded over the chart table in the corner, leaning on his folded arms with his cap tilted forward at a comic angle.

Carrington found the waiting more trying than anything he had experienced during the last week. He had no spirit for the job ahead of him.

After half an hour the captain came to the center of the control room and leaned casually against the steel ladder under the conning-tower hatch.

"Right," he said, "it should be light enough to see through the periscope now. But let's have some of these bright lights switched off, Number One. . . . Asdic transmission all-round sweep. Pilot, where should the *Black Pearl* be now?"

"If her course and speed have been steady, sir, she should be bearing about Red 20, range four miles."

Half a minute later the asdic operator reported an echo bearing Red 15, range 8,500 yards.

"That'll be her," said the captain. "Get that plotted, Pilot. Continue asdic sweep all round." He turned to the first lieutenant. "I shall need full buoyancy as soon as possible after surfacing, Number One, and I'll be staying on the motors until the operation is over. I'll want the signalman up at once with the Aldis, and the coxswain steering from the bridge."

"Aye, aye, sir."

"All-round asdic sweep completed, sir. All clear except for previous echo, now Red 17, range 8,000 yards."

"Right. Periscope depth, Number One."

While the hydroplane operators were bringing the submarine up from one hundred feet, the captain turned to the after corner where Carrington was standing with the third hand. They were both now wearing light rope-soled shoes and belts with loaded revolvers.

"Boarding party all ready? Where's the second coxswain?"

"Here, sir."

"Heaving lines ready?"

"All ready, sir."

"Good. Now I want you three to get down onto the fore casing as soon as we surface. Wait at the front of the bridge until we're nearly alongside and then go right for'ard to the bow. I'm aiming to approach the schooner on her port beam, which will be her lee side. As soon as you can jump, Carrington, jump. You'll have to be nippy—you may not get a second chance. Luckily the swell has calmed down a good deal."

"Fifty feet, sir," called the first lieutenant, "forty-five feet . . . forty feet . . ."

"Up periscope!"

As the periscope column slid upward the captain bent low, flicked down the folded handles at the lower end of the periscope and came up with it until it was in the fully raised position. With his eyes staring into the binocular lenses he pushed the whole periscope round in a swift circle, his legs gangling round the perimeter of the well. Then he began to search slowly down the port side, looking for the schooner.

"Steady on periscope depth, sir," said the first lieutenant quietly.

"It's still bloody dark," muttered the captain. "Ah, wait a minute . . . yes, there she is. Not much more than a vague blur at the moment, but she's got quite a lot of canvas flying by the look of her. At a guess I'd say I was about five degrees on her port bow. . . . Stand by to surface."

"Check main vents," ordered the first lieutenant.

Despite his anxiety, Carrington found himself listening to the surfacing drill with a half smile of almost affectionate recollection. In the "dim religious" light of the control room, the quiet orders and the routine replies sounded as unhurried, as punctual and as familiar as the reponses in a church service. "Ready to surface, sir," said the first lieutenant.

A moment later the peaceful tenor of the proceedings was interrupted by an exclamation from the asdic operator. He was sitting at the after end of the control room, listening intently in his earphones, his hand busy on the bearing pointer. "Captain, sir! I'm picking up a new echo now, Red 110, range 10,000 yards."

"What!" said the captain, quickly turning the periscope to the left and searching carefully on either side of the new bearing.

"It's a fairly small echo, sir, but there's definitely something there."

"Any propeller noise?"

"Not yet, sir. Range is closing slowly."

"Well, there's nothing in sight yet on that bearing. Pilot, start plotting this new echo and let me know its course and speed as quick as you can. It's just possible it may be a Russian submarine. If it is, Number One, we may be in for some fun. Well, the sooner we go up now the better." He had one more quick look all round the horizon, then flicked up the periscope handles. "Down periscope, half ahead together . . . *Surface!*"

"Blow all main ballast!"

Amidst the hissing and roaring of the compressed air bursting into the external ballast tanks, the captain climbed into the conning tower with the signalman hard on his heels. Carrington, next in line, standing with one foot on the first rung of the lower ladder and watching the depth-gauge needles steadily rising, heard the metallic "clunk" as the captain removed the safety clips on the upper hatch.

"Twenty-five feet, sir!" The first lieutenant was calling the depth-gauge readings up the tower. "Twenty feet . . . fifteen feet . . . *ten* feet, sir . . ."

The submarine began to roll in the trough of the surface swell. Looking up the tower, Carrington felt a little splash of water on his cheek. There was a flood of pale daylight as the captain thrust open the upper hatch and climbed out onto the bridge. Then Carrington was moving up, his hands gripping the rungs one after another under the soles of the signalman's shoes. Heaving himself through the hatch he stumbled onto the perforated deck of the bridge. In the hollow bridge casing below his feet he heard the foam surging over the pressure hull with the angry hiss of a breaker sluicing into a cave at high water. The smell of brine was strong in his nostrils.

The captain had already begun to shout orders down the voicepipe. At the after end of the bridge the signalman was breaking out the white ensign: it rippled free, snapping at the wind, standing out clean and sharp against the gray sky. Carrington clambered over and down the side of the bridge and gingerly worked his way forward along the handrail. A wave slapped up, soaking him to the crotch, and he swore, softly and deliberately.

At the foot of the bridge he was joined by the third hand and the second coxswain. The fore casing stretched slim and straight before them, gleaming with wetness, lifting and dipping to the swell, with the hydroplanes projecting horizontally like ridiculous ears and throwing up twin flurries of spray. From this level, only a few feet above the waterline, the tumbling edge of the swell looked swift and angry, but in the long gray valleys between the crests the surface was smooth. The wind had been easing steadily all night.

Over the top of the swell Carrington was startled to see the schooner—startled not by the fact of her being there, for he had known she would be there, but by the undeniable physical reality of her visible presence. Though she was still hull-down, there was a sense of imminence about this high, slender white ghost tilted against the paling sky, at one moment seemingly stationary, at the next yawing and dipping, nodding like a charger impatient of its curb. They were so nearly right ahead of her—ten degrees or so on her port bow—that the wind-hard curves of her sails were as slim as first shavings of the new moon.

Carrington had no time to admire her beauty. The second coxswain was securing a heaving-line under his armpits. This cheerful character was a stocky little man with a bashed-in nose and burly shoulders, knobbly, ugly, but quick and deft in his movements.

"Now, sir, I've given you a fairly slack loop so you can slip it off, easy-like, when you get aboard 'er. I'll give you plenty of slack when you jump. No need to worry, sir—I'll look after you if you fall in the drink."

"O.K.," said Carrington, grinning at him but wishing he shared his self-confidence. He would have given anything at this moment to be sitting quietly at his office desk in Lincoln's Inn Fields.

A lamp signal was blinking hesitantly from the *Black Pearl*, but Carrington's Morse was too rusty for him to read it even at slow speed. The range was closing fast now. The lines of the schooner were broadening out, and Carrington could see her lunging bowsprit, the deck canted over toward them, men running forward under the vast white mainsail, and the sea licking swiftly within inches of her lee rail. "She's moving much too bloody fast," said the third hand. But almost at once Carrington saw a fluttering of the fore topsail; a second later it came down with a run.

The submarine was coming round in a slow left-hand turn to bring the *Black Pearl* onto her starboard quarter. At the end of the turn the two ships were on nearly parallel courses, converging slightly, the submarine a length ahead of the schooner and waiting for her to come up. Meanwhile, by lowering all topsails, jibs and mizzen, reducing her canvas to main- and staysail only, the schooner had effected a noticeable drop in her speed. She had in fact come down to about five knots and was now riding the sea fairly comfortably, steering a course diagonally across the swell.

"We ought to be getting for'ard now," said the third hand. "You'd better go first, sir."

Carrington led the way along the fore casing, holding on to the taut lifeline. The two vessels were so close now that Carrington could recognize the Jamaican bos'un at the schooner's wheel, working hard to keep the course steady, and behind him the tall, bulky figure of Captain Gustavsen, standing calmly with feet apart, watching the situation with his experienced seaman's eye.

"Stand by, for'ard!"—the submarine captain was booming at them from the bridge through a megaphone—"I'm closing in now."

Having got the measure of the schooner's speed, the submarine was now running level with her, with about thirty yards of dark-gray, gently heaving water between them. Waiting unhappily on the narrow bow, Carrington watched the gap steadily closing; behind him, the second coxswain was holding the slack of the heaving-line looped in his left hand.

The two ships were rolling a good deal now, seesawing vertically in irregular swoops, and the waves, constricted in their passage between the hulls, were shooting higher and chucking up vicious little fountains of spray. The three men on the submarine's bow were getting uncomfortably wet.

They seemed to be drifting in on the schooner at an alarming speed. "He's coming in too fast," said the third hand, with a quick, anxious look aft. But the swing was checked; for a moment the submarine steadied on a parallel course, then began edging once more to starboard, feeling her way in.

Carrington braced himself for the jump.

As the submarine touched her bow against the schooner's rail there was a little jolt, but no more. Carrington and the third hand made their leap together, plunging through a wall of spray at the precise moment when the schooner began her upward roll. They landed on the deck with surprising ease. Carrington stumbled forward onto his hands, but immediately recovered himself, slipped out of the loop of the heaving-line and threw it clear. Someone was at his elbow, steadying him; he turned—it was Jan Isaaksen, the mate, recognizing him with astonishment. Over his shoulder Carrington saw the submarine dropping astern. He had to admit that it had been an extremely competent feat of seamanship.

He was about to follow the mate aft and make himself known to Captain Gustavsen when the sound of a familiar voice behind him made him turn swiftly on his heel.

"You've come for me, I suppose, Pedro."

Howard was standing at the head of the cabin companionway. He had pulled a navy-blue jacket and trousers over his pajamas, and he was standing with his hands in the jacket pockets, leaning against the weather side of the companionway to brace himself against the motion of the ship. His black-dyed hair was ruffled, and he had a weary, shrunken look about him. He had discarded the horn-rimmed glasses. The thin black mustache of his disguise emphasized the sardonic expression of his mouth.

"Is this the man we're after?" said the third hand at Carrington's elbow.

"Yes, but leave this to me for the moment," said Carrington, moving up the sloping deck to stand facing Howard.

"You've come armed, I see," said Howard.

"You're under arrest, Bill. I hope you're not going to make things difficult."

Howard said nothing for several seconds, but stared at Carrington with a bitter, twisted smile. In the silence between them, and above the sound of the sea, Carrington was suddenly aware of a confused shouting from the stern. He turned his head to see what was going on, and as he did so Howard moved quickly to the weather side of the deck and stood looking down into the water.

Carrington drew his revolver. "What the hell's happening?" he shouted to the third hand.

"*Accolade*'s flashing a signal—something about a periscope. . . . My God! . . . *Look,* sir!"

On the starboard side of the schooner, and so close that it seemed a collision was inevitable, a dark green monster was rising out of the sea: the conning tower of a large submarine, with the water draining off it in a cascade of boiling foam; the tower, moving forward at a speed slightly greater than that of the schooner and on a course parallel to it, was knocking up a confused white turbulence in its wake. A moment later the long deck casing emerged all at once from the water with a sound like surf receding on a shingle beach.

Clearly embossed on the side of the tower was the shape of a hammer and sickle in bronze relief.

"Holy smoke!" exclaimed Carrington, running to the weather rail. The Russian submarine, now nearly at full buoyancy, was so close that she was bumping and grinding her saddle tanks against the schooner. Gustavsen, beside himself with fury, came running along the starboard side of the deck, shaking his fist at two Russian officers who had appeared at the top of the conning tower.

Howard turned for a moment toward Carrington, his face radiant with bitter triumph.

"So you betrayed me after all!" he cried. "What price treason now? But you're too late, Pedro." Then he was climbing over the schooner's rail, poising himself for the leap.

"Bill, you bloody fool!" yelled Carrington, moving toward him—but Howard had jumped. He landed on the slippery, curving bulge of the submarine's saddle tank, lost his footing as a wave swept over him, recovered himself and caught hold of a projection at the base of the tower.

Carrington was shouting above the commotion of the sea. "Bill, come back, you crazy, crazy fool! For God's sake . . ."

Howard was already beginning to climb up the outside of the conning tower. The submarine was speeding up a little now, drawing slowly ahead. One of the Russian officers had disappeared down the hatch; the other was leaning over the side of the bridge in some agitation, encouraging Howard to hurry. As Howard's hand reached the top rung, there was a sudden roar of escaping air. The submarine had opened her vents.

"She's diving, sir!" yelled the third hand into Carrington's ear.

In a moment Howard would be over the top and climbing down into the upper hatch. Carrington, moving forward along the schooner's deck, fired three times. At the third shot Bill Howard turned, with his left arm already over the bridge rail. He looked at Carrington as though he was about to speak. But instead of words, blood gushed out of his mouth; his arm lost its hold and he pitched forward, pivoting on his feet, falling head first onto the saddle tanks. The Russian officer looked down from the bridge with horror, and then turned hurriedly away to get through the hatch before the submarine went under.

The sea, now washing green over the saddle tanks, seemed for a moment to be floating Howard clear. But at the next surge of the swell his body was sucked down and crushed between the two hulls.

A week later, Carrington rang the Admiralty from his office and after some difficulty managed to get through to Mrs. Day.

"Hullo . . . Jane?"

"Yes, who is it?"

"Peter Carrington."

"Oh . . ."

"Hullo . . . are you still there?"

"Thank you for your wonderful letter."

"I was wondering," he said, "if I could persuade you to come and have supper at my flat one evening this week. I'm not a bad cook as bachelors go, and I thought perhaps we might share another bottle of that Château Latour 1955."

There was a moment's pause before her reply.

"Yes, I'd love to. . . . It was a beautiful wine."

THE PERENNIAL LIBRARY MYSTERY SERIES

E. C. Bentley

TRENT'S LAST CASE
"One of the three best detective stories ever written."
—Agatha Christie

TRENT'S OWN CASE
"I won't waste time saying that the plot is sound and the detection satisfying. Trent has not altered a scrap and reappears with all his old humor and charm."
—Dorothy L. Sayers

Gavin Black

A DRAGON FOR CHRISTMAS
"Potent excitement!"
—New York Herald Tribune

THE EYES AROUND ME
"I stayed up until all hours last night reading *The Eyes Around Me,* which is something I do not do very often, but I was so intrigued by the ingeniousness of Mr. Black's plotting and the witty way in which he spins his mystery. I can only say that I enjoyed the book enormously."
—F. van Wyck Mason

YOU WANT TO DIE, JOHNNY?
"Gavin Black doesn't just develop a pressure plot in suspense, he adds uninfected wit, character, charm, and sharp knowledge of the Far East to make rereading as keen as the first race-through." —*Book Week*

Nicholas Blake

THE BEAST MUST DIE
"It remains one more proof that in the hands of a really first-class writer the detective novel can safely challenge comparison with any other variety of fiction."
—*The Manchester Guardian*

THE CORPSE IN THE SNOWMAN
"If there is a distinction between the novel and the detective story (which we do not admit), then this book deserves a high place in both categories."
—*The New York Times*

THE DREADFUL HOLLOW
"Pace unhurried, characters excellent, reasoning solid."
—*San Francisco Chronicle*

END OF CHAPTER
". . . admirably solid . . . an adroit formal detective puzzle backed up by firm characterization and a knowing picture of London publishing."
—*The New York Times*

HEAD OF A TRAVELER
"Another grade A detective story of the right old jigsaw persuasion."
—*New York Herald Tribune Book Review*

MINUTE FOR MURDER
"An outstanding mystery novel. Mr. Blake's writing is a delight in itself."
—*The New York Times*

THE MORNING AFTER DEATH
"One of Blake's best."
—Rex Warner

A PENKNIFE IN MY HEART
"Style brilliant . . . and suspenseful."
—*San Francisco Chronicle*

THE PRIVATE WOUND
[Blake's] best novel in a dozen years . . . . An intensely penetrating study of sexual passion . . . . A powerful story of murder and its aftermath."
—Anthony Boucher, *The New York Times*

A QUESTION OF PROOF
"The characters in this story are unusually well drawn, and the suspense is well sustained."
—*The New York Times*

THE SAD VARIETY
"It is a stunner. I read it instead of eating, instead of sleeping."
—Dorothy Salisbury Davis

THE SMILER WITH THE KNIFE
"An extraordinarily well written and entertaining thriller."
—*Saturday Review of Literature*

THOU SHELL OF DEATH
"It has all the virtues of culture, intelligence and sensibility that the most exacting connoisseur could ask of detective fiction."
—*The Times* [London] *Literary Supplement*

THE WHISPER IN THE GLOOM
"One of the most entertaining suspense-pursuit novels in many seasons."
—*The New York Times*

Nicholas Blake (cont'd)

THE WIDOW'S CRUISE

"A stirring suspense. . . . The thrilling tale leaves nothing to be desired."
—*Springfield Republican*

THE WORM OF DEATH

"It [The Worm of Death] is one of Blake's very best—and his best is better than almost anyone's."
—Louis Untermeyer

George Harmon Coxe

MURDER WITH PICTURES

"[Coxe] has hit the bull's-eye with his first shot."
—*The New York Times*

Edmund Crispin

BURIED FOR PLEASURE

"Absolute and unalloyed delight."
—Anthony Boucher, *The New York Times*

Kenneth Fearing

THE BIG CLOCK

"It will be some time before chill-hungry clients meet again so rare a compound of irony, satire, and icy-fingered narrative. *The Big Clock* is . . . a psychothriller you won't put down."   —*Weekly Book Review*

Andrew Garve

THE ASHES OF LODA

"Garve . . . embellishes a fine fast adventure story with a more credible picture of the U.S.S.R. than is offered in most thrillers."
—*The New York Times Book Review*

THE CUCKOO LINE AFFAIR

". . . an agreeable and ingenious piece of work."   —*The New Yorker*

A HERO FOR LEANDA

"One can trust Mr. Garve to put a fresh twist to any situation, and the ending is really a lovely surprise."   —*The Manchester Guardian*

MURDER THROUGH THE LOOKING GLASS

". . . refreshingly out-of-the-way and enjoyable . . . highly recommended to all comers."
—*Saturday Review*

Andrew Garve (cont'd)

NO TEARS FOR HILDA
"It starts fine and finishes finer. I got behind on breathing watching Max get not only his man but his woman, too." —Rex Stout

THE RIDDLE OF SAMSON
"The story is an excellent one, the people are quite likable, and the writing is superior." —*Springfield Republican*

Michael Gilbert

BLOOD AND JUDGMENT
"Gilbert readers need scarcely be told that the characters all come alive at first sight, and that his surpassing talent for narration enhances any plot. . . . Don't miss." —*San Francisco Chronicle*

THE BODY OF A GIRL
"Does what a good mystery should do: open up into all kinds of ramifications, with untold menace behind the action. At the end, there is a bang-up climax, and it is a pleasure to see how skilfully Gilbert wraps everything up." —*The New York Times Book Review*

THE DANGER WITHIN
"Michael Gilbert has nicely combined some elements of the straight detective story with plenty of action, suspense, and adventure, to produce a superior thriller." —*Saturday Review*

DEATH HAS DEEP ROOTS
"Trial scenes superb; prowl along Loire vivid chase stuff; funny in right places; a fine performance throughout." —*Saturday Review*

FEAR TO TREAD
"Merits serious consideration as a work of art."
—*The New York Times*

C. W. Grafton

BEYOND A REASONABLE DOUBT
"A very ingenious tale of murder . . . a brilliant and gripping narrative."
—Jacques Barzun and Wendell Hertig Taylor

Edward Grierson

THE SECOND MAN
"One of the best trial-testimony books to have come along in quite a while." —*The New Yorker*

Cyril Hare

AN ENGLISH MURDER
"By a long shot, the best crime story I have read for a long time. Everything is traditional, but originality does not suffer. The setting is perfect. Full marks to Mr. Hare." —*Irish Press*

TRAGEDY AT LAW
"An extremely urbane and well-written detective story."
—*The New York Times*

UNTIMELY DEATH
"The English detective story at its quiet best, meticulously underplayed, rich in perceivings of the droll human animal and ready at the last with a neat surprise which has been there all the while had we but wits to see it." —*New York Herald Tribune Book Review*

WHEN THE WIND BLOWS
"The best, unquestionably, of all the Hare stories, and a masterpiece by any standards."
—Jacques Barzun and Wendell Hertig Taylor, *A Catalogue of Crime*

WITH A BARE BODKIN
"One of the best detective stories published for a long time."
—*The Spectator*

Robert Harling

THE ENORMOUS SHADOW (*available 8/81*)
"In some ways the best spy story of the modern period.... The writing is terse and vivid ... the ending full of action ... altogether first-rate."
—Jacques Barzun and Wendell Hertig Taylor, *A Catalogue of Crime*

Matthew Head

THE CABINDA AFFAIR
"An absorbing whodunit and a distinguished novel of atmosphere."
—Anthony Boucher, *The New York Times*

MURDER AT THE FLEA CLUB
"The true delight is in Head's style, its limpid ease combined with humor and an awesome precision of phrase." —*San Francisco Chronicle*

M. V. Heberden

ENGAGED TO MURDER
"Smooth plotting."
—*The New York Times*

James Hilton

WAS IT MURDER?
"The story is well planned and well written."
—*The New York Times*

Elspeth Huxley

THE AFRICAN POISON MURDERS
"Obscure venom, manical mutilations, deadly bush fire, thrilling climax compose major opus.... Top-flight."
—*Saturday Review of Literature*

Francis Iles

BEFORE THE FACT
"Not many 'serious' novelists have produced character studies to compare with Iles's internally terrifying portrait of the murderer in *Before the Fact,* his masterpiece and a work truly deserving the appellation of unique and beyond price."
—Howard Haycraft

MALICE AFORETHOUGHT
"It is a long time since I have read anything so good as *Malice Afore-thought,* with its cynical humour, acute criminology, plausible detail and rapid movement. It makes you hug yourself with pleasure."
—H. C. Harwood, *Saturday Review*

Lange Lewis

THE BIRTHDAY MURDER
"Almost perfect in its playlike purity and delightful prose."
—Jacques Barzun and Wendell Hertig Taylor

Arthur Maling

LUCKY DEVIL
"The plot unravels at a fast clip, the writing is breezy and Maling's approach is as fresh as today's stockmarket quotes."
—*Louisville Courier Journal*

RIPOFF
"A swiftly paced story of today's big business is larded with intrigue as a Ralph Nader-type investigates an insurance scandal and is soon on the run from a hired gun and his brother. . . . Engrossing and credible."
—*Booklist*

SCHROEDER'S GAME

"As the title indicates, this Schroeder is up to something, and the unravelling of his game is a diverting and sufficiently blood-soaked entertainment."
—*The New Yorker*

Thomas Sterling

THE EVIL OF THE DAY

"Prose as witty and subtle as it is sharp and clear...characters unconventionally conceived and richly bodied forth .... In short, a novel to be treasured."
—Anthony Boucher, *The New York Times*

Julian Symons

THE BELTING INHERITANCE

"A superb whodunit in the best tradition of the detective story."
—August Derleth, *Madison Capital Times*

BLAND BEGINNING

"Mr. Symons displays a deft storytelling skill, a quiet and literate wit, a nice feeling for character, and detectival ingenuity of a high order."
—Anthony Boucher, *The New York Times*

BOGUE'S FORTUNE

"There's a touch of the old sardonic humour, and more than a touch of style."
—*The Spectator*

THE BROKEN PENNY

"The most exciting, astonishing and believable spy story to appear in years.
—Anthony Boucher, *The New York Times Book Review*

THE COLOR OF MURDER

"A singularly unostentatious and memorably brilliant detective story."
—*New York Herald Tribune Book Review*

THE 31ST OF FEBRUARY

"Nobody has painted a more gruesome picture of the advertising business since Dorothy Sayers wrote 'Murder Must Advertise', and very few people have written a more entertaining or dramatic mystery story."
—*The New Yorker*

Dorothy Stockbridge Tillet
(John Stephen Strange)

THE MAN WHO KILLED FORTESCUE

"Better than average."
—*Saturday Review of Literature*

Henry Wade

A DYING FALL

"One of those expert British suspense jobs ... it crackles with undercurrents of blackmail, violent passion and murder. Topnotch in its class."

— *Time*

THE HANGING CAPTAIN *(available 8/81)*

"This is a detective story for connoisseurs, for those who value clear thinking and good writing above mere ingenuity and easy thrills."

— *Times Literary Supplement*

Henry Kitchell Webster

WHO IS THE NEXT?

"A double murder, private-plane piloting, a neat impersonation, and a delicate courtship are adroitly combined by a writer who knows how to use the language." — Jacques Barzun and Wendell Hertig Taylor

Anna Mary Wells

MURDERER'S CHOICE

"Good writing, ample action, and excellent character work."

— *Saturday Review of Literature*

A TALENT FOR MURDER

"The discovery of the villain is a decided shock." — *Books*

Edward Young

THE FIFTH PASSENGER

"Clever and adroit ... excellent thriller ... — *Library Journal*

**If you enjoyed this book you'll want to know about
THE PERENNIAL LIBRARY MYSTERY SERIES**

Nicholas Blake

☐	P 456	THE BEAST MUST DIE	$1.95
☐	P 427	THE CORPSE IN THE SNOWMAN	$1.95
☐	P 493	THE DREADFUL HOLLOW	$1.95
☐	P 397	END OF CHAPTER	$1.95
☐	P 398	HEAD OF A TRAVELER	$2.25
☐	P 419	MINUTE FOR MURDER	$1.95
☐	P 520	THE MORNING AFTER DEATH	$1.95
☐	P 521	A PENKNIFE IN MY HEART	$2.25
☐	P 531	THE PRIVATE WOUND	$2.25
☐	P 494	A QUESTION OF PROOF	$1.95
☐	P 495	THE SAD VARIETY	$2.25
☐	P 428	THOU SHELL OF DEATH	$1.95
☐	P 418	THE WHISPER IN THE GLOOM	$1.95
☐	P 399	THE WIDOW'S CRUISE	$1.95
☐	P 400	THE WORM OF DEATH	$2.25

E. C. Bentley

☐	P 440	TRENT'S LAST CASE	$2.50
☐	P 516	TRENT'S OWN CASE	$2.25

Buy them at your local bookstore or use this coupon for ordering:

**HARPER & ROW, Mail Order Dept. #PMS, 10 East 53rd St.,
New York, N.Y. 10022.**

Please send me the books I have checked above. I am enclosing $ _____
which includes a postage and handling charge of $1.00 for the first book and
25¢ for each additional book. Send check or money order. No cash or
C.O.D.'s please.

Name _____

Address _____

City _____ State _____ Zip _____

Please allow 4 weeks for delivery. USA and Canada only. This offer expires
5/1/82. Please add applicable sales tax.

Gavin Black

☐	P 473	A DRAGON FOR CHRISTMAS	$1.95
☐	P 485	THE EYES AROUND ME	$1.95
☐	P 472	YOU WANT TO DIE, JOHNNY?	$1.95

George Harmon Coxe

☐	P 527	MURDER WITH PICTURES	$2.25

Edmund Crispin

☐	P 506	BURIED FOR PLEASURE	$1.95

Kenneth Fearing

☐	P 500	THE BIG CLOCK	$1.95

Andrew Garve

☐	P 430	THE ASHES OF LODA	$1.50
☐	P 451	THE CUCKOO LINE AFFAIR	$1.95
☐	P 429	A HERO FOR LEANDA	$1.50
☐	P 449	MURDER THROUGH THE LOOKING GLASS	$1.95
☐	P 441	NO TEARS FOR HILDA	$1.95
☐	P 450	THE RIDDLE OF SAMSON	$1.95

Buy them at your local bookstore or use this coupon for ordering:

Michael Gilbert

☐	P 446	BLOOD AND JUDGMENT	$1.95
☐	P 459	THE BODY OF A GIRL	$1.95
☐	P 448	THE DANGER WITHIN	$1.95
☐	P 447	DEATH HAS DEEP ROOTS	$1.95
☐	P 458	FEAR TO TREAD	$1.95

C. W. Grafton

☐	P 519	BEYOND A REASONABLE DOUBT	$1.95

Edward Grierson

☐	P 528	THE SECOND MAN	$2.25

Cyril Hare

☐	P 455	AN ENGLISH MURDER	$1.95
☐	P 522	TRAGEDY AT LAW	$2.25
☐	P 514	UNTIMELY DEATH	$2.25
☐	P 523	WITH A BARE BODKIN	$2.25

Robert Harling

☐	P 545	THE ENORMOUS SHADOW *(available 8/81)* $2.25	

Buy them at your local bookstore or use this coupon for ordering:

Matthew Head

☐	P 541	THE CABINDA AFFAIR	$2.25
☐	P 542	MURDER AT THE FLEA CLUB	$2.25

M. V. Heberden

☐	P 533	ENGAGED TO MURDER	$2.25

James Hilton

☐	P 501	WAS IT MURDER?	$1.95

Elspeth Huxley

☐	P 540	THE AFRICAN POISON MURDERS	$2.25

Frances Iles

☐	P 517	BEFORE THE FACT	$1.95
☐	P 532	MALICE AFORETHOUGHT	$1.95

Lange Lewis

☐	P 518	THE BIRTHDAY MURDER	$1.95

Arthur Maling

☐	P 482	LUCKY DEVIL	$1.95
☐	P 483	RIPOFF	$1.95
☐	P 484	SCHROEDER'S GAME	$1.95

Buy them at your local bookstore or use this coupon for ordering:

Austin Ripley

☐ P 387   MINUTE MYSTERIES $1.95

Thomas Sterling

☐ P 529   THE EVIL OF THE DAY $2.25

Julian Symons

☐ P 468   THE BELTING INHERITANCE $1.95
☐ P 469   BLAND BEGINNING $1.95
☐ P 481   BOGUE'S FORTUNE $1.95
☐ P 480   THE BROKEN PENNY $1.95
☐ P 461   THE COLOR OF MURDER $1.95
☐ P 460   THE 31ST OF FEBRUARY $1.95

Dorothy Stockbridge Tillet
(John Stephen Strange)

☐ P 536   THE MAN WHO KILLED FORTESCUE $2.25

Henry Wade

☐ P 543   A DYING FALL $2.25
☐ P 548   THE HANGING CAPTAIN *(available 8/81)* $2.25

Buy them at your local bookstore or use this coupon for ordering:

HARPER & ROW, Mail Order Dept. #PMS, 10 East 53rd St., New York, N.Y. 10022.

Please send me the books I have checked above. I am enclosing $ _____ which includes a postage and handling charge of $1.00 for the first book and 25¢ for each additional book. Send check or money order. No cash or C.O.D.'s please.

Name _____

Address _____

City _____ State _____ Zip _____

Please allow 4 weeks for delivery. USA and Canada only. This offer expires 5/1/82. Please add applicable sales tax.

Henry Kitchell Webster

☐ P 539 WHO IS THE NEXT? $2.25

Anna Mary Wells

☐ P 534 MURDERER'S CHOICE $2.25
☐ P 535 A TALENT FOR MURDER $2.25

Edward Young

☐ P 544 THE FIFTH PASSENGER $2.25

Buy them at your local bookstore or use this coupon for ordering: